The Land of Milk and Honey

Viktor Shel

I want to express a deep gratitude to my friend Carol Keller
for the invaluable assistance in the translation of this book.
Viktor Shel

ISBN 978-0-9890856-7-0

Editor: Cathy Reed.
Translation from Russian: Viktor Shel.

Cover Design: Iryna Spica.
Typeset at SpicaBookDesign in *Plantin*.
Printed and bound with www.createspace.com

Chapter One

It was the end of 1988, and people in the Soviet Union lived very poorly. Simple necessities were hard to obtain; government stores were famous for empty shelves; and work in foreign countries for Soviet citizens looked like an impossible dream.

One winter day, Daria was checking the homework of her students as she sat at the table in the staff room. She was interrupted when Nina Pavlovna approached her. Nina was an old friend; they had become buddies at the university and later worked together at the same school, for several years, as Russian language teachers. Looking at Nina, Daria immediately noticed that she was very excited.

"What happened? Why are you so excited?"

"I want to share something with you and ask for your advice. Yesterday, I received an unusual offer and I was so excited I couldn't sleep all night," replied Nina.

"Is he handsome?" Daria asked, smiling.

"He? I'm not talking about a man nor about marriage."

"If not about a man, why are you so excited?"

"How would you be feeling if you had been offered a job in America?"

"Whoa! Somebody offered you a job in America?" Now *Daria* was excited.

"Let me start from the beginning," said Nina. I was in the District Party Committee visiting with Sophia Andreyevna. First, I reported on the work of our school party cell, and then the conversation turned to life in general. I told her frankly that I was barely making ends meet, that I couldn't even afford to buy a new skirt. Sophia was very sympathetic. She said that even her job in the District Party Committee didn't pay enough, and she told me that the best way to make good money was to work abroad. She told me that just a year of work in the West would allow for several years of comfortable living."

Daria's eyes widened.

"And now there is a chance for me to get that kind of work," Nina continued.

"Sophia knows a person who can help me find a job in America. Even though I didn't believe that it was a real opportunity, I wrote down the phone number, and yesterday I called Igor Ivanovich, the man who Sofia recommended. He offered to meet me in the lobby of the Hotel Moscow. It turned out that Igor was a very handsome man, dressed in a dark blue suit, and with the manners of an English gentleman. He introduced himself as the representative of a company engaged in finding certain specialists for jobs in the United States, and he said he could help me find a job in America.

"His firm is looking for those who would be willing to work as a governess for a rich American family. In one year, I would be able to earn nearly ten thousand dollars! Imagine ten thousand dollars! That's forty thousand rubles of our money! Compare that with my school salary of two hundred a month! He is looking for competent workers, and the firm looks after obtaining the passport and visas. The contract must be signed for a year, but if you like the job, the contract can be extended."

"And what happens if you don't like the job?" asked Daria.

"What are you talking about? What nonsense!" exclaimed Nina. "Why wouldn't I like working in America? Why wouldn't I like working with kids? The position of a governess is quite a decent job – no worse than teaching school; just fewer students."

"Nina, are you really saying this? You, the chief of the party cell at our school!"

"This position doesn't satisfy me, Daria. Igor's proposal would open up the possibility for me to earn some much needed money. Think about it, in just one year I can earn a lot of money!"

Daria had doubts. "Don't you think that in America, they would have people who would want to work as a governess? Why is it necessary to look for people from the Soviet Union?"

"Oh! I forgot to tell you that we are talking about the rich immigrants who have emigrated from Russia to the U.S., and they want their children to learn Russian."

"Someone from the former Russian nobility, or what?"

"Of course...immigrants from the old aristocratic Russia. Aristocratic families historically hire a governess for their children. Igor said he was particularly pleased that I am a teacher of the Russian language. So...what do you think about this proposal?"

"Nina, this is an unusual proposal. I am doubtful about what Igor says. The proposal is too good to be true. How well does Sofia know Igor? Are you sure he isn't a crook?"

"I didn't ask her that," Nina admitted.

"How much money did he ask you to pay him for placing you as a governess?"

"He didn't ask for money. He just asked me to sign a contract for a year."

"It seems incredible! I just can't believe it!" Daria said.

"So, should I accept it?"

"I can't decide for you. It's too a big step in your life. You must decide yourself."

"You always refuse to advise me! I just asked for your advice, and you hide in the bushes. How would you decide, if you were to get such an offer?" asked Nina.

Daria thought about it. Her eyes swept the cramped staff room, the dusty shelves along the walls, and the old bald teacher of physics, Ivan Stepanovich, bent over children's notebooks at the far end of the table. How she, too, wanted to escape from this dismal environment! Just think, America! It would be a completely different world, like a dream! The country of Milk and Honey! How much she would love the opportunity to look at that world with her own eyes!

"I would sign!" Daria said frankly.

"You wouldn't be scared?" asked Nina

"I would first agree, and then I would start to panic."

"Why would you be afraid?" Nina insisted.

"I would be afraid that this Igor is a crook and a cheater; that he isn't what he claims to be."

"I thought that you'd be afraid of America! There are, in fact, problems in the capitalistic government there, the brutal exploitation of workers, and rampant crime. There is much to be feared in an unfamiliar world!"

"I would be afraid of your Igor much more," Daria said.

"He's a very handsome, intelligent young man. Why would you be afraid of him?"

"He could cheat us!"

"No, he is not a cheater. He wouldn't disappoint us. You should be afraid of America, not scared of Igor. You know, I could ask him if he needs more people. I could recommend you to him if you want," Nina said.

"Oh, my friend, how happy I would be to go to America!" admitted Daria. "I believe that I would succeed there and maybe even meet a young gentleman of the Old Russian nobility and marry him,"

"Don't be stupid!" admonished Nina. "Who would want you without money and a career? No, I just want to earn money and come back home."

"You're right. I'm dreaming too much. I have to finish checking my notebooks. Come and visit me this evening. We can chat about it and I'll bake a cake."

Chapter Two

Daria was excited about her conversation with Nina, and she finally decided to contact Igor herself. She phoned him, and he made an appointment with her in the lobby of the hotel Moscow.

Daria had to admit that Igor really was very handsome. In fact, his deep voice and impeccable manners were so impressive that Daria invited the young man to her communal apartment, where they drank a bottle of wine and ate some cake. Igor told Daria that wealthy Americans commissioned him to find tutors for their children. Daria was so carried away by his story that she ignored the fact that Igor didn't define this work by the term 'governess,' but used the word 'caregiver' instead.

Without hesitation, she agreed to all the terms of the contract. In 1989, a trip to the United States for a simple schoolteacher seemed like an incredible adventure. Such an opportunity, she thought, could only happen once in a lifetime, and she just couldn't let it pass her by. Let Nina worry and ponder; Daria was confident in her abilities. She was ready for any adventure in order to escape from the dreary life in her communal apartment and the endless long trips on the subway and on the bus. She was tired of the hundreds of school essays she had to check on a daily basis, seven days a week. She was ready to take a chance on this new adventure in order to get away from her uneventful life.

Nina was amazed at how quickly Daria had accepted Igor's offer. Didn't America scare her? It was the 'Country of the Yellow Devil!' Gangsters lured victims in every corner! There was banditry! There was capitalism! Soviet propaganda insisted that capitalism was the worst and the scariest thing that could happen to mankind.

"If you are afraid of wolves, don't go into the woods!" Daria explained. "A lot of people live there and nothing happens to them!"

Thanks to Daria's influence, Nina finally overcame her fear and decided to go too. She concluded that there were probably a lot of people as excited about the opportunity as Daria, and that if she didn't go now she might miss the opportunity to get work in America! Here, one could work for a century and not earn good money. She hurried to tell Igor that she had decided to go to America.

Nevertheless, making the decision certainly worried Daria. She understood that she was drastically changing her life and would be facing many unknowns. Yes, her life was hard now, but she was used to that hardship. On the other hand, what was waiting for her in America? She was afraid that the requirements for being a governess might be so high that her abilities would not satisfy the rich noble Americans. What would happen in that case? Would she immediately be sent back to Moscow? She had grown up in a village – did she know all the rules of etiquette? Or in which hand people should hold a fork? Or how to curtsy? She couldn't know what they had in their rules! How well did she have to know English? Would her knowledge be enough? She felt the urgency to practice the English irregular verbs!

The excitement of those days consumed the two women and they became inseparable. Now Nina spent all her spare time in Daria's room. Following Daria's lead, Nina constantly studied her English lessons, and she searched the library for books on the rules of etiquette.

Time passed quickly. In less than three months, with the help of Igor, all the necessary travel papers had been organized and their suitcases were packed. The two women didn't even have time to learn all their etiquette lessons before it came time to leave.

As they flew to the German airport in Frankfurt, Daria remembered that she had forgotten to write to her mother in the village about her decision to work in America.

"Don't worry," said Nina. "I didn't tell my relatives either. They are out there in the boonies, confident that only enemies live abroad. They would feel that we had betrayed our homeland by agreeing to work in the United States."

"I don't worry about that; my mom would understand."

"I am worried!" replied Nina. "My relatives would convict me. Of course, if I came back with money, they would forgive me, but if I didn't earn good money, they would remember and torment me the rest of my life for my hasty decision."

"I firmly intend to conquer America! I don't care what they think of me at home," stated Daria.

"Don't be so sure! Sooner or later, we will have to come back home," said Nina.

"I am not sure of that. If I like it there, I may stay forever."

"In America?" Nina asked with fear in her voice.

"Yes, in America. I would live there just like other immigrants from Russia!"

"Not me! I will return home for sure. I want to build a family. Soon I will be thirty and it will time to get married."

At the airport in Los Angeles, as they kept up with the flow of passengers, Nina and Daria noticed a fat, bald man with a placard. Two women had already approached him. Making sure that the placard had the name of the firm that brought them to America written on it, they joined the other women. After the group was joined by one more woman, the bald man said:

"Okay, so now you're all assembled. My name is David and I'll drive you to the office. There you can wait for the arrival of your employers."

David directed them to an old minivan and he drove them to the company office, which was half an hour away. The office was located in the back room of a store, and the old desk and chairs were the only furniture in the room.

"It doesn't look like a real office," Daria whispered to Nina, "and it smells of rotten vegetables." David asked the women to sit in the chairs along the wall and wait until their employers arrived. Daria sat down in the chair near the desk. She looked over the dirty room and thought that the firm must not be rich if they had such a shabby office. From the open door, she heard the loud voices of the store customers. They spoke in Russian. It seemed to her that she hadn't left Moscow.

It wasn't long before a full-figured, tall woman came to get Daria. The farewell happened so quickly that Daria didn't have time to find out where Nina was going. They barely had time to hug each other and say goodbye.

"My name is Tamara," said Daria's new mistress, in perfect Russian. "Let's go. I'm in a hurry."

Daria, bent under the weight of her suitcase, followed Tamara to a bright red car parked in the store parking lot. Tamara opened the trunk and Daria heaved her suitcase inside.

As Daria sat in the car, she examined Tamara and didn't find anything special about her. She was an ordinary woman with black hair that was graying, a hooked nose, and no particular signs of noble birth. Daria didn't know what status the woman held in America, but she seemed like an average woman, like the women who rode on the Moscow subway every day.

It took about twenty minutes before the car stopped at a three-story building. "Here we are," said Tamara. "My father lives on the second floor."

With difficulty, Daria lifted her suitcase out of the trunk, and she took the elevator with Tamara to the second floor of the building. The long corridor was covered with a thin carpet. Tamara stopped at one of the doors and rang the bell. An elderly woman opened the door and gestured them into the apartment.

"Come in," Tamara invited Daria. "I hope David from the agency explained your responsibilities."

"No. Nobody told me anything," replied Daria.

"My father had a stroke," explained Tamara. "Half of his body is paralyzed and my mother really can't handle caring for him by herself. I work, and my husband also works, so we need a nurse that can do the job of caring for my father. You'll be living with my parents in the apartment and taking care of my father. I don't live here; we have a house of our own, but we'll bring food and everything that you need."

Daria was shocked. "You need a nurse?" she queried.

"Of course, a nurse. Didn't David tell you?"

"I was told that I was going to work as a governess for children."

"Well, your agency wasn't telling the truth! Everyone knows that they bring domestic workers from Russia. Here, such workers are very expensive, and they are asking just eleven hundred dollars a month for the Russian workers."

"Why do they want workers with a higher education?" asked the disappointed Daria.

"I don't know about that. They are crooks and they deceive people. What have they promised to pay you a month?"

"Eight hundred dollars."

"That, I think, they will pay you. Come, I'll show you my father."

Daria was now beginning to realize what had happened. She had been brought here as a nursemaid, not as a teacher! Yes, the agency preferred people with higher education, but it wasn't because they needed teachers! Daria understood that she had made a big mistake! How could she have been so entrusting? What could she do now? Eight hundred dollars a month was certainly good pay, but what a humiliation it was to become a nursemaid! What have I done? I was so stupid!

Lying in a hospital bed, the old man with extinct eyes stared at Daria, who, in turn, looked at the helpless old man with fear and disgust. His face was pale, he had the aquiline nose as of his daughter, and his head of thin gray hair was scattered all over the pillow. He was breathing heavily.

"Dad, this is Daria. She will live with you and care for you," Tamara explained.

The old man tried hard to smile, but it came out as a grimace, and it was clear that even that effort took all his energy. He lisped through his teeth: "Excuse me."

"Hello, I came here from Russia," she said awkwardly, not knowing what else to say.

Daria was completely shocked at her new position. In Moscow, she had been suspicious of Igor's persuasive words, but a desire to change her life, and also her inherent opportunism, had overcome her suspicions. She had convinced herself that it would be an exciting adventure. How could she have known that Igor was recruiting domestic workers? There in Moscow, that possibility had never occurred to her.

But now she was a caretaker, a servant! What a humiliating position! Suddenly Daria could hardly keep back her tears.

Tamara didn't seem to notice Daria's feelings as she handed her a piece of note paper. "Here's my phone number," she said. "Call me if something happens."

As Tamara left, the old woman said to Daria, "He needs to use the urinal bottle. Help me with this and to change his diaper."

At first, Daria didn't understand what the old woman wanted from her; then glancing around the room, she saw the urinal bottle.

Daria picked it up and wanted to give it to the old man, but the old man was stricken with paralysis and couldn't use the bottle without help. She had to quickly learn a most unpleasant side of caring for such patients. With disgust, she unzipped the old man and placed the urinal bottle between his legs, but this was useless because the old man was wearing a diaper. She had to lift him and then try to pull out the smelly soaked diaper from underneath him.

After she succeeded in removing the diaper, she had to direct his penis into the throat of the urinal bottle. From inexperience and embarrassment, Daria coped badly with the task.

Then she had to put on a new diaper, which meant it was again necessary to lift the old man up and stretch the fresh diaper underneath him. His wife tried to help Daria with this task, but it was difficult for her.

As Daria raised the old man, she noticed the red bedsores on his back and buttocks. With horror, she realized that she could be accused of giving poor care to the elderly.

"Did you notice the bedsores on his back?" she asked the old woman.

"Yes, I saw them, but what could I do? I couldn't turn him. Now we'll try to fix the problem."

"How long has he suffered with those?" asked Daria.

"He returned from the hospital three months ago. They send a nurse once a week, and she told me something, but she said it in English and I didn't understand what she was saying. I think that some ointment should be used."

Daria called Tamara. She wanted Tamara to know about the bedsores to make sure she wasn't blamed for the problem in the future.

Tamara pounced on her. "Who told you to use the urinal bottle? We put him in a diaper so he wouldn't have to use a bottle."

"But your father asked for a bottle," Daria replied.

"It doesn't matter what he asked for! I explained to him long ago that he can pee in the diaper."

"Actually I'm not calling about the use of the urinal," said Daria. "I'm very concerned that he has bedsores. Also, I wouldn't want to be accused of causing him bedsores by not caring for him properly."

"Of course, he has pressure sores! He can't move! Tomorrow the nurse will come and she will take care of the bedsores with some ointments. But *you* don't need to handle it. Just wait for the nurse! Tomorrow morning wash him with a damp towel so he'll be clean for the arrival of the nurse."

The old woman invited Daria into the living room for lunch.

"My name is Anna Zalmovna," she said. "You can call me Anna. I was told that in the United States they don't use the middle name."

"My name is Daria Ivanovna," Daria said. "You can call me Dasha."

"Here, Dasha, you can see that my life is ending in such bad circumstances. My whole life is cut at the root! At the very root! All my support collapsed! How can I live without Fima?"

She said this in a trembling voice and the tears rolled down her cheeks. Daria looked at Anna, knowing that she couldn't complain to that unfortunate old lady about the deception that had led her to this house.

How she would love to express to someone the pain in her heart. She had been hoping for a decent job as an educator and now she had a nursemaid's duties at the house of a paralyzed old man.

"Your husband will recover," were the only words that Daria could squeeze out.

"I don't believe it. He is getting worse and worse. Look how he suffers! What will happen to me? I couldn't bear his death!"

"Don't bury him in advance! He will recover."

"No, he won't recover. I feel it!"

"I hope he will heal!" insisted Daria.

Anna didn't answer her. They sat in silence, each retreating into their dark thoughts. Then from the bedroom, there was a rattle. Anna hurried into the bedroom and Daria followed. The old man was unconscious; his face was even paler and his lips were blue. Every breath was accompanied by loud snoring, and then the snores became less frequent. Both women froze in horror.

Daria was first to react:

"We must call an ambulance!"

"Call 911. Hurry!" replied Anna.

Daria grabbed the phone.

"Help! Please help!" She screamed into the phone.

Daria didn't remember what she was asked or how she answered. In spite of her poor knowledge of

English and her frayed emotions, the English words must have somehow jumped from her memory.

God himself knows how they determined the address, but after five minutes, firemen had arrived and were crowding into the bedroom. They found that the old man had stopped breathing, and that there was nothing left to do except acknowledge his death.

Anna was in shock. Daria led her out of the bedroom and sat her down on the couch. The firefighters asked some questions, but neither Daria nor Anna could understand them. Daria called Tamara and asked her to come quickly. The firefighters didn't wait for her arrival; instead, they invited an official from the building office and he answered their questions. By the time Tamara arrived at the apartment, no one was there except Anna, Daria and the corpse of the old man.

Chapter Three

"*What do I* do with you?" David said, looking at Daria. "I found you such a good place, and you didn't last even one day! This Tamara immediately got rid of you. She could have kept you for one night, the bitch! So where do I put you? I have some clients, but they live in San Francisco. I'll contact them."

He dialed the number and said into the phone that he had a woman who was ready to go to San Francisco. Daria heard him demand extra pay for something. Then he turned to Daria:

"You'll have to spend the night in a hotel. Your new position will be in San Francisco, and it is impossible to send you there today."

Daria was so shocked by the change of circumstances that she didn't even ask what kind of work was waiting for her in San Francisco; but in her heart, she cherished the hope that this time she would get lucky and the next job would be more decent.

They drove up to the two-story hotel and parked the car. David took her to the lobby and told her to wait. Daria looked around and decided from the furnishings that it was a cheap hotel. She worried that she would be settled in a room with multiple beds, and that she would have all night to fear for her safety, and for the safety of her suitcase, her only possessions. She remembered the articles in Soviet newspapers about the predominance of robbers and rapists in America. Such people possibly inhabited this low-cost hotel. Daria was suddenly terrified; she was hounded with a sense of despair and the realization that she had made a fatal mistake.

David took her to her room, informing her that she must be prepared to travel to the airport at eight in the morning, and that she should meet him in the lobby at ten minutes before eight. Then he gave her ten dollars and told her to go down the street to the local deli to buy a sandwich for herself.

She asked him if it was dangerous to leave her suitcase in the room.

This question made him laugh. "This area is perfectly safe, and besides, you have your key to lock your door," he said reassuringly.

After David was gone, Daria cautiously looked around the room in which she would be spending the night. The room was clean and there was only one bed in the room. In one corner stood a table with a large TV, and there was a desk for writing.

There was also a door, and when she carefully opened it, there was a large bathroom. This surprised her. The room was equipped with a bathtub, a toilet and a washbasin. On one shelf were neatly folded towels; and on a shelf beside the sink, she found a tiny piece of soap carefully wrapped in shiny paper. Near the soap were two small bottles. "Are these for me?" she wondered aloud.

In contrast to the shabby lobby, the room looked decent, much better than Daria had anticipated, and it appeared to be designed for only one tenant. After the shock she had experienced in the apartment of Tamara's parents, she hadn't expected such a nice room.

Daria locked her apartment door, walked through the hotel lobby, and stepped outside. A breeze ruffled the leaves of the trees, and it was surprisingly warm for the middle of winter. Daria easily found the delicatessen. With some difficulty choosing the right words, she ordered the cheapest sandwich so as to save a bit of the money she had been given. At her hotel room she locked her door and quickly ate the sandwich. Then she decided to have a bath in her private bathroom.

While relaxing in the warm water and breathing a huge sigh of relief that she had escaped her first 'assignment,' Daria once more pondered her situation. She had mistakenly believed that a job as a teacher waited for her in America. The sweet words of

Igor had been a lie. But was her goal just to earn some money and return back to the communal apartment? No, she had come to achieve success in America, not just to earn some money.

Greedy David had settled her in a cheap hotel, but it turned out that America was so rich, that even a cheap hotel room was fabulous – a private room, a big bathtub, fresh sheets and towels.

She wanted to believe that she had made the right choice when she decided to change her life and go to work in America. She had left the little village, the communal apartment, and the miserable salary of a secondary school teacher. She believed in her abilities to fight for a better life. She would build a decent future in this rich country. She would conquer America, even if she had to work as a maid.

Daria knew there was no possibility of career development for her in the Soviet Union. The people in the country lived very poorly, and she didn't see a possibility for improvement because people with initiative were prohibited from getting ahead and were often prosecuted. In these circumstances, there was no hope for her personal success. Realizing this, she didn't want to return to Moscow.

In Russia, Daria had greeted perestroika with enthusiasm, with the hope that, at last, people would be able to achieve material wellbeing. Modernization allowed for more free speech, but it didn't bring any improvement in living conditions. Daria's personal life had been miserable, and her girlish dreams of family and children seemed extremely unlikely to materialize. Where, in the Soviet Union, could she meet the prince who would sincerely love her and take her away to his castle? Always busy at work, Daria didn't have time for any kind of personal life; and working in the team of women teachers was not going to lead to meeting a prince. In those circumstances it was impossible to achieve her dream.

Basking in the warm water, she decided that she had done the right thing by adopting the suggestion of Igor. Was it even possible to compare this room in a cheap American hotel to the conditions of hotels of the Soviet Union?

"America is indeed a rich country and you have to be a fool to pass up the chance to conquer it!" she told herself aloud.

When Daria reluctantly left the bathtub, she took a fluffy towel, dried herself, and enjoyed looking at herself in the mirror at the sink. What looked back at her was a beautiful woman with elastic breasts, a small waist and wide hips. Daria was pleased with herself. This woman was ready to conquer new territory! With enthusiasm and hope, she jumped into the wide bed and quickly fell asleep.

Chapter Four

At the airport in San Francisco, Daria easily found a young woman who was holding a homemade poster with an inscription in Russian: 'Daria Ivanovna.' The woman was wearing shabby jeans and a blue t-shirt with a 'San Francisco' on the front.

"Congratulations on your arrival in San Francisco!" the woman exclaimed enthusiastically. "My name is Tanya."

"I am Daria Ivanovna," answered Daria.

Tanya picked up Daria's heavy suitcase and asked her to follow her to the garage where the car was parked. Following Tanya, Daria decided that this young girl was likely working for her future masters as a maid. Her reasoning was based on the comparison between Tamara and Tanya. Tamara hadn't touched Daria's suitcase, whereas Tanya, without a word, had grabbed the handle of the heavy suitcase. In addition, Tanya was dressed too modestly; definitely she belonged to the working class.

Tanya sat in the driver's seat and offered Daria a place beside her. As the car moved, Daria wondered which way they might be traveling, but nothing she could see was questioning. The wide road was full of cars, for some reason, all of them rushing in the same direction. Fifteen minutes later, Tanya turned off the highway and crossed the overpass just to get on to a different highway. A few minutes later, the car drove onto a bridge.

"We are crossing the bay," explained Tanya.

Watching Tanya, Darya thought that, perhaps this time her future owners were very rich if they had sent this lovely girl to pick her up. Maybe this time Daria would be lucky, and her future employers really would be from wealthy former nobility.

It took almost an hour of driving, but the high-rise buildings of San Francisco were never seen. They passed by some of the mountains, changed highways a couple of times, and finally stopped the car near a two-story house. Daria got out, looked around and decided that she was somewhere in the countryside. It was not like the Russian hinterland, where there were only dirt roads overgrown with weeds and lined with shabby houses. An asphalt road led to a number of houses that stood apart from each other. Neatly manicured green lawns and big trees surrounded the houses. The house where they stopped had a lawn that was neatly mowed and trimmed. The concrete driveway led to the broad door of the garage.

"Welcome to the city of Pleasanton!" said Tanya.

The front door led into a large hall. Daria scanned the room and noted the high ceiling, shiny parquet floors, oil paintings, a beautiful chandelier, and a staircase leading to the upstairs rooms. The house made a deep impression on her. "Manor house," Daria thought.

A young man with a beard met the women. He took the suitcase from Tanya's hands, and offered Daria to climb the stairs to the second floor. He guided Daria to a room with a bed and bedside table. The floor of the room was covered with a thick, soft carpet in which Daria's legs were comfortably buried.

"This is your room." The young man said. "Here is a closet for you to use. Arrange your things in it. My name is Solomon. Now your pupils are in the home of their mother. I will bring them here after an hour, and introduce you."

"What about master of a house. Where is he?" Daria asked.

"We are the masters, Tanya and I."

"You are?" Daria's eyes widened.

"Yes, we are. We needed a nanny, and my parents helped us to contact your firm."

Daria couldn't believe that these two young people were her new masters. They were dressed too modestly and behaved too simply to be the mysterious wealthy Americans that she had imagined while riding from the airport.

"I was told that I would work as governess," said Daria.

"Who has a governess nowadays?" Solomon asked, surprised. "Our children are still very small. Our daughter is three years old and our little boy is only fifteen months. Tanya goes to work next month, so we need somebody to take care of the children when Tanya is at work – a nanny."

"I am a teacher of Russian language," Daria said.

"I told David from your agency about our needs. We didn't know that they were bringing educated people. We need a nanny to look after the children and help Tanya with household chores. Let us hope that the children will love you."

Tanya from downstairs called loudly: "Daria Ivanovna, Solomon, please come to eat."

During the meal, Tanya and Solomon spoke with Daria in a friendly manner, as they were not her masters, but friends. Daria learned that her bosses were not from the Russian nobility, but the children of ordinary Soviet Jews who had left Russia fifteen years ago. Solomon joked about an agency that fooled people, offering them prestigious work, when in reality, this was not the case. He was very sympathetic.

Solomon left house to bring kids later in the evening. Tanya suggested that Daria should rest and not to wait for Solomon to return.

Daria spun in a comfortable bed an hour now, and realized her dream still hadn't come true. She was hurt and offended to know that she, a respected teacher, had so easily believed Igor. The most annoying thing was that she had had convinced herself that she was going to work for a noble family. She remembered that in the nineteenth century, many educated women were hired by a rich noble family to work as a governess. For a girl from a poor family, it was a prestigious job, especially if she worked for a family from the very top of society. But times had changed, and princes, barons and wealthy nobles that had many servants and other domestic workers no longer existed. Nowadays, perhaps working as a 'governess' was a combination of parenting and household chores. She thought sadly about how much reality differed from her dream. But fortunately working for Tanya and Solomon was much better than taking care of a paralyzed old man.

The sun had hardly broken through the window when Daria opened her eyes. She looked at the clock. It was still very early. She quickly and quietly dressed, trying not to disturb anyone, and then went to the first floor. Glancing at the big room, she was awestruck by the new furniture, the clean walls with lots of pictures, and a wide glass door that led outside. She walked to the door. In the distance, she could see the mountains, covered with dark green. The door led to a veranda, which was furnished with white plastic furniture. She opened the door and stepped out onto the porch. The beauty astounded her.

The yard was small, but cozy. Along the fence, unknown bushes in bloom were emitting a light fragrance. Behind the bushes were pyramids of evergreen cypress. Colorful flowers surrounded a small pond in the corner of the courtyard. Daria walked down to the pond and saw that fish swam in it. She counted three fish: two were red, and one was white with red spots. She admired the beautiful fish, and while watching them she calmed down. Her experiences were on the backburner, giving way to peace of mind. If she was destined to perform the humiliating job of a house-keeper/nanny, then at least it was in this rich beautiful house.

A charming little girl appeared on the veranda. Seeing Daria, the frightened little girl stopped, looking curiously at the stranger.

Daria smiled graciously and asked in Russian: "What's your name?"

"Susana," answered the girl shyly. "Are you our new nanny?"

"Yes, my name is Dasha," said Daria smiling.

Daria's kind smile reassured the girl. She looked carefully at Daria and concluded: "Beautiful nanny Dasha."

Chapter Five

Three months passed. Daria was feeling much more relaxed and she had become friends with her masters. Tanya was friendly, cheerful, and generally behaved modestly. When she came home from work, she didn't give Daria directions; she cared for her children and did a variety of chores. Solomon also didn't hesitate to do housework and he helped the women to care for the home and the garden.

They treated Daria respectfully as if she was a member of the family. Daria felt comfortable with them and she truly loved the two children. Tanya had named her children the American way: the boy was called Michael, and the girl, Susana. Michael had just started to talk and he needed relentless supervision. Susana took her position as the older sister seriously, and she diligently helped Daria.

The children loved their nanny, and Daria was happy to take care of them. Clutching Michael to her chest, she dreamed that someday she would hold her own baby. Michael would stroke her face with his soft, plump little hands, and it made her feel blissful. "Oh, what a fool I am!" she thought. "Someone else's

Jewish child is as dear to me as my own. Why did I decide to move to America? Now my dream of having my own baby is impossible!"

Soberly assessing the situation in which she found herself, Daria came to the conclusion that she needed to swallow her pride, and that she needed to use the present situation to her advantage. She reminded herself that she had come to conquer America. The agency was paying her as promised, and working with the two young children was enjoyable. Nothing terrible had happened. Instead of working for an ancient noble family, she was living with wealthy Jews. How had they gotten rich so quickly?

In the evenings, when the children went to bed, Tanya and Solomon and Daria usually gathered in the dining room to drink tea and discuss the affairs of the day. The discussions were candid, and soon Daria learned almost everything about her young hosts. Solomon worked in a large company as a programmer, and Tanya worked in another company as a financial broker.

The word 'broker' in the Soviet Union meant a criminal businessman from the shadow economy. So when Tanya had said proudly that she worked as a broker, Daria had looked up in surprise.

"A broker is an adviser on investments in the securities market," explained Tanya. "I use data from our research analysts to advise my clients about the most favorable deals. They appreciate the advice, so it's pleasant work and I enjoy it."

"Are the earnings good from such work?" asked Daria.

"Yes, I make a good living. Everything depends on the number of shares that my clients buy or sell. I have a lot of rich clients and some of them are very active."

"To get to the position of a broker, what must one learn?" asked Daria

"I have a master's degree in finance. I graduated from the University of California in Berkeley."

"Is it a good university?"

"One of the best."

On one such evening, Tanya asked Daria if she was planning to go back to Moscow when the contract with the company was finished, or would she like to stay in America?

"Is there such a possibility?" asked Daria with caution and hope.

"By law, it isn't possible, but as far as I know, these laws are not strictly enforced. Immigration agencies don't have enough personnel to check each and every immigrant, and many government agencies deliberately conceal data regarding illegal immigrants. So we have a huge number of illegal immigrants, especially from Mexico."

"How do they live? Who employs them and is it legal to employee them?"

"Actually, the law doesn't allow the hiring of illegal immigrants, but the rules are often broken or bypassed. For example, the agriculture industry needs seasonal workers, but working in the fields is hard and very poorly paid, so the Americans typically don't take these jobs. That means the farmers are forced to hire illegal immigrants; and it's so important for the US economy that even Immigration Services pretends that they don't know about the illegal seasonal workers on the farms."

"I don't want to work on a farm," said Daria. "In my youth, I ran away from the farm to the city, and I never wanted to go back to the village."

"I don't suggest that you become a seasonal worker. You have a higher education and you can find a better job than weeding cabbage."

"I am an educator, a teacher of Russian language and literature. Is there a need for this specialty in America?"

"Maybe in some schools that teach Russian as a foreign language, but not many schools offer Russian. I don't think it would be easy to find a job as a teacher of the Russian Language – maybe impossible. You need to be retrained for a job where there is a demand."

"Retrained? In my thirties?"

"The thirties isn't old age. Here people are learning in their fifties or sixties. You have to begin with improving your English language skills. We have Las Positas College here in the valley, where they teach English to people for whom English is a second language. We need to get you into these classes. Solomon, what do you know about this college?"

"To tell you the truth, I know nothing about this college," Solomon said. "But I can easily find out about it. If Daria wants to study there, we will do everything possible to help her. I can even take on the responsibility of driving her to class."

"That isn't very convenient. Daria, have you ever driven a car?" asked Tanya.

"I have a driver's license, but I have never owned a car, so I have very little driving experience."

"We will solve the transportation problem somehow," said Tanya.

Once the couple discussed a wish to get rich. Daria was very surprised when she learned that Tanya and Solomon didn't consider themselves rich. They claimed that they were not rich in spite of owning an expensive house and being able to afford to pay more than a thousand dollars a month for a nanny! Daria couldn't believe it, but Tanya explained to her that they were not poor, but on the other hand they couldn't claim to be rich. They belonged to the middle class. Yes, they lived in a nice house, but the house had been bought on credit, for thirty years. Until the house was paid off, it belonged to the bank. If they, for whatever reason, couldn't make their mortgage payments, the bank would take the house away from them. Also, the new car that Solomon had bought had to be paid for in installments, on a monthly basis, to another bank. However, they earned enough to pay for all their expenses. The whole wealth of Tanya and her husband was founded on good earnings and not on inherited money.

Listening to Tanya, Daria realized that in America anyone who worked hard at a good job could achieve a lot. She must also find a way to achieve this possibility. The desire to succeed in life had always been Daria's goal. She, of course, would like to achieve the simple female happiness of being married and having children, but she didn't believe that happiness would include living in a tent. She knew only too well how financial difficulties could bring strife and suffering into a family's life. Her older sister had loved a handsome young man and she had married him. Their love lasted long enough to have two children and four years of marriage; but then her husband escaped from the poverty-stricken life of the collective farmer to well-paid work in Siberia as a construction worker, leaving behind his wife and lovely children in the village. No, poverty would not bring happiness! It was necessary to achieve material success, and then begin to think of building a family.

Solomon kept his promise and enrolled Daria in a special class to learn English at the local college. Classes for adults began at seven o'clock in the evening and they were only two hours long.

Tanya came home from work before six. She packed the kids into their car seats, and the three of them drove Daria to class. To get to the college took no more than five minutes. The problem was that the children's bedtime fell during Daria's class time, and Tanya couldn't leave the children alone in the house to pick up Daria. Therefore, they had to rely on Solomon to drive Daria home after class. Solomon rarely came home before eight in the evening as he often had to stay late at work. Daria realized how inconvenient it was for Tanya and Solomon to have to drive her to and from the college, and she decided to figure out how to walk home. After studying the route on a map, Darya informed Tanya one evening that she was going to return from the college on foot.

Tanya began to dissuade her: "Do you know the names of our streets, Dasha? Each street in our city is called a road, or a drive. Why is it so? Because people drive along those streets; they don't walk. Streets are designed for cars, not pedestrians. You don't find pedestrians walking along our streets, especially at night; and some streets don't have normal sidewalks, only narrow paths."

"I'll find a way! I cannot expect Solomon to pick me up every night." Daria said.

Their disagreement changed one evening when Solomon called to say that he had to stay late for a meeting and wouldn't be able pick up Daria from college on time. Reluctantly, Tanya agreed to permit Daria to walk home from college that evening. Pleasanton was a quiet town, no crime, nothing to fear; but the walk was long and would take about forty minutes.

Daria left college after the lectures. Some students hurried to their cars and some to the bus that connected the college with the subway station. The bus left only once in the evening, and those who used it had to hasten in order not to miss it. For Daria, the bus route wasn't on her way home, so she walked briskly towards home on the concrete walkway along the road. Sometimes there were lights that dimly lit her way. She figured that she needed to walk alone for two miles, and she walked steadily.

Suddenly, out of the dark bushes that separated the walkway from the road, a large black dog appeared, and she stopped in fright at the sudden appearance of the animal, at which point the dog came up to her and sniffed, happily wagging its tail.

Daria breathed a sigh of relief and continued her walk. The dog followed her, so they walked together for a few blocks. Then as suddenly as it had appeared, the dog disappeared into the roadside bushes. She worried that, like the dog suddenly appearing out of the dark, thick bushes, a person, taking advantage of the darkness and seclusion, could attack her. The attacker wouldn't know that she didn't have even one dollar in her bag! Terrified, she quickened her pace, trying to get past the dark spaces between the streetlights as quickly as possible.

Fortunately, in the distance, she saw a light shining from a small shopping area, and as she came closer, its brightly lit shop windows beckoned invitingly. When she got to the area, she immediately calmed down. There was a large grocery store; it was open, and people were coming out pushing carts full of groceries. Daria crossed over to a lighted area of the street and continued walking. She crossed a wide street with traffic lights, walked down this street, and then once again turned onto to a dark side street. Finally, she reached Tanya and Donovan's home.

"I was very worried!" exclaimed Tanya, hugging Daria.

"I myself experienced fear, but as you can see, I am home unharmed." Daria said smiling. She was happy that the long walk was over.

"Solomon isn't home yet. He called to say that the meeting was over, but it takes him about forty minutes to drive home from his office. Sit down, dear Dasha. I'll treat you to something."

At the college, Daria was successful in her English studies. She refreshed her knowledge of English grammar, and by studying every day, she quickly increased her vocabulary. Solomon spoke to her exclusively in English and insisted that she answer him in English. Therefore, Daria was able to practice what she was learning at the college. In her spare time, she watched TV shows, and soon she was pleased to follow some of the developments in the soap operas that frequented the TV screen.

Then Tanya kindly bought a TV set for Daria's bedroom so she could watch programs at night. Daria looked forward to her favorite programs, and every day she understood better what the characters on the shows were talking about. She was very happy with the friendly environment that she lived in, and she was grateful. She loved the kids and enjoyed taking care of them; and they had become very attached to her.

Sometimes on weekends, the parents of the young couple would come to visit. Solomon's parents treated Daria in a friendly manner, but as an outsider. On the other hand, Tanya's mother, Elizabeth

Isaakovna, treated Daria as if she were her second daughter.

"May I call you Dasha?" Elizabeth asked when they first met.

"That is what my mother called me," said Daria.

"You can call me Lisa. Here in America nobody uses last names."

"Mom, how can we help Daria with solving her immigration issues?" Tanya asked. "Daria would like to stay in the United States at the end of her contract."

"There is a Mexican man working at our company. He said something about the fact that one can pay money to acquire papers in Los Angeles. These are actually false documents, but many firms accept them as real. For starters, Daria may want take advantage of this. I will ask the man to tell me more about it."

"Isn't it dangerous, Mom?" asked Tanya.

"Yes, it's dangerous, but living *without* papers is dangerous too. The worst thing that could happen is that Daria would be sent back to Moscow."

"They wouldn't immediately send her back; they would first put her in prison."

"The same punishment awaits any illegal immigrant, even if he doesn't have false documents."

"My visa ends soon," Daria chimed in. "In several months I'll be living here illegally."

"It's true," Tanya agreed.

"We have nothing to worry about." Elizabeth intervened decisively. "Nobody will come to check whether you are living legally in America. In America, there is no registration or district police officer to check on you. In general, immigrants are almost never checked. Millions of people live for years in the United States illegally. It is certainly wrong, but America attracts people like a magnet. Not only are there Mexican seasonal workers; there are also quite a number of other people among the illegal immigrants. And there are offices of full of lawyers who specialize in legal assistance to illegal immigrants."

"What can help?" asked Daria.

"An application for political asylum, or something similar. Consider that your case could take a long time, and it could be delayed. Until your case comes up in an immigration office, you can live and even work in the country. And some illegals are waiting for a time when Congress will announce *amnesty* for illegal immigrants. Typically, the amnesty would cover those who have lived in the country for several years."

"How often does Congress declare this amnesty?" Daria asked.

"Over the past twenty years, I think it has happened twice. No one knows when the next time will be, or whether it will be or not be. But people hope."

"It's like waiting for weather at sea. Not very reliable," Tanya explained.

"There is another option," said Elizabeth, smiling. A beautiful woman can marry a US citizen. In your case, it is possible."

"To arrange a false marriage one needs to have lots of money. Who would agree to a false marriage without money?" said Darya sadly.

"Why a false marriage? You are a young and very pretty woman. It wouldn't be difficult to meet a young man who will marry you."

The conversation ended, but this conversation left a deep impression on Daria's heart. She thought about a possible job. What decent job was she ready for? Was it possible to find a job as a teacher of Russian language and literature? If it was possible, could she find such job? Tanya said that nurses were needed, but Daria didn't want to become a nurse. She dreamed about an interesting job as a broker. Tanya was right in saying that in order to find a good, interesting job, she needed to be retrained. Retrained to what job? How could she organize this retraining? These thoughts occupied her mind all day, every day.

Chapter Six

Elizabeth called after several days. She said that she had arranged a meeting with the Mexican man from their firm. She told Daria that the meeting was scheduled for Saturday, at a Mexican restaurant in San Jose. She explained to Daria that there was no need to dress up, as was customary in Russia. Being dressed casually would be fine for this restaurant.

The evening after Elizabeth called, Mr. John Packard, Daria's college teacher, asked her to stay after class. He was interested in her life story. He told her that he was writing an academic paper in which he was studying the typical participants in his 'English as a Second Language' Courses. All the participants were immigrants and each of them had an interesting history. He was studying their situations and trying to make generalizations that could be used in his doctoral dissertation in Sociology.

Daria didn't know what to do. She was afraid to refuse, but it would be dangerous to admit to Mr. Packard that she would soon be an illegal immigrant. Who knows – maybe he would rush to report this to the immigration office? On the other hand, it was uncomfortable for her to refuse. What to do? Of course, it would be interesting to get acquainted with this American; he was an interesting and ambitious young man. She even allowed herself the luxury of thinking there could even the possibility that she might seduce him, and legalization in the country would be provided! She blushed with embarrassment as the thought crossed her mind.

In her position, it wasn't easy to get acquainted with Americans. How to proceed? Should she take the chance? Yes, she should! Such a chance she would be foolish to miss.

"I'm ready to tell you my story, but not now," she said.

"Could we meet somewhere where nobody will interfere and we could talk quietly?" he replied.

"Where?"

"There are two places to choose from: my office at the college, or at my house in an informal setting," said Mr. Packard.

"I think it would be better at your house," said Daria.

"I have Sunday evening free. Could you spend Sunday evening with me?"

"Yes, I can; I'm free on Sunday. The problem is I don't have transportation. Could you pick me up?"

"Agreed. Give me your address."

Daria didn't dare to tell Tanya about John's invitation. In her heart, she was troubled. She was worried that perhaps she was asking for trouble. Could she trust this handsome American? Could she open her soul to him? She decided to discuss with Elizabeth how she should behave with Mr. Packard. Tanya's mother was a serious woman and she would understand Daria's dilemma.

On Saturday, on their way to meet with the Mexican immigrant, Daria began to talk about Mr. Packard. She wanted Elizabeth's advice on what to reveal to him and what she should hide. Should she talk to him about her legal status?

Elizabeth listened to Daria attentively. They were traveling south, on a wide highway, towards the mysterious city of San Jose.

"I wouldn't worry. In American colleges, most teachers hold left-wing views. If he is writing a paper on immigrants, he probably relates to immigrants with compassion. By the way, Dasha, is he an interesting young man?"

"He is bearded and long-haired, but nice looking," replied Daria, smiling.

"Nice looking? This is good! Go ahead, Dasha! The proletariat has nothing to lose but their chains!"

"You think so?"

"Don't rush to open up; he probably will not ask about your legal status. He will be interested in why people immigrate. Tell him about your childhood, about studying at the university, about the attitude towards the policy of the Soviet Union. His type likes to be the brains of slaughtered ideology. They happily support immigration as the result of a political decision, not an expression of mercantile interests."

"Thank you for your advice."

"Listen Dasha, don't use perfume; Americans don't like the pungent smell. And before your visit, be sure to take a shower. Americans cannot stand the smell of sweat. And smile."

"I will try."

"Dress modestly. Do you have tight jeans?"

"Yes, I do."

"That is great. You have a lovely body and jeans would make you look very attractive."

At the Mexican restaurant, a stocky dark man met them. He smiled at Elizabeth and invited them to his table.

"My name is Jose," said the Mexican man. "Lisa told me that you need documents. My cousin in Los Angeles knows people who can help. It will cost $300 for a driver's license and $150 for a social security number. They cannot sell them any cheaper. If it suits you, I can arrange the deal."

"And how reliable are these documents? Where can I use them?" asked Daria.

"I can honestly say that you should not show the documents to the police. They would immediately check their validity on the computer. But these documents can be used at almost any company for a job application. Companies don't check the authenticity of the documents."

"I need to think about it," said Daria carefully.

"Thank you for the information," Elizabeth said to Jose. "My friend needs to seriously think about it. It's a big risk. If she decides to buy the documents, I'll let you know, and we'll figure out how to implement it."

On the way home, Daria was tormented by the question of how to understand Elizabeth's desire to help her. She broke down and asked her about it.

"I am a good judge of people, and I liked you from the first day I met you," said Elizabeth. I'm sure you're a good person, and it is my duty to help a good person in need. I came to the United States with a young daughter, and strangers – good people – helped us. Now it is my time to help. You won't have an easy road ahead, but remember my prophecy: you will achieve happiness. The main thing is to do everything possible on the road to happiness, and do it with all your strength. Seek, and you will achieve all."

"I don't know how I can thank you enough for your concern."

"I'm not doing this for gratitude. The best reward for me is to watch your success," replied Elizabeth.

Daria couldn't believe it. In real life, back in Moscow, no one helped you just because you were a good person. The rule of thumb was: "I will help you if you pay me." Daria thought that Elizabeth must need something. She didn't believe that such unselfishness was possible.

Chapter Seven

All day Sunday, Daria was apprehensive. It was difficult to decide what to wear; her wardrobe didn't offer her much to choose from. She had brought just one decent dress from Russia and a pantsuit of fine wool, and both pieces of attire no longer fit correctly. She pulled on her shabby jeans and an embroidered silk blouse, and asked Tanya if it was okay to go that way. Tanya looked her over and approved her outfit, saying that it was very sexy.

Tanya's remark confused Daria. "What do you mean 'sexy'? Do you mean immodest?"

"No, it doesn't mean immodest! Sexy is very attractive."

"I would like to look attractive and modest at the same time," said Daria.

"Don't worry. You have achieved this."

The doorbell interrupted their conversation. With a sinking heart, Daria opened the door. John stood in the doorway. He was dressed very simply, apparently to emphasize the informal nature of the meeting. Daria welcomed the thought that Elizabeth had been right in recommending that she dress modestly. It would have been challenging to be dressed in an elegant pantsuit. She didn't want to make a bad impression on John.

John's apartment was located in a large residential complex just one mile from Tanya's house. He parked and they walked up a path to the nearest house, climbing the stairs to the second floor. The front door opened into a small living room, and John indicated that Daria should sit in the leather chair near the fireplace. Daria looked around the room with curiosity. A round floor lamp with a large shade lit the freshly painted white walls that were decorated with colorful photos in simple wooden frames. A computer desk, located in the corner of the room, was lit with a simple lamp. A large sofa and a coffee table took over most of the living room, making the room seem even smaller.

"Tea or coffee?" John asked.

"I'd prefer sweet coffee."

"I'll make it now. I've prepared a questionnaire for the interview. Is it okay if I ask you the questions while I make the coffee?"

Daria was afraid of embarrassing questions, but she didn't dare to refuse. She stiffened and said, "Okay. I'll try to answer."

"Why are you so nervous? Relax. I'm not examining you. This is meant to be a friendly conversation. Is it hard for you to answer in English? Forgive me, but I don't speak Russian, so it is necessary to speak in English. The exercises will be useful to you, and I will try to speak slowly. Don't worry ... you are perfectly capable of answering the questions, and I'll help you."

"Go ahead," said Daria.

"First question: Where were you born and where did you spend your childhood?"

"I was born in the village of Oaks in the Ryazan region of Russia. The village was part of a large collective farm called 'Way of Ilich.' Do you know of such a farm?"

John nodded.

"My mother was a teacher. She taught in the lower grades of the local school, and my father worked as a truck driver for a collective farm. I spent all my childhood in the same village and I was the second child in the family. When I was three, my father had a bad accident and my mother buried him in the village cemetery. I don't remember him, but my mother and I often visited his grave. So I grew up without a father in the village."

"You see? You did an excellent job with the story," John said approvingly. "More coffee?"

"No thanks."

"Tell me about the living conditions in your village.

"The village was like all villages in rural Russia – not better, not worse. The water in the well was located about a hundred yards from our home. The toilet was outdoors, in the yard. There was no shower. Electricity didn't appear until I was ten years old, and the electricity for the houses was supplied only at nighttime. People used it only for lighting."

"What about working conditions?"

"All the villagers belonged to the collective farm. I had to work in the fields when I was fifteen years old. It was a lot of work, and I earned nothing."

"If they don't pay people for the work, why do people work?"

"The peasants have no choice. Farmers, like slaves, cannot leave the farm. To work in the city requires registration as a city dweller on one's passport, and this is very difficult to obtain. The boys can hardly wait for army enrollment, so as to be able to leave the village. I chose to study in the university in order to leave the village."

Daria didn't explain to John what kind of tricks she had to use to convert her student registration to register as an inhabitant of Moscow. He wouldn't understand how important it was for her residence to be in Moscow. Here in America, because there was no registration, it was easy to change cities. How to explain the Russian registration problem to an American man?

"I enrolled at a university in Moscow, and I remained there to work after graduation."

"What kind of work did you do?"

"I taught children in school."

"Which class?"

"I taught Russian language and literature in high school."

The doorbell interrupted their conversation. John opened the door. A tall, broad-shouldered young man stood at the door in a sports shirt and jeans torn at the knees.

"Hi John! I'm sorry that I didn't warn you," the man said. "Are you busy?"

"I invited my Russian student for an interview. I'm using her interview for my doctoral work."

"If I'm quiet, can I be present and listen?"

"If she doesn't mind and you promise not to interrupt us."

John turned to Daria and looked at her questioningly. Daria smiled tightly and said,

"I don't mind."

In her heart, Daria wasn't pleased that she had to answer in front of *two* Americans. The presence of this observer confused and frightened her. Her English wasn't good enough to allow her to feel at ease. However, she felt that John regarded this visitor with great respect, and it would be uncomfortable to deny the request of the stranger.

John was a little frazzled. He had planned a frank

interview, which might not be possible in the presence of an outside observer. John's work required meeting with immigrants from different countries. His task was to investigate the root causes of immigration and the difference in the motives of representatives from different countries. To understand this, it was necessary to achieve the full confidence of the person being interviewed. Having a visitor could interfere with the sense of trust.

Meanwhile, the visitor addressed Daria: "My name is Tom. I'll sit quietly and try not to interfere with your conversation. I felt lonely at home."

Daria looked at Tom with curiosity, assessing the young man. He was handsome and he had a clean face and kind eyes. He looked young. Daria thought that Tom was too young to have any interest in her. She must make an impression on John, not on Tom. Looking at John, she said quietly, "We should continue. What is the next question you are interested in?"

"We stopped at the fact that you taught children the Russian language in high school. Was this work interesting for you?"

"Very interesting. I like kids and I like Russian literature. The one thing I didn't like was that the program required teaching in a highly politicized manner."

"What do you mean?"

"I had to give the students an analysis of Russian literature from the viewpoint of communist ideology. I love literature, but I don't like ideology. Teaching in the school is formalized to such an extent, that even such an interesting subject as literature becomes dry and nauseating to explore."

The conversation lasted a long time. John tried to strictly follow his questionnaire. The questionnaire didn't have direct questions about immigration status, and John didn't ask. By the end of the evening, Daria was exhausted. It was very difficult to respond in English to the questions, making sure that the answers were impressive, and making sure to divert John away from the discussion of her status. To Daria's delight, she was successful at the task. She didn't know how she had managed to remember her English and find the right words to answer each question, but she had.

John offered her a cup of coffee before driving her home. Tom, who had been silent all this time, asked for a bottle of beer instead of coffee. Daria declined beer. While drinking his beer, Tom looked at Daria with curiosity. He was definitely interested in the young Russian woman. After drinks, Tom offered to take Daria home. John was clearly delighted with the proposal, and Daria concluded that she had failed in charming her teacher.

"Where do you live?" Tom asked, as they got into his car. Daria told him the address.

"That's an expensive area," remarked Tom.

"I live with relatives," lied Daria.

"What do you do in your free time?"

"I study English."

"You speak well enough. My grandfather lived in America for seventy years, and he couldn't speak so well."

"From what country did he come to America?" Daria dared to ask.

"From Russia. He lived in the small town of Lida, near Minsk."

"Maybe he came from Poland. Prior to the Second World War, Lida was a Polish city."

"He came to America from Russia in 1903," said Tom.

"If it was 1903, then you are right. It was Russia before the First World War."

"I would like to meet with you some more, but not at John's house," said Tom. "Do you like the theater?"

"I do."

"I have two tickets to the show 'Cats' for next Sunday. Would you go with me?"

"I am somewhat embarrassed because I just don't know if I'll be free next Sunday. If you give me your phone number, I'll call you on Friday."

"Good. I'll wait for your call."

Daria appreciated Tom's invitation, but she was embarrassed about his age. Tom looked very young, so Daria felt that he wouldn't be interested in her as a woman. Meetings with him could be a waste of time. The boy's grandfather was from Russia, so he had become interested in her; and he had been interested immediately, as soon as he met her. Could his interest be serious? She doubted it. On the other hand, she very much wanted to see the show. It could be a rare chance to go to the theater in the USA. She could work for Tanya the whole year and not have the opportunity to go to the theater. She decided to accept Tom's offer. What was the risk?

Chapter Eight

Daria's plan to visit the theater with Tom did not materialize. Tanya was going to be busy on Sunday and she asked Daria to stay with the children. She promised she would compensate by giving Daria time off her regular duties.

Daria called Tom and apologized that she couldn't go with him to the theater. As she hung up, she thought sadly that her acquaintance with the young American was probably over.

Suddenly Elizabeth called. She said that she had a plan that could be interesting for Daria, and she promised to come on Saturday to discuss the plan.

Elizabeth's plan seemed frivolous to Daria. Elizabeth offered to introduce her to a distant cousin, whose mother wanted to marry him off. Daria replied by saying that she didn't believe that an adult son would listen to his mother. The establishment of family was very delicate, and Daria believed that the intervention of the mother usually hindered more than it helped. Elizabeth responded to this argument by saying that Daria's beauty would convince the young man, and that the delicate pressure from his mother would help expedite his decision.

"Tell me about this cousin. Maybe he is sick or ugly?"

"What are you thinking, Dasha! I wouldn't be telling you about him if he were a freak! He is tall, handsome, and very sensible. I'm sure you would like him, and he earns a very good living. The trouble is that he's passionate about his work, and nothing other than work interests him. So he doesn't have time for courting girls. He needs somebody to bring him his bride on a silver platter."

"It's very strange, but rather intriguing. I have little faith in the success of this venture. However, in my position, I must take advantage of any opportunity."

"That's good. I phoned my cousin and agreed that this weekend we will meet her son in Los Angeles."

Elizabeth fulfilled her promise. She made the appointment and then drove Daria to Los Angeles. She had called her older cousin in Los Angeles and they would be able to stay with her. The trip was long and tiring. Leaving Pleasanton at six in the morning, they arrived at Elizabeth's cousin's house in the afternoon. She lived in a four-storey house built especially for elderly people who were in public care. Elizabeth tried to open the door to the lobby, but it wouldn't open. The door was locked. What to do?

"Are you visiting somebody?" asked an old woman sitting on a bench near the house. She spoke in Russian.

"Yes, Mirra Novozhilova, in apartment 2A."

"It is necessary to pick up the phone and dial her code."

"I don't know her code," Elizabeth said.

"You press the X on the phone, and the display will show the name and the code. Press X until you reach the surname Novozhilova."

With the old woman's help, they found Mirra's apartment code and were able to get through to Elizabeth's cousin. There was a nasty lingering alarm and then Elizabeth opened the door to the lobby. They went up to the second floor, where Mirra was waiting for them.

"Welcome, my dear," said a short, fat woman dressed in a flannelette dressing gown. She gave Daria a friendly smile and Daria immediately felt comfortable. She and Elizabeth followed the old woman into her apartment where a table with plates of food was waiting for them.

"I've been waiting for you for two hours already," said Mirra. Unfortunately, the soup has gotten cold, so we must reheat it."

"It was a long drive, so we only just arrived," Elizabeth explained.

The old woman turned to Daria. "Sweetheart, they said that you are from Moscow. Tell me about Moscow; I miss it so much. Where did you live there, darling?"

They spent all evening chatting with the old lady. Mirra was delighted at the opportunity to talk with Elizabeth and Daria. Having immigrated in her old age and not having mastered the English language, Mirra's ability to communicate with people was very limited.

Her children and grandchildren were always busy with their own lives and didn't have time to pay attention to the lonely grandmother. The ability to talk the whole evening seemed like a holiday to her, and because of this, Daria heard, in detail, Mirra's entire biography. She also learned about her children and her close and distant relatives. By late evening, Darla knew more about Mirra's family than she did about her own family.

Daria asked Mirra if she knew of people with the surname Mogilevich, explaining that her friend from Russia was working for them. But Mirra didn't know them.

In the morning, Daria was surprised to find Mirra smartly dressed and wearing bright lipstick. And she was wearing beautiful gold jewelry. The old lady explained that she was going to visit her cousin

Harry, who lived in the Russian-speaking part of Los Angeles – North Hollywood. Harry was the father of the young man that Elizabeth wanted to introduce to Daria. Elizabeth called Harry and said that she would join Mirra on her visit to help Dora, Harry's wife. She asked Daria to wait in Mirra's apartment until they were ready, and somebody would pick her up. Daria didn't understand what she meant by 'ready.' It turned out that Elizabeth's departure had been designed for Daria to meet Michael, Dora and Harry's son, who would be sent to drive her. Elizabeth wanted the young people to get acquainted without spectators.

Soon, Misha came for Daria. She didn't expect that he would come for her and she was confused when he knocked.

"Who do you want?" Daria asked fearfully.

"I was sent for you. Are you Daria Ivanovna?"

"I am," confirmed Daria.

"All right. I was asked to pick you up. My name is Misha."

On the way to his parents' apartment, Misha entertained Daria with jokes of Odessa. The jokes flew out of him like water spilling from a bucket. Daria had never laughed so heartily in her life as she did in those fifteen minutes as Michael drove her to his father's apartment.

Daria was greeted as a dear guest in Harry's house. Harry's wife, Dora, asked her to sit down and said, "I am very glad to have you with us in Los Angeles. Are you from Moscow?"

"Yes, I'm from Moscow."

"You are a teacher?"

Yes, I am a teacher," confirmed Daria. "I see that you know everything about me."

"Not really. You could tell us a lot about yourself. We are relatives of Lisa, but we are not from Moscow. We are from Odessa. In Odessa, teachers are greatly respected. Were you born in Moscow?"

"No. I am from the Russian hinterland. My mother works as a teacher in the village."

"You are from the village, but from an educated family. I thought so. Your mother works as a teacher, and what about your father?"

"My father was a truck driver."

"Why 'was'?"

"He passed away when I was three years old."

"I'm sorry, I didn't know this." Dora was embarrassed.

"It's okay. I'm used to it."

"Lisa told me that you came to work here and would like to stay in America ... forever."

"I myself am not so sure. On the one hand, I would like to live like a human being, as Tanya lives.

On the other hand, it is a foreign country for me. I don't know anybody here, whereas there, in the Soviet Union, I have my mother and my sister," Daria said frankly.

"But that is not really a problem. If you arrange to obtain U.S. citizenship, you will be able to help your mother and sister. You can even bring your mother here, and in her old age she wouldn't be lacking for anything."

"It's impossible. I am here illegally and there is no chance to obtain legal status. As soon as my contract is over, I have to go back to Moscow."

"I like you. Come, I'll show you our apartment." Dora said to Daria, smiling.

Dora guided Daria into a bedroom and closed the door. She sat on the bed and offered Daria a chair.

"I don't want Misha to hear our conversation, so I'll talk quietly. How do you like my Misha? He is a very good boy, very talented. You know, he got the highest scores in school, he graduated from the University, and then he got a great job! But I cannot be happy! Judge for yourself: the guy is thirty-five years old, and he has no family, no woman to spend time with. I want grandchildren! He is so interesting, and such a fine man, so why doesn't he have a girl? He knows how to make people laugh! And he's handsome too, don't you think?"

"He really is a very interesting man," Daria said.

"So, if you like him, do you agree to marry him?"

"What? How can I do that?"

"With my help. He is an American citizen, and by marrying him, you would be able to gradually get US citizenship. You would be able to help your mother and sister. Do you like Misha?"

Daria was confused. She didn't know what to say! She hadn't even had time to get to know Misha, let alone be ready to link her life with him! She badly needed marriage, but she had thought it would be a false marriage, not a real one with a strange man. But Dora wanted her to agree to a real marriage. Daria wanted to marry a man, but one she would fall in love with, not one she had just met. She dreamed of a man who would love her too. She was ashamed to admit, even to herself, that at her age she still was dreaming of a magical prince from a fairytale.

"Dear Dora! I have just met Misha for the first time. I didn't even know him an hour ago.

I'm really looking for a marriage with an American to get the right to stay and work, but I thought about a false marriage with a natural born American, not an immigrant. Why would an immigrant need to marry me?"

"Honey, I understand everything. It's the best case for you. It is difficult to seduce Misha for marriage. We must start from afar. I need to convince Misha that it is necessary to rescue a beautiful woman by entering into a marriage of convenience. He is kind. He would go for this. After the marriage, you would gradually become close to him and turn the relationship into a real marriage. I think that such a plan seems the most realistic."

"What if he wouldn't want to go along with your plan?"

"It is my duty to convince him that his civic duty is to assist you in obtaining US citizenship," Dora insisted.

"I don't think I want use deception to lure your Misha. Opening up to him would be better. What if he has somebody and hasn't told you?"

"He doesn't have anyone. Do you agree with my plan?" Dora asked nervously.

"I don't know what to think."

"You go home to Tanya and think about my plan. Misha is an eligible bachelor. You will not find this anywhere else. He would be earned good earner. He would be dedicated and caring. You will love him when you become more familiar with him, I am sure."

Daria understood that Dora's proposal was meant to be very tempting. What she couldn't understand was why Dora would want her as her daughter-in-law.

In the living room, Daria asked Dora if she knew people by the name of Mogilevich. Dora didn't know them, but she asked Misha to find the phone number of Mogilevich in the phone book.

Less than ten minutes later, Daria was talking with Nina on the phone. Nina complained to her about the difficult conditions of her work. She was taking care of an old lady, sick with Alzheimer's disease. It was a tough and thankless job. Nina wanted to end her contract in a hurry, and she missed Moscow. Daria didn't have a chance to meet with her girlfriend as Nina was tied to the old woman, and Elizabeth was in a hurry to get home.

Chapter Nine

On the way back from Los Angeles, Elizabeth asked Daria about her impression of Misha.

"He is funny, and good looking, but did I receive enough knowledge about him in ten minutes to build a family? I am very worried. For legalization in America, it would be good to get married, but in order to have a good life, I would like to fall in love."

"Learn more about Misha. He's a good guy."

"Is he divorced?"

"No. He never married. The impression is that the girls have never been interested him."

"Maybe he's gay?"

"What does that mean?"

"That he doesn't love girls, only boys."

"I don't know," Elizabeth hurried to answer. "He's never had a relationship with anybody as far as I know. He's just choosy, or perhaps has never been interested in finding a bride."

"Where is the confidence that he will like me?"

"There is no certainty. But there is definitely a chance. You are good, intelligent and kind. And what a beauty!"

"You flatter me." Daria was embarrassed.

"The children think the world of you too. When I talked to Tanya, she told me that her Michael has been asking about you non-stop since we left. Children have a good feel for people; they can't be fooled."

"I love the children. Michael is a little angel."

"And Tanya said that an American guy called to speak to you. His name was Tom."

"That is the young man I met at my instructor's house. He wanted to date me.

However, I doubt that he can be seriously interested in me. He looks very young."

"Is Misha better?"

"Misha, at least, is older than me. Tom is very young. Young and good looking," Daria said frankly.

At Tanya's house, Elizabeth asked Daria once more to think about Dora's proposal.

Tom turned out to be a persistent man. He called a few more times. Daria was embarrassed when Tanya handed her the phone each time he called. She didn't know what to say to him. Would be it proper if she dated this guy while thinking about Misha? Tanya nudged Daria to go for it.

Tom invited Daria to go with him on Saturday to Calistoga, a small resort town north of San Francisco. Such a proposal put Daria in a difficult position.

Could she be away from home for that amount of time? Tanya might need her help.

"Tom invited me to Calistoga. What should I say?" she asked Tanya.

"You must agree. You can't refuse. Misha hasn't offered you anything yet. I wouldn't count on Misha. What if he won't accept Dora's plan? You can't refuse Tom. Go with him!" insisted Tanya.

Influenced by Tanya, Daria agreed on a trip to Calistoga with Tom on Saturday, and Tom promised to call her with details. After she hung up the phone, Daria thought about her life. The flow of her life was changing from a wide, quiet river into a fast mountain stream. It was scary and exciting. What would happen when she reached the waterfall? Would she break her neck on the stones? She realized that she loved the risk! Wasn't it the love of adventure that had brought her to America?

Chapter Ten

Tom arrived early in the morning. Daria barely had time to eat breakfast before his arrival. When Daria was already sitting in the car, Tanya asked her whether she had taken a swimsuit.

"What for?" Daria asked, surprised.

"What will you do in Calistoga without a swimsuit? How are you going to bathe in the mineral pool?"

"Don't worry! We will buy one on our way," said Tom.

"I don't have swimwear and no money either," said Darya sadly.

"Don't worry, I have a credit card." Tom pulled out a small rectangular plastic card. "We will survive."

The car rolled down the road, leaving Tanya on the doorstep of her house. Daria sat in the front seat and watched the scenery on their way to the unknown resort town of Calistoga, which was apparently rich in mineral springs. Suddenly, their pace slowed and the road was flooded with cars moving at a snail's pace.

"It's the bridge," explained Tom. "Once we pass over the bridge, the traffic will be faster. Travel over the bridge requires a fee, and people move slowly at the pay booths. Did you eat breakfast?"

"Yes, I had breakfast."

"I haven't had anything to eat. Let's stop at the winery and have lunch."

"Why not, if you are hungry," replied Daria. She didn't understand the part about the winery.

She thought that a winery was just for producing and selling wine. It turned out that the winery had a big shop that sold not only wine, but also a variety of snacks. Tom ordered two sandwiches and a bottle of mineral water. They sat on a bench at the entrance to the store and enjoyed the scent of the flowering shrubs that surrounded them.

Daria was surprised. She had already eaten breakfast; where did she get such an appetite?

A phone call interrupted their breakfast. Tom talked on his cell phone for a long time about a particular program. Listening to his quick, firm answers, Daria had the thought that her young admirer was not a simple man; he seemed to be bright and assured.

Finishing lunch, they continued on their way, and an hour later, the road brought them to the center of a small town. Tom turned off the road and parked at the door of a small shop.

"You can choose a swimsuit," he said. They have a very large choice here." Tom summoned Daria to the racks where a variety of colorful swimwear was on display.

"What type of swimsuit do you want? A two-piece or a one-piece?"

"I want an inexpensive and modest swimsuit," said Daria.

"All the suits here are the same price. Choose the one you like the best."

Daria removed a black and white bathing suit from its hanger and examined it. The bottom of the two-piece was tailored as a triangle, designed to barely cover the immodest places. She was terrified of the swimsuit and quickly hung it back on the hanger.

Tom watched with curiosity and appreciation of her quest. He enjoyed watching her reaction.

With difficulty, she finally found a more modest swimsuit.

"Let's buy a bathrobe too," said Tom. It's convenient when you walk to the pool."

"No. It's a lot of money," replied Daria.

"Don't worry about that. I won't use money; I'll use a credit card." Tom smiled.

"That doesn't exempt you from having to pay," insisted Daria. "I have no extra money, I and won't have spare money to ever pay you back for the robe. See, the robe costs ninety-nine dollars. With that much money, people in Moscow live for two months."

"We're not in Moscow, and I'm not saying that you have to pay. I'm buying."

"But that is inconvenient."

"Don't worry. I can afford it."

Daria didn't know what to say. She was scared. What would he want for this? Did he think that he had bought her? She was afraid that with this trip she might fall into a moral abyss, and she didn't know what to do.

Tom felt her mood.

"Don't worry," he said quietly. "You won't always be so poor. I believe that you will achieve great success in this life. You can pay me back when you earn your first million."

Daria smiled sadly. She dreamed about being able to have a decent independent life. It would be nice to live like Tanya and Solomon.

"I am an educator!" Daria said. "In Moscow, I taught Russian language and literature to children in school. There is no need for people with my experience here in the U.S., and I don't have skills or training in other types of work. So there is no chance of me making a million dollars."

"You should learn something that is needed in America. I recommend that you take some courses at the university. You need to first pass the language exam for foreigners, and after that you can enroll in a class at the university."

"Can I? No. Studies at the university are expensive."

"Not cheap, but you could maybe get a scholarship. Many universities help poor students. They can give you a job."

"What kind of job?"

"For example, the workshops with students studying Russian, or some other work. You can definitely get help."

Finally, they reached Calistoga. At the traffic lights, they turned right onto the main street, and after one block, they turned into a cross street and parked the car.

"We've arrived." Tom gave Daria his hand.

Registration took no more than ten minutes. Tom took the key and led Daria to the room.

The room was a large dark room in which the furniture consisted of a large double bed, a table with chairs, and a TV. Heavy curtains sealed the room from outsiders. Observing the room, Daria thought with horror: "Cheap room for lovemaking. How should I react if Tom insists on sex? What to do?" Daria regretted that she had agreed to make this trip.

With dread, she anticipated aggressive action from Tom. But Tom didn't do what she was so afraid of. He pulled out his bathrobe and swimming trunks from his backpack. "I'll go in the bathroom to change," he said.

Tom slid into the bathroom and Daria prepared her new swimsuit and bathrobe. She looked at herself in the mirror. She moved closer to the bathroom door and listened. The peaceful sound of running water was coming through the closed door. She turned on the TV. There was a soap opera, and the transmission quality was not very good. Her worries died down a bit when suddenly the bathroom door opened and Tom appeared in the room, wrapped in his white bathrobe.

"It's a great shower," he said. "I recommend it."

Daria grabbed her swimsuit and bathrobe and went into the bathroom, where she first of all locked the bathroom door. Then she undressed, found a clean towel, and turned on the shower. The hot water felt wonderful but she couldn't take too long. When she put on the swimsuit, it was much more revealing than she had hoped, especially from behind. But she couldn't do anything about it. She came out of the bathroom wrapped in the fluffy bathrobe.

"Okay, let's go to the pool," said Tom.

Near the pool, they found a white plastic chair, threw their robes on it, and walked into the pool. The water was warm.

Tom swam slowly and Daria followed him. For her, it was a great pleasure to swim in the warm pool.

"Do you like it here?" Tom asked.

"Very much."

"I was sure you would enjoy it."

Hanging on to the edge of the pool, they lightly swung their legs in the water and watched the other visitors. Another young couple, embracing each other, sat at the opposite edge of the pool. Some noisy teenagers were diving in the center. Suddenly Daria heard people speaking Russian behind her. Daria looked back and saw an elderly couple slowly swimming across the pool and talking.

"I was told that immigrants from Russia have chosen the Calistoga area as their place of residence. Some say that the Russians breathed life into this backwater," Tom said.

"Why?"

"They believe in the healing properties of the local water."

"That is why you brought me here?"

"Partly, but also because I have Russian roots and I believe in this water."

"You have Russian roots?" Daria asked.

"I told you that my maternal grandfather was from Russia. He was from a small town named Lida. Have you heard of it?"

"It is in Belarus."

"No, my mother said that it is in Russia. Her grandfather was a rabbi there. He fled from the

Bolsheviks to Poland. I am not sure if he ran from the Bolsheviks or from the pogroms."

"Are you Jewish?" Daria asked.

"No, I belong to a Baptist church. My paternal grandfather was a Catholic from Ireland, but he switched to a Baptist church in the beginning of the century because he wanted to marry my grandmother. Her father was a Baptist preacher."

"It is very complicated. It is something very difficult to understand," Daria said frankly.

"America has always been a melting pot, and I'm a mixture of many peoples and religions. I'm proud of that."

"The USA is a strange country."

"You will love our America when you know it better."

Daria thought that most likely she wouldn't have time to get to know America. The contract with the company was ending soon. Would she get an agreement with Misha? It was difficult to believe that this would happen. It looked as if Tom liked her, but she couldn't imagine that this good-looking young man would think about her seriously. He might want to have a short love affair with her...be her lover. All guys were up for that. But it didn't mean that he would want to offer a long-term relationship. She watched Tom swimming in the warm pool. He really was a very attractive, very nice young man. What a pity that he was so young.

No, to solve her problem, she needed to use all of her charms to attract Misha. Besides, his mother was nice, and she was willing to help. The fact that she wasn't thinking about a real romantic relationship suddenly dawned on her. She urgently needed to solve her immigration problem. She must now think of marriage as a business relationship, and not a romantic one. She had no hope for that kind of love.

They returned to the room, where Tom suggested that Daria use the bathroom first, asking her to quickly change because he was very hungry. Then he changed and joined Daria. There was no hint of an invitation to share the bed with him, and Daria was grateful that Tom had behaved decently and been respectful of her. They returned the room key and left the hotel.

As the car picked up speed, Daria was surprised to realize that she felt a tiny bit disappointed. Yes, she had been terribly afraid that Tom would force himself upon her, but at the same time, he was such an attractive guy! It had been so long since she had been so close to a good-looking young man! Daria couldn't understand herself. Why was she so attracted to him? He was too young and she should not encourage his advances in any way.

After driving for about an hour, Tom stopped at a restaurant and they went inside. He handed her the menu and when she looked at the names of the dishes, she was embarrassed that she didn't know what any of the dishes were. She had to ask Tom to order for her the same thing that he had ordered for himself. Tom smiled and ordered steak. When the waiter brought the steak, Daria noticed that the meat was only half ready. Daria ate cautiously, watching as Tom ate the pink meat with great pleasure.

When they returned to Daria's house in the evening, Tom stopped the car at the edge of the sidewalk and said, "See you soon."

He moved his face close to hers; and without thinking about what she was doing, Daria bent toward him and their lips met in a kiss. Tom breathed heavily.

"May I call you?" he asked.

"Yes," whispered Daria.

Chapter Eleven

Daria couldn't stop thinking of her discussion with Tom about the possibility of attending an American university. She had always loved to learn; it was in her blood. Obtaining a specialty that would provide both financial security and a meaningful life in the future became an obsessive dream.

Tanya was an example of the possibility of having a good job. Strangely, Daria no longer associated the word "broker" with something illegal. Tanya worked as a broker and she was very proud of it.

Daria thought of what kind of work she would like to do. She decided against being a teacher. It was interesting work, but even in America, it was a low-paying job. It didn't make sense to live from paycheck to paycheck in the USA; she wanted to earn a good salary and be able to buy a nice house like Tanya's.

"Tanya, what specialty in America is the most popular?" Daria asked.

"The biggest demand is for computer programmers."

"It doesn't suit me. I'm not that crazy about computers. What else?"

"Marketing. But you need to be proficient in the English language."

"That I could master. What else?"

"Finance."

"That suits me more. Could I enroll in the university in this specialty?"

"Do you have a transcript of your marks from your university?"

"Yes, I brought my diploma and transcript with me."

"In that case, you can take a Masters degree in economics."

"It can't be! Are you not mistaken?" asked Daria.

"I know for sure," replied Tanya. "You must first pass the language exam, and if you do, you'll be able to enroll at the university."

Daria almost forgot about her trip to Los Angeles and about the request of Elisabeth's cousin Dora. She was only thinking about the possibility of enrolling in the university, being busy with housework, and caring for the kids. Her dreams were about how to free herself and live independently. They were impossible dreams for illegal immigrants.

However, Dora hadn't forgotten her plans. Three weeks after Daria returned from Los Angeles, Dora called her to inform her that Michael was coming to San Francisco for a conference. Dora asked Daria if Michael could call her and arrange a rendezvous with her.

Daria checked with Tanya and then agreed on a date. A day later, Misha called. He asked Tanya how to get to Pleasanton from San Francisco. She encouraged him to take the subway, which was called BART, and promised to meet him at the BART station in Pleasanton.

Misha was boisterous, noisy, and full of jokes. First thing, he picked up little

Michael, put him on his shoulders, and ran with him around the house. Michael was delighted. Looking at them, Daria smiled and thought that life was becoming very interesting …and scary somehow.

I just spent the weekend with one guy and now here comes another, she thought to herself. Is Misha interested in me? He is a handsome guy, funny and intelligent, and he seems to love little kids. It looks like he really needs a wife. Why is he not married, I wonder. Couldn't he find a woman he could love? Is he too picky? Am I any better than other women?

Tanya called them for lunch. Over lunch, Solomon and Misha talked a lot about politics. They discussed the situation in the Soviet Union. Something unusual had happened there. It was hard to believe, but the Supreme Soviet (the parliament)

of the Russian Federation (one of fifteen republics of the Soviet Union) had announced the sovereignty of the Federation, and the former first secretary of the Moscow City Party Committee, Boris Yeltsin, had become the first president of the Federation. This was shown to the world on CNN. It turned out that the main republic of the Soviet Union had escaped the authority of the Party Central Committee and its Politburo. It was a crack in the unity of the Soviet Union, and such an unusual event that it was a wonder to the former Soviet citizens living in the U.S.

Daria listened to the men's conversation and believed that this was the collapse of the Soviet Union. What would happen to the people? How would it be for those who living in this sinking ship? No, there was no hope to wait for better living conditions in the Soviet Union. How wonderful it would be to settle in this country, the U.S.! She looked closely at Misha, listening to his conversation with Solomon. She liked his intelligent and sober reasoning. She liked him more and more. It would be good to marry him.

A phone call broke the conversation and Tanya gave Daria the receiver. It was Tom and he wanted to meet. Daria politely told him that she couldn't meet him today. He asked to call the following Saturday and she told him that it was better on Sunday, which he agreed to.

She had just hung up with Tom when Tanya once again answered the phone and handed her the receiver. This time it was her friend Nina.

"Dasha! I'm returning home!" Nina told her.

"The year has not ended yet!"

"My old lady gave her soul to God, and so I am going back to Moscow. They offered me a new contract, but I refused. I want to go home! I'm tired of being a servant."

"Nina! Wouldn't you like to stay in America?"

"What good is it here? I want to go home. Thankfully they paid me for two months ahead. I'm taking home ten thousand dollars!"

"I definitely want to stay in America," Daria said with conviction.

"Is your work good? I hated my work. It is not for me." Nina insisted.

"When do you fly to Moscow?"

"Tomorrow."

"I wish you a pleasant flight. I will stay! I like it here."

"Be happy!"

Misha stayed in Pleasanton for the night. In the morning, he had to attend a seminar in the heart of San Francisco, a few steps from the subway station. He asked if Daria was willing to go with him on the subway to San Francisco. The seminar would last for only one hour, and then he would be free the whole day. They would be able to walk around the city and in the evening go to the theater. Daria wanted to go, of course, but for such a trip she would have to leave the children. She felt that it was impossible to leave them for a day. Tanya smiled and explained that her mother was already on the way to Pleasanton to give Daria a free day.

Soon Elizabeth arrived. She brought homemade cakes and toys with her for the children. She took Daria aside and explained, "Don't be surprised. Dora asked me to replace you for the day so Misha would be able spend the day with you in San Francisco."

Now everything is in your hands. Seduce him! I hope you will!"

"Aunt Lisa! I'm afraid."

"Why be afraid? He won't bite you; he is very well mannered. But it is necessary to shake things up a little. I know you can do it. Just look at him! Is he not hand-some? And he is a very kind and sympathetic man."

"Yes, he's very good looking," confirmed Daria. "But look at me. What interest can he have in me? I am unsettled and illegal."

"You are a beauty! You're a very good looking, educated, attractive woman," Elisabeth said.

Daria blushed. "Thank you for the compliment. Oh, I'm very nervous!"

Solomon drove Misha and Daria to the BART station. Accepting Misha's invitation to spend the day with him in San Francisco worried Daria. It was not a trip to Calistoga. The date with Tom had been simple because it hadn't imposed any obligations on her. But too many people had their hopes up regarding this trip to San Francisco. Misha's mother, Dora, Aunt Lisa, and Tanya were all counting on Daria's success in enticing Misha. Even Daria herself had high expectations. How should she behave? To what extent to allow courtship on the first date, so as not to seem too anxious or, conversely, too disinterested? She was very worried.

On the train, they stared out the window at the landscape. The train quickly passed the homes and then paralleled the highway in a gorge between two mountains where there were only hillsides covered with dry grass. Misha began to entertain Daria with anecdotes about Odessa. She was not really up for the jokes; it was easy for him to laugh, living carelessly in America, but the jokes weren't really funny for her.

Misha saw that Daria was not enjoying his jokes and that she seemed sad. He too was caught up in an awkward situation, and he had made jokes only to hide his embarrassment regarding this meeting that had been set up for them. He was doing this for his mother, but personally, he did not want this woman.

What for? Marriage would be a shame and a terrible change in the rhythm of his life. His mother had said that she wanted grandchildren, but did she care what *he* wanted?

"Daria Ivanovna, I know that my mother planned all of this. Don't worry. We will have a good time. This I promise you."

"Misha, it would be better if you called me simply Dasha. Calling me by my name and patronymic is uncomfortable."

"I agree. It is necessary to drink some Brüderschaft to reinforce our friendship," Misha said.

"I don't drink; I am afraid of being drunk. Let us assume that we have already shared wine."

Misha nodded. "Well, Dasha, tell me a bit about yourself,"

"What is there to say about me? I am a very simple person – born in the village, graduated from high school and then the Pedagogical Institute. At the Institute, I met a solid, interesting man. He was twenty years older than I was and looked like a reliable partner for life. We dated for a couple of months, and then he made an offer and we got married. But the marriage was short-lived. The first attraction passed and love never came. Besides, I was convinced that under his external solidity was a hidden pettiness and jealousy, and a complete lack of intelligence. I left him.

I worked as a teacher of the Russian language and literature in a high school – with a miserable salary. Then I was offered a job in America and I accepted it. That's my biography."

"So, you came to America to work."

"Frankly, you're right. I hoped to earn some money and then go back."

"In that case, why did you agree to date me?"

"Aunt Lisa persuaded me. The Soviet Union is falling apart, and there are opportunities here, so my plans have changed. In Moscow, I knew very little about America, and my dream was limited to income. Now I have learned more about America, and I have bigger dreams. I love America and I would like to arrange my life here. So I decided to listen to the wise women, Aunt Lisa and your mother, and date you. In addition, you seem nice and you are obviously intelligent. Why refuse to spend time with an interesting person?"

"Thank you for your frankness. You made a mistake once. With this decision, you may be making a mistake again. Are you not afraid? Maybe I'm worse than your ex-husband?"

"I'm very afraid," said Daria frankly. "My problem is that I have no choice. Time is running out for me. The term of my contract ends soon, and I will be sent out of the USA."

"I like your openness. Mom assessed you

immediately, and she is well versed in human nature," said Misha.

The train pulled around to the back of the industrial district. The view from the train's window was industrial buildings, building materials, and a car cemetery.

"America is rich. See how many cars are thrown away," said Daria sadly. "I don't want to return to poverty-stricken Russia. I would like to stay here. It is my dream to enroll in a university, and get a good profession to make a living in America."

Misha nodded. "I understand."

He told another anecdote. Daria was relieved that she had opened up to him and she was very pleased to ride on the train with this kind person. She made an effort to laugh at his jokes.

The day turned out to be a lot of fun. They visited the attractions of the city and rode on the cable car. Misha treated Daria to dinner at a restaurant on the rooftop of a high-rise hotel, where it was possible to see a panoramic view of San Francisco. They settled comfortably at a table by the window.

"I don't want to deceive you, Dasha. You're a very good person and I really like you. My mother insisted that I make you an offer. I realize that it is silly to make a proposal at the request of my mother, but I have decided to follow her advice. Marry me."

"Misha! Are you really making me an offer for a false marriage?!" Daria couldn't believe her ears.

"Yes and no. You are very beautiful and certainly a suitable woman, but our acquaintance is so short that we might need some time for our marriage to be considered as real. The problem is that you don't have the time to wait. So today I am asking you to marry me. We will arrange a marriage and wait together for a future decision. If the marriage isn't acceptable to us, we will divorce."

"But marriage and divorce require a lot of money!" Daria exclaimed.

"You need not think about the financing of this deal!"

"How can I not?"

"The money is not a question. I propose to you seriously; I am not kidding. I offer you my hand – take it as a sincere offer of help."

"If you really like me, I have no choice. I am very pressed for time. But I don't like this situation and I am afraid!"

"Stop being afraid! For you it is a sure ticket and I promise to help you with your legal status. Then if you don't want to continue the marriage, I will divorce you at your first request."

"Why do you want the marriage?" Daria asked.

"I can't deceive you," Misha replied seriously. "I

have a reason to offer you marriage. I could hide my reason now and open up to you after the registration of our marriage, but I don't want to do that. I don't want to start with deceit. The truth is I can't promise you the love that you undoubtedly deserve."

"Why? Don't you like me?"

"It's not because I don't like you! Not at all! You are charming, and I want to treat you with the utmost respect. The problem is with *me*. I'm gay!"

"What!?" exclaimed Daria. "Why?"

"I don't know. For some reason, men attract me, not women. That's just the way it is. I can and I want to be your friend, but I can't become a real husband. You need to carefully think it over and decide whether you want to accept my proposal or not. I really want you to agree. I can make it very, very desirable for you, and I'll certainly help you enroll in a university!"

"I want to study at an American university! It is my absolute dream!"

"I like you more and more! I'll help you to realize your dream! We'll make it happen! Honestly!"

All the way back to Pleasanton, Daria thought about Misha. She wanted so badly to stay in America and the marriage proposal was perfect for this. But why would Misha want this marriage? What should she do? Should she throw herself into this adventure or was it better not to risk it? How to proceed? Misha couldn't love her, but it seemed that she wasn't repugnant to him. It was not clear why he had made her the offer. How long would it last? Would he kick her out on the street when he became tired of her?

Daria was so worried that when Tanya met her, she asked Daria if she was sick. Daria reassured Tanya, saying that if she was sick it was only mentally. She told Tanya that she had received a proposal of marriage from Misha.

Tanya laughed. "Why are you worried? Was this not the purpose of dating him?"

Chapter Twelve

At home in Pleasanton, Daria anxiously pondered the situation. Being a simple Soviet woman, she had the idea that homosexuals were a type of criminal, who for the sake of satisfying their criminal perversion, were willing to do any crime.

She was afraid to make a decision. Misha didn't look like a criminal. Why was such an intelligent-looking man engaged in homosexuality? She didn't dare open up to Tanya. Why slander Misha? She would make the decision herself so that, later, nobody else would be blamed for her errors.

In the end, the proposal to marry Misha deceptively was a dangerous but tempting adventure. Wasn't the trip to America an equally dangerous adventure? She had believed that cheater, Ivan, at his first word. Why be afraid to take risks now? She was scared because she didn't know what unknown danger might lie ahead in this adventure with a gay man. But Misha seemed like a good person, as did his mother. After much agonizing, she decided to accept Misha's offer.

Daria asked Tanya's permission to make a call

to Los Angeles. Tanya didn't object, saying that success was waiting for her.

Misha was delighted by Daria's decision. Now he would work on organization the marriage ceremony. He explained that he would try to make the ceremony and the reception as modest as possible. He didn't want a noisy celebration, but a party would be expected. If there wasn't one, his mother wouldn't understand and the relatives would be offended. It would be best to have the wedding in Las Vegas because many of his relatives would not be prepared to go there. He told Daria that he would try to organize everything as soon as possible.

"I see, Daria, that you are doing well," said Tanya. "It is necessary to look for your replacement. I can't be without help."

"You must call the company," said Daria. "They'll send a replacement from Moscow."

"I don't want to use them. They would again send a woman telling her that someone from the old nobility was looking for a governess. I don't like cheating. I was lucky with you; you love children. But they might send a woman who would take it out on the children, after learning that she had been deceived. I'll put an ad in the Russian newspaper and ask the shopkeepers of the Russian delicatessens to ask their customers who might want to work as a nanny. My friend found a babysitter in three days this way."

"I will miss the children. I'm so attached to them!"

"The children will miss you too! But remember that the door to our house is always open to you, and besides, you are going to be our relative."

"Yes," confirmed Daria, thinking sadly about little Michael and his delicate hands.

Daria had become very attached to the children. Over the past few months, Michael had started to talk, and he had learned to use the potty and even become Susana's partner in games. Susana, for her part, enjoyed being the older sister and the boss.

Daria had been very happy to play with the children, read them stories, and teach them songs and rhymes, and they were also very attached to her. It was sad to leave such engaging children. But life goes on, and nannies cannot stay forever.

A week later, Misha called and said that he would arrive on Sunday to discuss an important issue. Daria waited anxiously, worrying that Misha might have changed his mind.

Misha came in a rented car and invited Daria for lunch at a restaurant. On the way, he explained that he hadn't changed his mind and that he wanted to introduce her to his partner, with whom he had lived for ten years. Near the restaurant, a gray-haired man in a formal dark suit walked toward them. He introduced himself as Ken. To Daria, he seemed old, but he proved to be relaxed and enjoyable. At lunch, he was mostly quiet, listening attentively to the conversation between Daria and Misha.

When Misha and Daria drove back to Tanya's house, Misha told Daria that he was very pleased that Ken seemed to like her.

There was one task that Daria needed to complete before leaving Pleasanton, and that was to pass the language exam for foreigners. Her teacher, John, helped her to sign up for the exam. He considered it to be his duty to help students who wished to continue their education.

The exam was set for a Saturday morning in the city of Oakland. Solomon took Daria to the BART station in Pleasanton and explained how to get from the subway to the school where the examination would take place.

Daria stepped out of the subway car in Oakland and immediately noticed that she was surrounded by a mass of dark-skinned people. Having heard about the high level of crime among African-Americans in Oakland, she was truly afraid and hurried to leave the BART station. In her excitement, she forgot Solomon's directions regarding how to find the school, and she had to ask passers-by. Apprehensively, she asked directions from a black woman on the street, and the woman politely and willingly pointed her in the direction of the school.

At the school, she easily found the room where the examination was provided. The examiner, a black woman, after finding Daria's name on the list, gave her the exam paper. Daria had a relatively easy time answering the exam questions, and with gratitude she thought about Antonina Nikolaevna, her first English teacher. Daria proudly handed her completed exam back to the examiner. She was sure she had answered all the questions correctly.

On the street, a whistle from a car drew her attention. Parked at the edge of the sidewalk was Tom.

"John told me that you were taking the exam today. I've come to drive you to Pleasanton."

"You're embarrassing me. I can use the subway."

"Why use the subway when you can travel by car? Besides, you must be hungry, and I am too. We can go to a restaurant."

"But my mistress will be waiting for me in Pleasanton."

"Please call her and tell her about the delay. Explain to her that you are having lunch in the city."

"Do you think that she would believe me that I have the money to spend to go to a restaurant?"

"In that case tell her the truth that I invited you for lunch."

Daria, with confusion, agreed to have lunch with Tom. She wondered how to tell Tom that she was getting married and that she couldn't date him any longer.

How was she to explain this to him without hurting his feelings? She didn't want to lose such a good friend. She felt she couldn't openly tell him of her desire to succeed in life and to someday be in a similar situation as Tanya, and that to do this, she needed to live in the US legally. She didn't have time to wait for Tom and hope that he would one day be interested in marrying her; she urgently needed to get married right away. Tom was young; he could afford to date and not marry for a long time. He was an American citizen, but for her, it was necessity to fight for citizenship. How could she explain to him why she had consented to a false marriage?

Tom took Daria to an Italian restaurant, and they sat in a corner away from prying eyes. Tom ordered some Italian dishes that were unknown to Daria, and he began to ask her about her exam. She sluggishly responded to his questions, not daring to start the necessary conversation.

"What's wrong? Are you afraid that you did poorly on the exam?" he asked.

"No, I handled the exam just fine, but I am

troubled about our courtship. I decided to enroll in a university in Los Angeles, and most likely, I will soon leave Pleasanton."

"I'll visit you in Los Angeles."

"You shouldn't visit me."

"Why?"

Daria worked up the nerve and blurted out, "Because I'm getting married."

"Did I hear you right? You said that you are going to get married?"

"Yes, that's what I said. A Russian made me an offer, and I agreed."

"Married?" Tom looked at her with the eyes of a beaten dog. He didn't want to take her seriously.

"I would like that we part as friends. Would you agree?" she asked.

"Friends?"

"Of course, friends. There was nothing serious between us. You are clearly a very good man. I would like you to not to be angry with me."

He didn't answer. His mood was black. Since childhood, he had trained himself to restrain his emotions, and he tried not to show Daria that the news hurt him to the core. Wearing a phony smile, he silently finished off his meal. Daria also ate without a word, afraid of saying too much. She wanted to maintain good relations with her handsome admirer.

101

In front of Tanya's house, Daria reached out her hand to Tom. Tom gently shook it and said, "I wish you happiness. I take no offence. I hope that you will have a happy marriage. Farewell."

He looked into Daria's eyes with suffering in his own. Daria, feeling guilty, looked into his eyes. Tom couldn't stand it; he looked away and started the car. Daria stared at his car for a long time as he drove away. Although she was pleased that the difficult conversation was over, she felt heavy in her soul.

Chapter Thirteen

Misha was a little nervous when he left to meet Daria at the Los Angeles airport. How could he not be nervous when his partner had expressed to him everything he thought about the boy's venture into a shameful marriage? Misha's decision to marry a woman was like a stab in the back for Ken. Why should Misha pretend that he was a normal man? Ken was sure that everyone had known about Misha's homosexuality for a long time, and he thought that Misha had long been open with his mother and her relatives. This marriage was a fraud! Anyway, sooner or later the fraud would be revealed, and Misha would not be able to avoid explanations.

It was hard for Misha to persuade Ken that his mom was elderly and had been brought up in the morality of those times when the love of man to man was considered a crime against the state and against the morality of a socialist society. His mom would suffer and it would elevate her high blood pressure; and this could cause unexpected consequences. He would never forgive himself if he caused something to happen to his mother. Ken, gripping his heart, agreed with the plan of the arranged marriage to a woman, but the sediment remained in the hearts of both him and Misha.

Misha saw Daria in the crowd of passengers leaving the airport and couldn't help but admire the tall, slim woman with long blond curls falling to her shoulders. She was very beautiful. No wonder his mother was so fond of her. It was a pity that she was not destined to give his mother grandchildren. Misha picked up Daria's suitcase and placed it in the trunk of his car.

"I'm going to drive us to the apartment that my cousin, Lily, found for us," he said. "I hope you will like the apartment. It is in North Hollywood, and many immigrants from the Soviet Union live in that part of the city. There are many shops selling goods for Russian immigrants. You'll like it there."

"I feel uncomfortable."

"The apartment has two bedrooms and each bedroom has a bathroom. We will share the apartment with my American partner Ken. There's plenty of room."

"Is the rent very expensive?"

"Yes and no. It is not your worry. We will only be sharing the living room and kitchen, and Ken and I will try not to embarrass you. Today you can rest until the evening, and then we'll go to Las Vegas and register the marriage there. My mother is already there, waiting for us at the Caesar's Palace hotel. Ken will take part in the ceremony; he'll play the role of your father and give you away. It is a well-accepted American custom – symbolically giving you to me. It is a rite of marriage, and he wanted this role so it looks as if he is your only relative."

"Is he old enough to be my father?"

"He's nineteen years older than you are, so you could have been his daughter."

"How will your relatives accept that you, a Jew, are marrying a Russian woman?"

"Don't worry. No one will care about the difference in ethnicity or religion."

"Why do you live with Ken?"

"I love Ken. He's my partner."

"Business partner?" Daria didn't understand Misha.

"No. He is my love partner."

"Do you love men?"

"Yes I do. I love men."

"How can that be?"

"I love men as others love women."

"Are you a pervert?"

"I'm a homosexual. I don't want to admit my homosexuality to my family, and that is the reason for me to arrange a marriage with you, so my family will think that I am a normal man. Do you understand?"

"What am I to do? I'm scared."

"Don't be scared. You have nothing to worry about. We will live in one bedroom and you in another. No one will hurt you. Ken is a very kind, warm-hearted person."

Daria was very disappointed. She had to portray being a married woman and at the same time continue to be alone! Everything was fake! She was even getting a fake father!

It seemed that this was her destiny. In the Soviet Union, she had to say one thing while thinking another; and here she had to be single and play the role of a happy wife. She would have to lie to all the members of the family! How terribly tired she was of lying! Would lies always surround her?

"Don't worry, Dasha. Ken is a very gentle and caring person! We'll never hurt your feelings." Misha's voice was soft and sincere.

Daria felt sorry for herself, for her female destiny. She had driven herself into a blind alley from which there was no turning back! She didn't know anything about homosexuals. She was scared and she didn't see a way out of this mess. She had to accept her destiny, such as it was.

Misha realized that he had shocked the woman. Driving to North Hollywood, he didn't utter a single word. He wanted Daria to calm down and absorb the information.

The entrance to the apartment was directly into the living room, without the mandatory hall as in the Soviet Union, and the kitchen was part of the same room.

Ken was waiting for them. He looked jealously at Daria and held out his hand to her. She fearfully took his hand. His handshake was gentle as his chubby fingers squeezed hers. She looked into his kind eyes and found sadness in them.

Daria liked the apartment. Of course, it wasn't like Tanya's house, but her room was spacious and she had her own bathroom. She was pleased that the bathroom had a lock and that it was possible to lock the bedroom door. That was good! The living room was small but cozy, furnished American-style with a large sofa, a coffee table and a huge TV.

"Welcome home!" Ken said calmly.

Tall Ken looked tired. His smile was friendly and not forced. He didn't look scary.

Daria went to her bedroom to rest, as Misha had advised her.

As she sat on her bed, her thoughts were gloomy, but not for long. Misha's cousin, Lily, who had found the apartment for them, distracted them. She burst noisily into the apartment and immediately rushed to get acquainted with Daria.

"Hello, my dear! I'm Lily. My mother and Aunt

Dora are sisters. I am very glad that I will be at the upcoming ceremony presenting myself as your first girlfriend. I really hope that I'll be your girlfriend, not only at the ceremony, but also after. Mirra said that you are beautiful, but it seems to me she was being careful with her description. I see that you are a real beauty! How did it happen that men didn't scoop you up in your Moscow? Misha is very lucky."

Daria, listening to this woman, thought about how hard it was going to be to take part in this masquerade where many eyes would evaluate her every step. Would she be able to keep up the pretense?

"We will drive to Las Vegas by car," continued Lily. "Have you been there?"

"Never."

"Oh, you will like Las Vegas! It's so beautiful, just amazing! You'll love it!"

"Why Las Vegas? Why wasn't it possible to hold the ceremony here in Los Angeles?"

"Dasha dear, you can't compare a wedding in Las Vegas to the weddings in Los Angeles. There's no comparison. Las Vegas is so chic; your wedding will be remembered for a lifetime."

"I wanted a modest wedding," said Daria.

"No way! Misha is getting married!" Lily said proudly.

"Did you invite a lot of people?"

"We sent invitations to all the relatives. I'm sorry we couldn't invite anyone from your side."

"Yes, I don't have any relatives in the United States," Daria confirmed.

"It turns out that not many people from our family will be coming. Tanya refused to come. Good thing that Aunt Lisa accepted. There will be about twenty people, including you and Misha."

It was necessary to use more than one car for the trip to Las Vegas. Misha promised to drive Lily, her son, and two old women who were distant relatives. There was no room for Daria and Ken, so they would use the second car. Daria was a little confused about the necessity of having to travel with Ken, and while they traveled, she tried to strike up a conversation with him. She wanted to understand the man with whom she would have to share her husband and an apartment, knowing that much of her life and her future depended on having a good relationship with this older man. How to establish a decent friendly relationship with him? She figured that she needed to be honest and speak with him openly.

"Ken, I don't know you at all. I would like to know more about you." Daria began the conversation as the car rolled down the highway.

"I also know very little about you," replied Ken. The trip to Las Vegas was long, and Daria managed to tell Ken a lot about her life. She spoke in detail about her childhood in a poor village, where there was no running water or central heating, and where fresh vegetables were on the table only in the summer and autumn. In the other seasons of the year, people had to be content with bread and potatoes.

She told him about her dream to escape the poverty of collective farm bondage and acquire a place in the city where there was everything that one needed: tap water, a warm apartment, and sometimes there were even sausages to buy in the store. She told him how hard she had studied so as to get an education and get a job in the city. Then it seemed that she had achieved her dream.

However, as soon as she became a city dweller, she realized what a miserable life it was to live as an ordinary Soviet citizen. Yes, they did not travel down muddy roads as on the collective farm, or toil in the country fields. Instead, they stood in long lines trying to buy just the essentials, and they worked for a miserable salary that was often lacking from payday to payday. No, it was not her dream.

Once here, in the United States, she saw for the first time, living with Tanya and Solomon, how common people can honestly achieve a good life. Her goal was to learn a profession that would ensure a good life for her.

Ken listened in silence, but Daria saw that he listened to her with interest. For Ken, everything that Daria told him seemed like a story from another planet. It was hard to imagine that there were countries in the twentieth century where part of the population lived without the right to freely change their address. The living conditions that Daria described seemed to belong in the Middle Ages. Was she specifically exaggerating in order to justify her desire to gain a foothold in America?

"You know, it is not a free lunch here in America. Do you know that in America, in order to secure a comfortable existence, one must work very hard?" he asked.

"I'm not afraid of hard work. I have a plan. I'm going to enroll in the university. In Moscow, I worked as a teacher of the Russian language at a high school, but this specialty is of limited use in America. I want to learn a profession that I can put into practice here. I want to get a Masters degree in finance and economy. Tanya said that with my education I could enroll directly in the Masters program, but I have to check it out."

Ken respected Daria's plan of getting an education and the conversation took on a friendly business-like character. If a woman wanted to go to university, it meant that she would have a chance to succeed in life, and Ken approved of her desire to learn.

They talked about Daria for a couple of hours, and by the end of the conversation, Ken began to trust Daria. He decided to divulge his opinions and feelings about what he didn't like concerning this venture into a fictitious marriage.

"It is difficult to imagine the life of the three of us in one apartment."

"I'm also worried about that," said Daria frankly. "And I hate that I'll have to constantly lie about the success of my life with Misha."

"Why did you agree?"

"I had to. My contract was expiring and I would have had to return to Moscow. I had no other way to obtain a legal residence permit in this country and everything depends on this document. Without legal status, I could not go to the university and I could not get a job. My entire life depends on it. I didn't ask Misha; he offered me this marriage. Could I refuse the only chance to fulfill my dream?"

"But this is unethical!" Ken insisted.

"I agree. But can you understand that I have no other choice?"

Ken thought. They drove in silence for a long time, each thinking their own thoughts.

Chapter Fourteen

They arrived in Las Vegas late in the evening and the shining lights of the city gave the impression of a fairy tale. Caesar's Palace greeted them with brightly illuminated fountains at the entrance. Daria was amazed at the hotel's splendid architecture, the lavish decorations, and the employees dressed in Roman style.

Misha met them in the hotel lobby. He said that he had rented two interconnecting rooms in the Roman Tower on the ninth floor. He asked Daria and Ken to change clothes and join him in the cafe for dinner. The ceremony was scheduled for the next day at five o'clock in a small chapel near the hotel, and after the ceremony, there would be a gala dinner.

Daria and Ken took the elevator to the ninth floor. The spacious room that was Daria's had a large bed, a desk, and a TV with a huge screen. Daria opened the door to the bathroom; it featured polished marble and lavish bronze decorations. The luxurious room made a big impression on Daria; it was if the room had been designed exclusively for royals. She couldn't believe that ordinary Americans could afford such luxury. In this mansion, one wouldn't be ashamed to lodge a king. She thought of her old room in her communal apartment and she felt very sorry for her friends and relatives who remained in the country of victorious socialism. What had socialism brought to the people of Russia?

Lily, Misha, Ken and Daria dined together in the café, which was essentially a business setting. They discussed all the details of the ceremony and Lily took over the purchase and preparation of the bridal dress. She explained that all the necessary purchases could be made without leaving Caesar's Place. There were plenty of different shops located inside the hotel.

Ken said that he had purchased the rings in Los Angeles. However, he didn't know the size of Daria's finger so he had bought the ring in his finger size. Daria smiled, understanding Ken's hint. In Ken's mind, she didn't have to wear a ring after the ceremony, and Ken was planning to wear this ring himself for a long time.

"My finger is big. I think that the ring will be just right," said Daria, looking into Ken's eyes.

"If the ring is a little big, we can take it to the jeweler's back in Los Angeles. The ring can be easily sized," said Misha.

Daria thought that Ken and Misha understood her. The wedding was false and she didn't need a ring.

She just needed the ring here in Las Vegas to show Misha's relatives. But unlike Daria, Misha wanted the ring to fit her finger. His mother would immediately suspect that something was wrong if the ring didn't fit. He decided to buy her another ring, with a stone, so as not to resemble the Soviet engagement ring. Such a ring would be for Daria even after they got a divorce.

They were busy all the next day preparing for the ceremony. Daria and Lily found the perfect cream-colored dress with bare shoulders. Being the practical woman that she was, Daria chose the cream dress because it could be worn not only at the marriage ceremony but also at other occasions. Misha bought Daria a beautiful gold ring with a small diamond and they bought a large bunch of flowers. They finished their shopping adventures just in time for the ceremony.

The guests were waiting for them in the small chapel. They were seated on long benches facing the low trestles where the ceremony was to take place. Misha's appearance was greeted with applause. A tall man in a dark suit stepped up beside Misha and announced that he would be conducting the ceremony. The music began.

Ken took Daria's arm and led her down the aisle to the stage. He was very serious and solemn and he seemed sad. Daria did not remember the next twenty minutes. Although she knew that the whole thing was false, the experience made her feel as if it was real and that the bonds of marriage had tied her to Misha forever.

Dinner at the restaurant went from tense to solemn. Daria found that it was hard to feel at ease celebrating when they were surrounded by a group of strangers eating their dinner at restaurant tables all over the big dining room. Misha's father, Harry, was the only person who allowed himself to relax and even to get drunk. It was he who suddenly stood up and shouted "Bitter! Bitterly!"

Daria was stunned; she was terribly confused. Ken looked at her first, then at Misha, but then someone kindly explained to Ken the meaning of the call "bitter" at a wedding. By Russian custom, this was a request for the bride and groom to publicly kiss each other.

Ken's face was gloomy and Misha was more confused than Daria. A demonstration of his ardent love for his young wife was not in his plans. On the other hand, he couldn't show everyone that he had not married for love. With anguish, he looked at Ken and Ken looked away.

Misha stood up and said, "There are too many strangers around. It is uncomfortable to kiss in front of strangers." He motioned with his hands in the direction of the tables where people were dining.

"They are not looking at you," Harry insisted. "Bitter!"

Daria realized that she needed to save Misha. In truth, she was an actress playing the role of the bride. She stood up, pulled Misha's face to hers, and with the applause of the entire table, kissed him passionately on the lips.

Daria boldly looked into Ken's eyes. Ken smiled condescendingly, and Daria sat down with relief. It was not easy when Ken was being jealous.

Ken really was jealous. This beautiful young woman had changed their lives. And these Russians didn't understand what was going on. Why not open the eyes of the parents to the true state of affairs? If they loved their son, they would forgive him. If they didn't love him, then was it worth it to arrange this masquerade? And looking at another side of the issue, this woman really was very attractive – beautiful and intelligent. What if she would suddenly wake up feelings in Misha that he didn't know he had? It all made Ken feel anxious.

In the middle of dinner, Elizabeth summoned Daria.

"Are you happy? Isn't it the truth that Misha is a very nice guy?" asked Elizabeth.

"So far I am happy," said Daria.

"I'm very happy for you," Elizabeth said.

"I don't know yet how good my future will be. I am very happy that I didn't have to immediately leave the country, but on the other hand, I'm totally unsure of the future."

"Is this because of the gloomy American who played the role of your father?" asked Elizabeth. "Where did Misha find him?"

"He is Misha's friend," Daria explained.

"Cute, but terribly joyless. He sits with such a look as if it's not a wedding but a funeral."

Daria came to Ken's defense. "Don't judge him. How would you feel sitting in the company of everyone speaking a language you didn't know?"

"I wish you happiness as a wife!" concluded Elizabeth.

Daria wished herself luck. She couldn't expect to be a happy wife.

Chapter Fifteen

All the way back to Los Angeles, Daria thought that now she was left alone with the two men. Both men looked like intelligent people, but the thought that they were perverts scared her. What if they pounced on her at night and began their ugliness? In her soul, she remained wary and anxious about the two homosexuals.

The first night in the apartment, Daria couldn't sleep out of fear. All night she tossed and turned in her bed, listening to the rustles and waiting for an attack. The night passed and no attack happened.

In the morning, Misha noticing Daria's tired face, and he asked, "What's wrong? Are you not feeling well?"

Daria reassured him, saying that she was simply not used to sleeping in a new place.

"You'll get used to it," Misha advised.

It took a few anxious nights, but no one hurt Daria and she gradually got used to the fact that in the next bedroom lived two men. She felt as if she lived in a communal apartment with helpful and polite neighbors.

To get married was easy, but to organize a legal residence permit was difficult. The line at the State Agency of Immigration was unimaginably long. Daria and Misha took their place in line at seven in the morning and by noon they finally reached the window. A dark-skinned girl at the window listened to Misha's explanation, gave him a lot of papers, and told him to fill them out. There were so many forms that Misha had to take them home to work on them.

At their apartment, Ken looked through all the papers and recommended hiring an immigration lawyer to help fill out the forms. Misha went to the Yellow Pages and found the telephone numbers of five such lawyers. Meanwhile, Dora called and asked if they had been successful at the agency.

Misha told her how long they had to stand in line to receive a pile of papers that were very difficult to fill out. Dora said she had made inquiries and learned that it would be best to turn to the son of her friend. He was an American law attorney and had five years of experience in immigration issues. She told Misha his name was Alex Brodmann, and that with his help, her friends had already received a green card. She gave Misha his phone number, and he noticed that among the phone numbers he had taken from the yellow pages, Alex Brodmann was one of them.

Alex was a young man. He listened to Misha,

took his papers, and set up a meeting for two weeks hence. Misha asked whether it was possible to meet sooner, but Alex said he was all booked up until then. When Misha asked how much it would cost, Alex replied that it would be about ten thousand dollars.

Daria instantly became depressed. So much money! She had worked for a year as a nanny and not earned that kind of money. She realized that they had started all this in vain. She looked at Misha fearfully, and he said, without batting an eye, that they would be there on the day of the meeting.

"You and I had the wedding in vain," said Daria upon leaving the lawyer's office. "All of this is so expensive that it isn't worth it. Tomorrow I will buy a ticket to Moscow."

"Are you serious?" Misha smiled.

"And what is there left for me to do? Obviously I don't have that kind of money."

"Don't worry. This is what I expected. I understand that you don't have that kind of money. I started all of this, and I will pay."

"I cannot even imagine where and how I can give you back the money."

"You will not have to. We will overcome this barrier, don't worry."

Ken saw that Daria was concerned about something. Upon learning that it was the unreasonably high price of the lawyer that upset her, he explained that in America all the lawyers charged high fees, and that ten thousand was not very expensive. But he did ask if this lawyer was known for his successes. Misha calmed him, explaining that he had used this lawyer because he was recommended. In truth, he did not know how reliable Alex was. His mother's recommendation was not very comforting.

Daria's new situation in life started very slowly. She tried to be helpful, understanding her role as a housekeeper. She wanted to cook meals and clean the apartment. However, the men declined her meals, preferring to eat out in a restaurant. Housekeeping turned out to be even worse. Ken forbade her to touch anything in his and Misha's bedroom. He was used to taking care of himself and certainly didn't want help from Daria. She had to restrict her cleaning to just the living room, the kitchen, and her bedroom.

Misha explained to her that Ken was an older man and he had well-established habits that he didn't want to change. Daria was upset; it seemed that her help was useless. Although the men treated her very politely, she felt like an unwanted dependent. She couldn't wait to get the paper authorizing her to work. She was not used to sitting around.

To occupy herself somehow, Daria asked Misha for permission to use his computer when he and Ken were at work. Misha not only didn't object; he was very happy. He believed that without the ability to use a computer, there was no future in America. He bought a small computer table for Daria's bedroom and installed his computer on the table.

"Now it's your computer," he said. "I have long wanted to buy a new one for myself."

He brought some books explaining various computer programs and placed them next to the monitor. Daria unexpectedly discovered a wide range of activities. To her surprise, she found that computer work was interesting and did not require special talents. On the second day, Daria learned to open Microsoft Word and she wrote letters.

Daria was cleaning the bedroom when the phone rang. Alex Brodmann's secretary said that one of his customers had postponed his meeting that was scheduled for the next day, and this opened the opportunity to have an earlier appointment. Daria was delighted and she called Misha at work. He promised to take time off work and go with her to the lawyer.

At the lawyer's office, a female assistant asked them many questions and recorded all the details. She was interested in everything: when Misha had met Daria, when he had proposed to her, the address of their joint property, and of course, all the documents. One of the questions was about whether Daria was in the ranks of the Communist Party. The question was raised in the present tense. Although Daria had been a member of the party before her departure, she replied in the negative, believing that she would by now have been excluded for non-payment of membership fees.

Alex grimaced when he learned that Daria's visa had actually expired a couple of months before, but he didn't say anything. At the end of the meeting, the assistant made copies of all the documents, and Daria wondered how long it might take for the entire procedure. Alex explained that he would try to get a temporary residence permit in the next few days, and that the final decision could be delayed for a year or more.

Fortunately, Alex got the permit to her within a couple of days. The paper was a temporary document, valid until she received the consideration of her requests for the status of permanent residency. The temporary paper permitted her to work in America. It was the first small victory on the way to her goal.

Chapter Sixteen

This victory inspired Daria. Now her goal was to get at least some type of work so she wasn't wrapped around Misha's neck all the time. She longed for the freedom of being somewhat independent. Misha never showed her even a hint that she should go to work, but she felt guilty. She had tried to give Misha a portion of the money she had earned while working for Tanya, but he didn't accept it.

"You need the money more than I do. Don't be in a hurry to spend it. I don't need your money; I knew what I was getting into when I made you the offer. And Ken also knew," Misha said.

"Don't scare me. I am scared enough without that."

She was actually terrified. She hated the feeling of being completely dependent on others. She didn't want to depend on Misha, but she had to. So she dreamed of finding work that would bring enough money to make her feel independent. Now that she had permission to work, she wanted to find a job as soon as possible.

Looking for work proved to be not an easy task. First of all, she needed a resume.

Following the advice of Misha, Daria wrote up a resume and sent it to many schools, but she received no answers. She bought the Sunday paper and carefully examined the Help Wanted ads, figuring out whether or not she was capable of carrying out the work described. When she assumed that she could do the work, she visited the company and applied for the job. She visited many companies, but at all of them she received a polite refusal.

The Human Resources officials always said that they had no work available currently, but that they would keep her in mind if an opening came up.

Tired of her failures, Daria was deeply depressed. Was there no work for her? Without Misha's help, she could vanish in this strange world.

Ken noticed her depressed mood. "What happened?" he asked with concern. "Did we offend you?"

His attention, and the warmth emanating from his kind smile, had a relaxing effect upon Daria. She pressed her head to his chest and cried like a little girl. Ken was taken aback by her reaction. Not knowing how to calm the sobbing woman, he sat her beside him on the sofa and began to stroke her head, like he would a child.

"What happened?" he repeated.

"I'm a loser!" said Daria through tears. "No one wants to hire me. They treat me like a stranger and

126

they don't let me take on a job. I know that they have work open, and they tell me that there are *no jobs*. It is what everyone says."

"Not in America!" argued Ken.

"You believe that because *you* are an American and you are not faced with the same problem."

"Don't be discouraged. Tell me, have you applied to the university?"

"No. Is that allowed?"

"You see! You haven't done the most important thing! Work can wait, but you have to hurry to enroll at the university if you don't want to lose a year. Tomorrow you should go to the university. The trouble is that you have no experience or relevant education. I could have arranged for you to work with our company, but it requires education. Don't be discouraged; graduate from the university and then you will find a good job. You will find that America is welcoming and friendly."

Chapter Seventeen

Daria went to the university the next day, and the person in the Office of Student Admission sent her to a counselor. The counselor proved to be a pretty young woman named Patricia. With an affable smile, Patricia scanned the documents that Daria gave her. She took a while to study the translation of Daria's diploma and her scores at the Moscow Pedagogical Institute. The list of Daria's accomplishments impressed Patricia, and she noted with approval that Daria had recently passed TOEFL, the foreign language exam.

"You have excellent scores. We would be happy to enroll you, but we don't offer a master's program in Russian literature. Why did you choose our university?"

"I didn't come for a master's degree in Russian literature. I would like, if possible, to study business."

"Our university offers a number of programs in business management. You can take any of these programs."

"If I understand you correctly, there is no problem for me to enroll in courses to study business management?" asked Daria.

"You'll also have to study a few subjects that you

didn't study in your bachelor's program. If you agree to do that, then there is no problem."

"I agree," said Daria, scarcely able to contain her excitement.

"In that case, I'll give you some questionnaires and you can fill them out. Come back with the completed questionnaires and bring a check for sixty dollars. The payment is for the consideration of your application in our office."

"Tell me, how much will it cost me to study for my Master's Degree?" asked Daria.

Patricia told her the cost and Daria was horrified.

"I don't have that kind of money," said Daria. "I am not working."

"In that case, you must complete an additional application for financial assistance. The university helps underprivileged students. What is your legal status in the United States?"

Daria showed her the paper she had received from the lawyer.

"This paper isn't sufficient for admission to the university. Foreign students require a student visa. If we consider you as a resident of the United States, a green card is required. We can take you only provisionally until you get a green card. When filling out the application for financial assistance, don't forget to include your husband's salary."

Daria returned home depressed. She felt that there was no luck for her in America. Where to get money for her education? Again depend on Misha? Wasn't it enough that he had already spent so much on her! The lawyer fee alone would cost him dearly! No, she could not and did not want to turn to Misha. What to do? Who would have thought that an education in America was so expensive?

At home, she found only Ken. He sat in the living room, dejected about something.

Looking at him, Daria didn't dare burden him with her problems.

"Excuse me Ken, but maybe I can help you?" Daria asked sympathetically.

"Thank you, but you cannot help. I just received news that my mother has died. I was remembering my childhood and I felt sad. Mom was only eighty years old."

Daria thought that eighty was an extremely old age! She didn't say it, though, knowing that for a son, his mother was always young and the dearest person.

"I don't know how to help you to feel better; it is always painful when a mother dies. But you have Misha who loves you, and you have a good job..."

"You're right. I was feeling guilty. She always rejected me for my lifestyle, and because of this, I had not seen her in the last twenty years. I knew that I couldn't become straight. I could not change myself and suddenly fall in love with a woman. My mother didn't want to understand me. She wanted grandchildren."

"I can understand her. There wasn't anything unnatural about her wishes," said Daria.

"That's true, but I could not remake myself. I was born this way."

"Is it possible to be born homosexual?"

"I know that people are born this way. Whether it is their hormones that are wrong, or chemicals in their brain that are different from normal men, it is their drive to have sex with a man, not a woman. They cannot remake themselves. Each time a woman tried to seduce me, I felt no desire for her. I don't even care for the female form – and no other sexual anatomical differences. But Misha excites me. How do you explain that?"

"I don't know; I cannot understand it," replied Daria. "I used to think that such a union was a non-sensical perversion. But you explain it clearly and I don't know what to think. I have no reason not to believe you, but I cannot understand it. People were created to have offspring. I know that when I hold the hands of someone else's child, like Michael's hands, my heart trembles with joy."

"Yes, children delight the soul. But it is too late for me to think about children. It isn't enough to give birth to a child; you also have to raise one. That requires twenty years. I don't have that long."

"You are not so old. You will live twenty years and many more."

"Maybe I would live, but I wouldn't be able to work for that long. A child needs financial support."

"Yes, they do," confirmed Daria thoughtfully.

She thought about how she, though far from a child's age, required financial support to get on her feet in this country. Was this whole sham marriage thing in vain? Where to get money for university?

Ken felt the sadness in her response. He was sensitive to Daria's mood; it seemed that something was depressing her.

"How was your visit to the university?" He asked sympathetically. "You must hurry.

According to my information, the admission for this year ends soon."

"I cannot go to the university. It is too expensive to get an education in the USA. I don't have the money for it."

"Have you applied for financial aid?"

"Help depends on the financial situation of the family. I'm classified as being married, so with Misha's earnings, I am not eligible for financial help. And I cannot ask Misha to pay for my studies! He has already squandered so much on the lawyer's fee to obtain legal status for me, and for the wedding! No, I cannot ask him."

Ken contemplated. He respected the fact that Daria didn't want to ask Misha to pay for her studies at the university. It seemed that she was a responsible woman, even though she had agreed to a false marriage. He had watched her closely. During all this time, Daria had never asked Misha for a gift, and she spent money economically, buying only what they needed. Nor had she ever bought a single thing for herself.

Ken respected her and he felt himself partly responsible because he had not stopped Misha. He had even agreed to take part in the fictitious marriage, posing to Misha's relatives as just his friend. Ken remembered the wedding ceremony and his role in it, that it was he who had given Daria to Misha. This was usually the role of the bride's father. Should he continue his role as her father to help her now?

"Of course I should!" he exclaimed to himself. "Participation in deception imposes obligations! I should help Daria." Once Ken came to that decision, he felt gratification in his heart.

"I'll help you," he said to Daria. "I'll lend you the required money. I have saved money for my old age and I don't need this money until I retire. Use it for your education. I am unable to give you this amount as a gift, but I can give it to you as a loan without interest. You will graduate from the university, and then in three years you can gradually pay me back the debt. Do you agree?"

"I cannot accept such a proposal," Daria said decisively.

"Why not?"

"I'm not sure if three years after graduation I would be able to repay you the loan. I don't want to deceive you."

"If you couldn't repay me in three years, you could repay me in four years," said Ken. "To my regret, I cannot afford to *give* you the money, because I will need it when I retire. Believe me that I would give you the money for your education with pleasure if I didn't need it for my old age."

Daria didn't know what to do. She decided to talk with Misha. She felt the need for his approval. After all, he was her husband, even if it was a fiction.

Misha was upset when he learned that Daria had talked to Ken about tuition money, but he had no money and he knew that there would also be additional expenses for her education. She would have to spend a lot on books and she would need transportation. Finally, Misha approved what Ken had proposed.

Chapter Eighteen

The lobby in their apartment contained a mailbox that was sectioned off for each tenant.

Daria walked down to the lobby to retrieve the mail. She was waiting for a response from the university. It had been more than a month since she had taken all the papers to the admissions office, and now she was expecting a decision from the university. Every day she checked the mail, but the answer hadn't come yet, and she was starting to worry.

There was no response from the university, but there was a letter from her mother. Impatient, she opened the envelope in the elevator. Her mother wrote that after the upheaval in August, the life of the people had not improved. They lived poorly, and they were in need of all the essentials. In the village, people were depressed, and the school was having problems. Her mother was happy that her daughter lived in rich America, and that she didn't have to witness the desperation with in which Russia's population was now living. She didn't write about her own situation, but Daria knew how her mother lived and she was sure that she didn't have even the essentials.

Daria showed Misha the letter from her mother, and Misha reacted to the description of the situation in Russia with sorrow.

"Listen Dasha, we need to send money to your mother."

"How? How would we send money to my mother in the village? Is there now a way to send it to her directly?"

"I don't know how to send it to the village, but in Moscow, it is possible. Maybe your mother could go to Moscow to pick up the money?"

"Maybe. But who would give her the money there?"

"It is possible to organize it. Often we can't, but now there is a way to easily arrange this."

"How?"

"My distant relatives are coming to the States. They have sold their dacha and would like to transfer the money here. The easiest way would be for them to give some money to your mom there, and we'll return it to them when they arrive here."

"I don't have as much money as they will have gotten for the dacha," Daria said.

"It's not your concern. They will be happy to transfer it in parts. Let's have them give your mother five hundred dollars."

"Five hundred? Why so much?"

"We'll send three hundred. There's no sense in sending less. She will need money in order to travel to Moscow. We should arrange for at least six months now."

"Misha, you're my guardian angel! I'm so worried about my mother! As soon as I get a job, I will begin to repay you."

"It is better to save for tuition for next year. It is better not to ask Ken for help in the future."

Daria knew that next year she should pay for the tuition herself. For now, it was important for her to get a confirmation of admission from the university.

The next day, Daria finally received a letter from the university. What a joy it was for her to find out that she had been admitted!

She jumped up and down in her bedroom like a little girl, holding the welcome letter to her chest. For the moment, she didn't think about the borrowed money she would need to return, or about the forthcoming challenges with her studies. She was happy and filled with hope!

During her first month of study, Daria had to overcome various organizational difficulties and struggle with her English. But gradually Daria developed a study routine and even began to enjoy the lectures, the assignments and her new acquaintances. She loved being able to spend almost all of her time learning new subjects.

Toward the end of her first year of study, Daria was sitting in her room preparing her thesis when Misha rushed into her room without knocking. He was pale and agitated.

Daria knew immediately that something bad had happened.

"My mom is in the hospital. She had a stroke," he said.

"Let's go to the hospital!"

"I was just there. The doctors don't promise anything good. Dad is on duty."

"Take me to the hospital. I'll take care of her."

"While she is in the hospital, your care isn't needed, but when she is discharged, she will definitely need your help."

The next day, Misha and Daria went to the hospital to visit Dora. She was in intensive care and therefore visitors were not allowed. The doctor on duty told Misha that his mother's condition was very serious, and that treatment would not help. Misha and Daria returned home upset.

It turned out that Daria's help was not needed. Dora died in the hospital without regaining consciousness. Daria wanted to take part in the arrangements for the funeral, but in the US, special funeral homes take care of the dead, and no assistance of relatives is required. Misha and his father made arrangements with the funeral home, and Daria sat down at the phone and informed all the relatives when and where the funeral would be.

Daria was depressed. She understood that now there was no need for Misha to continue this marriage. He had done it to appease his mother. With his mother dead, he no longer had a reason to hide the truth about his relationship with Ken. With fear, she expected that Misha would want her to terminate the marriage before the government issued her legal status. Just as everything was almost settled, it could now all fall apart.

As the days passed, and then weeks and months, Misha didn't mention anything about divorce. Not knowing how to behave, Daria tried to be helpful. She took on the duty of caring for Misha's father. Once a week, Daria cleaned Harry's apartment and cooked dinner for him.

Realizing the tenuousness of her situation, Daria applied all her energy to succeeding in university. Learning was very hard because she often lacked knowledge of the English language, especially the technical terms. Without previous technical education, Daria didn't even know the Russian terms. But she was gradually becoming more familiar with the English language and with the technical jargon. Another burden, however, was having to take the Master's program at the same time as taking several business subjects from the Bachelor's program because she hadn't studied them at the Pedagogical Institute.

She studied hard, trying to get the highest scores on every subject. Her diligence was noticed at the university and she felt the respect of both the students and the teachers.

This dual workload prevented Daria from looking for a job. Only after successfully passing the exams of the first year, was she able to look for work. On the advice of fellow students, she asked a consultant to help her find a job working at the university. It turned out that the university had need for teachers who could conduct conversations with the students studying the Russian language to help them practice. The head of the department of Russian language offered Daria a teaching job considering her reputation as an excellent student. The wages were poor, but the offer came with an important benefit – the exemption from tuition fees.

It seemed that everything was settled. Daria was studying business and she had successfully found a job that could be combined with her studies. But it only *seemed* settled. Daria felt with all her being that the men were waiting for the time when she would be out of the house, leaving them free from her constant presence. It hindered them, preventing them from freely expressing their feelings.

Yes, and she felt abashed every night when she heard lovemaking noises behind the wall. At such moments, it seemed to her that she was the most miserable person on the whole of God's earth. Plus she slept on a wide bed yet was not able to feel the warmth of a man's body nearby. How she wanted to stroke her fingers against the hairy chest of a beloved man and press her lips to his!

Tossing and turning in bed at night, she wisely told herself that it wasn't anything to regret or to worry about. Everything was going well, everything was settled with her education, and she must not to think about having a man. It was necessary to suppress the urge, to live celibate as if she were a nun. However, it was difficult to suppress the call of the flesh when behind the wall, the bed creaked! It was so hard not to think about love. Hugging the pillow, she longed for love, so desirable and so unavailable. She knew it was best not to admit her desire, but sometimes she felt deprived and miserable.

Daria wanted to move away from her men, but it could be difficult to obtain a green card. Officials must not know that her marriage was fictitious. Ken would have to endure until she obtained her green card. She always feared that he might be bothered by her presence and ask Misha to find her an alternative shelter. While living with the men, she didn't need to pay for housing, and that allowed Daria to save money, but from her meager wages, she certainly couldn't afford to pay for even the cheapest tiny apartment.

Chapter Nineteen

The Green Card came unexpectedly. During the two years of waiting, Misha had repeatedly called the lawyer, asking him to speed up the preparation of the document. The answer was always the same: "We are doing everything possible to accelerate the process; you will need to wait." Then it finally happened, and Daria received the long-awaited document.

Now she was in the country legally! More so, she had all the rights of a US citizen, except the right to vote. It was a victory!

Ken suggested that they celebrate by going out for dinner. He even suggested they go to a Russian restaurant where a famous Russian singer performed with an orchestra. But Misha didn't want to celebrate. Because his mother had died recently, he was not up for a party.

So they decided to have a humble celebration at home. Daria baked meat pies and sweet cheesecake for the occasion, and the table was lined with dishes that Ken had brought from the Russian restaurant. Misha poured the wine and proposed a toast to Daria.

Ken wanted to speak. "Dear friends! I believe that the time has come to discuss our plans. Daria, how long before your graduation?"

"Only a short time. If I successfully pass all my exams, in six months I will get my Master's degree in business administration!"

"And for you to successfully complete your education, I propose this toast!" declared Ken.

"Thank you," said Daria. "And I want to tell you both that I have decided after graduation to go back to the San Francisco Bay Area to live. I don't want to bother you with my constant presence."

"I have thought about that," said Ken. I also think that the time has come for us to think about how Misha should open up to his relatives about our relationship. I no longer want to hide in the closet from the world. I am sure that the majority of Misha's relatives are aware of his orientation. Why live a lie?"

"I cannot," declared Ken. "My dad will be worried. He would not understand."

"I can no longer lie!" Ken exploded. "No more hiding! Be open, or I'm gone. I'm tired of playing the role of another man. I have nothing to hide. I didn't steal anything."

Daria intervened. "Boys, don't quarrel! I also believe that you need to open up and not to hide your relationship, Misha. Your mother didn't understand this, I agree, but this does not mean that you have to live all your life hiding in a shell. Sooner or later, the truth will come out."

"What am I to do? All my relatives will despise me!"

"Yes, it is possible that some members of your family will not understand you and maybe even condemn you. I myself still don't really understand the nature of your union," Daria said frankly.

"There, you see, even you don't understand me!" Misha exclaimed. He looked at Daria with the hope of support.

"I don't understand you, but I certainly don't blame you. I got used to your relationship and I have treated you with respect, and so will your relatives. They might not understand, but they will respect you. And maybe there will be somebody who won't, but then they're not your friend, and you shouldn't care about their opinion."

"I fully agree with Daria," Ken said in support. "You don't need anyone who doesn't accept you for who you are."

"I'm not thinking about my relatives," said Ken. 'My worry is about my Dad. He's an old man; he will suffer."

"Here you are very wrong!" Daria said gently. "I have the impression that your father guessed about your relationship with Ken long ago."

"Why did you decide that?" Misha asked in dismay.

"He asked me a question about how the men were treating me, and he wanted to make sure they weren't hurting me. After all, he knows that Ken shares an apartment with us. He is wise and he understands everything."

"It cannot be. Dad does not know."

"Well, I guess you think your father is stupid! He understands that there must be some reason that a stranger is living in the family nest. Where in America does a strange man share an apartment with a married couple? Single people can share an apartment, but not a family, especially newlyweds. Even I feel shy living in the same apartment with the two of you. But I have no choice."

"Is Dad pretending?" Misha asked with fear.

"Don't worry. He is playing his role perfectly just for you."

"What should I do? Did he actually say this to you?"

"No," said Daria. "I am sure he would not discuss your situation with me. He didn't discuss it, but he knows the truth. You are asking me what to do. My opinion is that you should come with Ken to the next family gathering. Everyone will see you together and draw conclusions."

"It is easy for you to give advice. I haven't made up my mind on this."

"You have to decide. The time has come to open up," replied Daria.

"I support Daria's opinion," stated Ken. "I believe that we need to open up to Misha's family. It would strengthen our relationship. We are adults and we have the right to live as we like."

"Easy for you to talk," retorted Misha. "I cannot even imagine everyone knowing my secret. From an early age, I have kept my attraction to men a secret. How do I open up now?"

"Was it always so easy to hide the truth?" Daria asked. "Did you never get into a mess?"

"Don't mock me. Only God knows how hard it was!"

"Uncover the truth, and you will immediately feel better in your heart," Daria said gently. "You will become free and easy."

They ended the miserable discussion. Unfortunately, the celebration for Daria was spoiled. Misha finished dinner in a bad mood, and Daria was troubled by the state of Misha's mind. She was heartily sorry for him. Hiding for so many years, it wasn't easy for him to suddenly announce to everyone that he was a homosexual. She was sure he was especially nervous about relatives who had grown up in the Soviet Union, where same-sex unions were considered a crime.

From the time that Daria had settled with Misha and Ken in the same apartment, she couldn't understand the reason for such unusual love between two men. In her mind, the nature of all living beings was aimed at procreation, and this was a natural reason for love. The union of two people of the same sex was against nature; it was perverted behavior. At least she had thought this to be so, until she read a couple of books belonging to Ken. The authors of these books argued that such a deviation is found not only in humans, but also in animals; and that it is not caused by perverse criminal behavior, but by natural variations in the human brain. In other words, these people were created by nature.

After Daria read the books, she hadn't necessarily believed what the authors had written, but she began to treat her roommates without prejudice. What if their brains really did work differently? They certainly didn't look or act like criminals, and they never tried to involve her in any kind of criminal behavior. No one was getting hurt by their union. They were hardworking, kind and polite people. They respected her privacy, and they were doing everything possible to help her.

Chapter Twenty

The university held a job fair, and Human Resources managers came from various companies to select those graduates who had the skills for the positions they needed to fill.

The university counselors had explained to the students how they should perform at an interview and had told them to prepare resumes to be given to the company representatives. This event was very important for Daria because she needed a job and she desperately hoped for an offer.

Daria thought long and hard about how to create her resume. The task was complicated because she had never held a position remotely similar to those in which she was interested. She needed to come up with a resume that would be impressive enough to spark the interest of the company representatives. Obviously they wouldn't be interested in her experience as a nanny, or in her experience of teaching Russian language and literature to high school students. Basically, she had no useful experience to share with these companies.

Fortunately, Ken offered to help Daria with her resume. "But how do I create a resume?" Daria asked him. "What can I write? My experience is not suitable for these companies. Who needs a former teacher of the Russian language?"

Ken didn't agree with Daria's opinion that she had no useful experience. He recommended describing first her work as a teacher, and then her administrative experience as the head of the Russian language department of the school. The combination of these two elements, according to Ken, proved her value. A teacher and a leader of the language department must have organizational skills and be able to lead people.

Ken helped her complete her resume and Daria was grateful for his help and support, but she still doubted that her resume would interest the employers. Still, she had a resume, bad or good, and she would hand it out at the fair.

At the fair, Daria was intending to distribute her resume to the attendees who represented firms from Silicon Valley. She knew that Silicon Valley, located south of San Francisco in the Bay Area, was the home of many High Tech companies. Her dream was to work for one of these companies, knowing that they represented the future of technology. Plus she wanted to get out of Los Angeles where she would always be reminded of her false marriage. She had been forced to deceive the authorities, and she wanted to get away from this page of her life.

She wasn't going to break off her friendship with the pair of gay men with whom fate had connected her, but she didn't want to live in the same city with them.

The job fair attracted the attention of all the university graduates. The University of California, Los Angeles is a very large school, so there were several thousand graduates ranging from Bachelor of Science to Doctor of Science, and all of them were looking for a job. In fact, there was such a crowd in the hallways designated for the fair that it was very difficult to reach the tables where the representatives of the firms were sitting.

The crowd made a painful impression on Daria. How could she attract the attention of the firms in these conditions? The young, energetic students lingered at the tables and didn't depart from them until they had talked to a company representative. She felt helpless in such a crowd. Who needed a woman speaking with a heavy Russian accent that had no experience in the field of semiconductors?

But she knew she must to do something. At least she had to make her way to the tables and leave her resume with the representatives.

Each representative took her resume and put it in a folder, but she wasn't able to have a conversation with any of them. She left the fair disappointed, certain that the fair had not been a success for her.

In spite of the fact that she tried hard to hide her disappointment, Ken knew immediately that Daria was depressed, and he tried to console her.

"If you were hoping that it was going to be 'I came, I saw, I conquered,' your hopes were wrong; it doesn't happen that way," said Ken. "The companies collect the resumes, they read them and analyze them, and then they choose someone who attracts their attention. Only then do they contact the university and collect additional information about that person. If you are lucky enough for one of them to contact you for an interview, that's when they might make you an offer. So you need to continue to study, and meanwhile the company doesn't have to rush with an offer either; they may not be hiring for a month or two."

"So you think I have a chance?"

"It's always a possibility. But I wouldn't *expect* an offer. It's important to keep searching."

"I thought that I might have a *little* chance."

"No more and no less so than before you visited the job fair. You are looking for a job that matches your education. Such work is hard to find, especially if you have no experience, or acquaintance with the industry, or people who know your work ethic."

Ken thought for a moment. "Basically, you don't have someone to *recommend* you," he said. There is no one within a company who can put in a good word for you. So I would recommend contacting an employment agency."

"And what exactly is that?" asked Daria.

"There are many agencies that specialize in the selection of employees for companies. The higher the requirements are for the employee, the more likely that a company would hire an agency who specializes in finding workers."

"Is it very expensive to ask an agency for help?" asked Daria, afraid that she wouldn't be able to afford it.

"My rule is: if the agency asks you to pay for help, the agency is worthless. Agencies that are worthy of attention never demand money from the prospective employee," explained Ken. "They get their money from the company that will employ you. You should deal only with such agencies."

"How do I find such an agency?"

"I will help you. Here in LA, I know several agencies. Through them, we will find an agency in the San Francisco Bay Area."

"I would be very grateful to you," said Daria.

Misha came home from work. After learning about what Ken and Daria were discussing, he said that he had a few phone numbers of such agencies in Santa Clara.

Daria calmed down a bit. Misha explained that the search for employment is very hard work, and that it should be addressed but not feared.

Chapter Twenty-one

Daria was in her bedroom preparing her last essay on the subject of economics when the phone rang. The telephone was in the living room on the coffee table and she rushed out of the bedroom.

"Allo!"

"Hello. I would like to speak to Miss Stepanoff," a man's voice said in English.

"Speaking," said Daria.

"I represent the firm Lokteh. We have reviewed your resume that you left with our employees at the university job fair in Los Angeles, and we would like to meet with you. Would you be willing to meet with us tomorrow at the Hilton Hotel?"

"I'll be glad to meet you," Daria answered.

"Can you come to the meeting at eleven in the morning?"

"Yes, I can."

"Our room is 4008 at the Hotel Hilton. Do you need directions to the hotel?"

"I will find it. Thank you." Daria was delighted.

"We will see you at eleven."

"I am looking forward to the meeting," said Daria.

The call elevated Daria's spirits. It turned out, after all, that she had handed out her resume at the fair for a purpose. She tried to remember what she had learned about the company 'Lokteh' while she was at the fair, but no matter how hard she strained her memory, she didn't remember anything. She scanned the list of companies for which she had gathered a prospectus before distributing her resume, but there was no such company among her papers.

Bewildered, she waited for the men to return from work. Maybe they would know something about this company. She forgot all about the essay she had been working on before the phone call.

Misha came first and she told him about the phone call.

"What did you say is the name of this company?"

"Lokteh."

"I don't know this company. And from what city?" Misha asked.

"I don't know. They didn't say."

"Don't worry. You will find out about the company at the meeting."

"How can I prepare for the meeting if I don't know anything about the company?"

"Don't worry! The less you worry, the better it will be."

Ken had no knowledge about the company

either. He told Daria not to think about the meeting, and that it would be better to finish her essay.

It was easy for him to talk, but Daria couldn't stop thinking about the upcoming meeting, and that night she couldn't sleep. All night she kept thinking about how to explain her story to the interviewer, about how to dress and how to wear her hair. A woman needs to think a lot about such things before an important meeting. She didn't fall asleep until morning.

Stepping onto the plush carpet of the Hilton Hotel, Daria kept thinking about how to behave at her interview. Room 4008 was on the fourth floor. She read the inscription "Lockheed" printed on a sheet of paper that was attached to the door.

She then realized that she made a mistake with the name of the company. It became clear why neither Misha nor Ken had known anything about the company 'Lokteh.'

"Miss Daria Stepanoff?" the young man sitting at the desk asked. "Very nice.

Please, sit down here. Would you like a cup of coffee or tea?"

"Coffee please."

"Milk? Sugar?"

"Yes please."

The young man gave Daria her coffee, handed her a packet of papers, and asked her to fill them out.

"There is no hurry. Please take the time to fill them out carefully. When you are finished, pass the papers back to me."

Daria looked around. The room had a few more people filling out papers. She wasn't the only one who had been called for an interview. It became immediately clear that she was in competition with the others and probably had little chance of getting work. Why had they called her?

The questionnaire contained many different questions and Daria regretted that there was no Misha or Ken to assist her. Their assistance would have been very useful, but now she had to rely only on herself. While answering the questions, she thought about what she remembered about the Lockheed Company. She knew that it was a large company in the business of developing space rockets. Probably very secret. Why would they need her, Daria Stepanoff, a Russian, not having US citizenship? She calmed herself down. Why worry about work which she probably couldn't get?

The young man took the questionnaire after she was finished and asked her to wait for her invitation to be interviewed. He suggested that she read the magazines lying on the table while she waited.

After only a short time, a pretty woman, dressed in a professional looking pantsuit, came through a door off of the waiting room and invited Daria into the office for a chat.

The conversation was very friendly. The woman was interested in Daria's teaching activities, her duties as a class teacher, and as the head teacher at the school. Then she asked her what she did in America. Daria told her about her teaching experience at the university. She spoke calmly and convincingly, and the English words flew out of her mouth. The woman listened carefully to her and wrote in a notebook. When the conversation ended, the woman told her that if they found her suited for the company, they would invite her to the city of Sunnyvale, where their company was located, for an additional interview.

At home, Daria told Ken about the interview. Ken wasn't surprised to learn that Lockheed had invited her for an interview. He believed that in order to work in some areas of the company, having a green card was enough, but Daria didn't believe him.

She firmly decided that it was necessary to contact the employment agencies that he had previously suggested. The men were right; it was necessary to pay more attention to the search for work.

Chapter Twenty-two

Daria received a letter from her mother. The main part of the letter was devoted to the plight of the country. In contrast to the feelings of hopelessness and despondency that had been experienced in the village after the fall of the Soviet regime, her mother was surprised to find out that in Moscow, the residents were glad of the coming changes. "What are they waiting for?" questioned her mother. "The era of frank selfishness, which is aimed at the immense enrichment of a handful of crafty and dishonest people, and the impoverishment of the rest of the population? What has become of the patriotism that is taught in schools?" Her mother was deeply worried about Russia, which in her opinion, was headed for a decline of morals and ideals.

Daria showed the letter to Misha. Misha said, "It is not so simple. Here in America, capitalism is thriving. The goal of every capitalist is enrichment. Selfishness really does rule the world of a capitalist. But in capitalist America, ordinary people live much better off than in the camp of developed socialism."

Daria didn't understand the higher standard of living of ordinary Americans, and it was hard for her to explain to Misha her mother's concern.

"The Soviet person believes that capitalists don't care about ordinary people," said Misha. "It is somewhat true, but not the whole truth. The economy is driven by initiative. It is not enough to invent something miraculous; to become a capitalist, this miraculous something must be produced and sold. To whom can be it sold? To people, of course! If people become poor, then who is going to buy everything that capitalists produce? Development would stop. Capitalists need people to be able to buy their goods. The whole mechanism of development in a capitalist society is objectively aimed at the steady growth of the economy and at improving the material well-being of the people, regardless of the wishes of individual capitalists."

"What prevents a socialist economy from growing for the benefit of the people?" asked Daria.

"Lack of material interest. In the Soviet Union, initiative is always punished. You know that in the Soviet Union there are no private enterprises; everything is done under the state plan. Private initiative is criminalized. In these conditions, there cannot be economic development. Do you understand this, now that you are living here?"

"It's just much more visible here," said Daria. "So do you think my mother is worried in vain? Will everything end up being like here?"

"No," said Misha, "she is not worrying in vain. It could take a long time for the economy to settle, and while everything is settling, the people will suffer. Russia is not ready for capitalism yet. Did your mother get the money?"

"Yes, she got it."

Ken looked at Misha and Daria; the conversation in Russian between them was irritating him. Daria noticed this and tried to speak only in English, but Misha didn't pay attention to Ken's discontent and he spoke to Daria in Russian. Daria unwittingly answered him in the same language. Ken felt left out, and he grew even more irritated. And this time, an innocent conversation about a letter from Russia he took as a discussion about him.

"What did I do that you discuss me?" he asked with indignation.

"The conversation was about my mother's letter," Daria explained soothingly. "I received a letter from Moscow."

"I know that you have something to hide from me. I see that Misha has grown cold to me."

"Why are you making this noise? It is so hard to live with you when you're always jealous. Daria received a letter from her mother and showed it to me. That's all," said Misha.

The men left the room. Daria felt that something

was wrong. She had noticed recently that Misha had begun to treat Ken somewhat aloofly. She didn't know what the reason was, but she knew that Ken noticed Misha's distance. She didn't like that she had been involuntarily drawn into a quarrel between the two men.

Daria thought that, most likely, the misunderstanding stemmed from the fact that Misha was in no hurry to open up to his relatives. While Misha hid his relationship with Ken, Ken did not feel confident. Ken wanted a lasting relationship. If a marriage between a man and a woman, supported by civil and ecclesiastical institutions, didn't guarantee the strength of a union, what could one say about a same-sex relationship that was not recognized by either society or the church? Naturally Ken felt insecure. He needed constant confirmation of the strength of their relationship to calm his soul, especially at his age. Daria could see that Misha sometimes forgot to provide Ken with those signals of love that Ken expected and needed. It wasn't because he didn't love Ken, but simply out of forgetfulness. In such cases, Ken was offended. And that certainly couldn't help to strengthen the union. Daria assumed that Misha was cooling his affections due to the unpleasant residue in his heart that had been caused by the unwarranted insults from Ken regarding Misha's reluctance to admit to others his homosexuality.

Daria felt that the tensions between her

roommates were without any serious reason. She kept pondering over how to behave so as not to cause unnecessary friction between the men. She completely switched to English and she began actively campaigning for Misha to announce to his relatives his relationship with Ken. This led to a deterioration of the relationship between her and Misha.

These months in Los Angeles were very hard for Daria. She felt that she was constantly caught between the discontent of the two men.

Her classes at the university were very successful. Before the end of the course,

Daria had a conversation with a consultant. He strongly recommended that she, being such an excellent student, continue her studies and go for the Doctor of Sciences program. To ease her financial situation, she was promised a job at the Department of Economics in addition to working with the students studying the Russian language.

The offer was very tempting, but Daria couldn't agree to it. It was impossible to continue her studies, particularly because she could no longer live with Misha and Ken in the same apartment. She had to break away from them. She longed for the freedom that she could achieve only by living separately and independently, and she was determined to go back to the San Francisco Bay Area.

Chapter Twenty-three

Daria received a letter from her mother, and the main part of the letter was devoted to the plight of the country. In comparison to the feelings of hopelessness and despondency that had emerged in the village after the fall of the Soviet regime, her mother was surprised to find out that, in Moscow, the residents were happy about the coming changes. What were they waiting for? The era of frank selfishness, aimed at the immense enrichment of a handful of crafty and dishonest people? The impoverishment of the rest of the population? What had become of the patriotism that was taught in schools? Her mother was deeply worried about Russia, which in her opinion, was headed for a decline of morals and ideals.

Daria showed the letter to Misha. He said, "It is not so simple. Here in America, capitalism is thriving. The goal of every capitalist is enrichment. Selfishness really does rule the world of a capitalist. But in capitalist America, ordinary people live much better off than in the camp of developed socialism. Why...?"

Daria didn't understand the higher standard of living of ordinary Americans, and she certainly couldn't explain it.

"The Soviet individual believes that capitalists don't care about ordinary people," said Misha. "It is somewhat true, but not the whole truth. The economy is driven by initiative. It is not enough to invent something miraculous; to become a capitalist, this miraculous something must be produced and sold. To whom can it be sold? To people, of course! If people become poor, then who is going to buy what capitalists produce? Development would stop. Capitalists need people to be able to buy their goods. The whole mechanism of development in a capitalist society is objectively aimed at the steady growth of the economy and at improving the material well-being of the people, regardless of the wishes of individual capitalists."

"What prevents a socialist economy from developing for the benefit of the people?"

"Lack of material interest. In the Soviet Union, initiative is always punished. You know that in the Soviet Union there is no private enterprise. Everything is done according to the state plan. Private initiative is criminalized. In these conditions, there cannot be economic development. Do you understand that now that you live here?"

"It's just much more visible here," said Daria. "So do you think my mother worried in vain? Will everything be as here?"

"No," said Misha, "not in vain. It could take a long time for the economy settle, and while it is getting settled, the people will suffer. Russia is not ready for capitalism yet. Did your mother get the money?"

"Yes, she got it."

Ken looked at Misha and Daria. The conversation in Russian between them was irritating him. Daria noticed this and she tried to speak only in English. But Misha didn't pay attention to Ken's discontent, and he spoke to Daria in Russian. Daria then answered him in the same language. Ken felt left out and he grew even more irritated. And he believed that the innocent conversation about a letter from Russia was a discussion about him.

"What did I do that you discuss me?" he asked with indignation.

"The conversation was only about my mother's letter," Daria said soothingly. "I received a letter from Moscow."

"I know that you have something to hide from me. I see that Misha has grown cold toward me."

"Why are you making a fuss?" said Misha. "It is so hard to live with you when you're always jealous. Daria received a letter from her mother she and showed it to me. That's all," said Misha.

The men left the room. Recently Daria had noticed that Misha was being somewhat aloof with

Ken. She didn't know what the reason was, but she knew that Ken noticed Misha's attitude. Daria didn't like the fact that she was involuntarily drawn into the quarrel between the two men.

Daria thought that, most likely, the misunderstanding stemmed from the fact that Misha was in no hurry to open up to his relatives. While Misha hid the fact of his relationship with Ken, Ken did not feel confident. He wanted an open and lasting relationship. If a marriage between a man and a woman, blessed by both civil and ecclesiastical institutions, didn't guarantee the strength of a union, what's to say about a same-sex relationship, which wasn't recognized either by society or by the church?

Naturally, Ken felt insecure. He needed continual confirmation of the strength of their relationship to calm his soul, especially at his age. Misha sometimes forgot to provide Ken with those signals of love that Ken expected and needed. It wasn't because he didn't love Ken, Daria believed, but simply out of forgetfulness. However, Ken was offended, and that certainly couldn't help to strengthen the union. Daria assumed that Misha was cooling his affection due to the unpleasant residue in his soul from Ken's unwarranted insults.

In these last months of living in Los Angeles, Daria felt that the tensions between her roommates were without any serious reasons. She kept pondering intensely over how to behave so as not to cause unnecessary friction between the men. She completely switched to English and she began actively campaigning in favor of Misha announcing to his relatives his relationship with Ken. However, this led to a deterioration of the relationship between her and Misha. These months in Los Angeles were very hard for Daria. She felt that she was constantly torn between the two men.

Her classes at the university, however, were very successful. Before the end of the courses, Daria had a conversation with a consultant. He strongly recommended that, being such an excellent student, she continue her studies and go after the Doctor of Sciences program. To ease her financial situation, she was promised a job at the Department of Economics in parallel with helping the students who were studying the Russian language. The offer was very tempting, but Daria couldn't agree to it. It was impossible to continue to go to school because she could no longer live with Misha and Ken in the same apartment; she needed to work and live independently. She longed for this freedom and she was determined to go back to the San Francisco Bay area.

Chapter Twenty-four

The day of graduation was approaching, and Daria realized that in American universities this event was a solemn occasion. She was interested to find out that, in America, graduates wore robes and a special hat with a flat top and a tassel, just like university graduates in the Middle Ages. Also, at these ceremonies, a number of famous people were invited to speak to the graduates, and the best students were entitled to make a speech.

She also realized that graduates could invite parents and close friends to the celebration, so Daria invited Misha and Ken to the ceremony. Ken was delighted and promised to come. Misha, looking away, told her that he would be busy that day and so wouldn't be able to come. For Daria, this was a blow that she hadn't expected. She had asked him over a month before to mark the day on his calendar. Was she guilty of doing something wrong? Why didn't Misha want to go to the ceremony?

At the graduation ceremony, Daria listened enthusiastically to the speeches. She was happy. Her initial apprehension had been replaced by jubilation. Receiving her diploma meant that she had achieved her first goal toward a successful future. How could she not enjoy it?

She was very pleased that Ken was there to share her joy. She was grateful to him for everything: for the fact that he suffered through the disadvantages and humiliation that had plagued the three of them, for the financial support in her first year of hard study, and for his moral support.

After the ceremony, they went to a restaurant to celebrate. Daria was still full of excitement when Ken suddenly decided to pour out his soul to her. Perhaps it was a result of the amount of spirits he had consumed.

"Daria, why do you think Misha didn't go to the graduation?" Ken asked. Then without waiting for her reply, he continued: "He has recently lost interest in me. There has been something missing. He frequents the bars, looking for casual encounters. What did I do to displease him? I only wanted one thing: that he would open up to his family. I did everything he wanted; I went through with that shameful spectacle of a fake wedding. Why has he lost interest?"

"Dear Ken, I think you need not worry," replied Daria. "Most likely, Misha is busy at work. I don't think he has replaced you."

"I suspect that he goes to the gay bars without me."

"Calm down. On what is this suspicion based? Did you see him at a bar?"

"I haven't seen him, but I feel that it is so. He has lost interest in me."

"I don't believe it. He loves you."

"You are a good woman," Ken said.

Ken was very upset, and the celebration dinner was not merry. Her dear friend was such a kind person and Daria was sympathetic. He explained to her frankly how difficult it was to live with uncertainty. Together, Ken and Misha lived as a family, but how did they form a union if it didn't have formal recognition in society, and they had no common successors as a normal married couple would. There was nothing but mutual respect and love that bound them.

But how much is enough love? Ken always feared that his partner would get bored with him, an older man, and would go after a younger lover. He realized that no couple ever lives with the continuous excitement and attraction that first brings them together. For happiness, Ken needed confidence in the future, but he had no such certainty. He explained all of this to Daria. She, being engrossed her own affairs and beliefs, didn't expect such candor from Ken. She was shocked, and she couldn't believe that Ken's suspicions were correct. She was convinced that his turmoil was simply based on ordinary, groundless jealousy.

At home, there was a letter from Elizabeth for Daria. It was an invitation for Daria to take a break from her studies and visit them in the San Francisco Bay area. Daria mentally thanked Elizabeth for the invitation and decided to grab at the chance of a much needed vacation. She felt more and more uncomfortable in the company of Misha and Ken, and a trip to Northern California was just what she needed.

On this night, Misha didn't come home all night. It was the first time he had been away from home overnight. Daria went to bed, but she could hear Ken pacing and pacing in his bedroom. Daria listened to his steps nervously and couldn't sleep. At about three in the morning, she threw on a bathrobe and went into the living room. From the bedroom came muffled sobs. Daria knocked on the door. Ken opened it and followed her into the living room. He was pale and could barely hold back his tears.

"I hate him. What decent lover could he find at a bar? A chance meeting could lead to any disease. What have I done wrong? What did I do to offend him?"

"Get this nonsense out of your head. Misha said that he was busy. He couldn't even go to my graduation. He is probably working late."

"No. His company is at a standstill right now. I know him; he is not at work," Ken said.

"And I'm sure that nothing terrible has happened. He is just late."

With great difficulty, Daria managed to somewhat calm Ken. She put him to bed and went back to her bedroom. She was very upset. Why should she get involved in the disillusionment of the men? In such cases, a third party is unwanted. What a pity that the day had begun so beautifully and ended so badly.

Was Misha, good Misha, really unfaithful to Ken? She felt sorry for Ken. Very sorry. She worried as she would worry about a close girlfriend if her husband had left her. She tossed and turned in bed all night, thinking sad thoughts. It wasn't until morning that she finally fell into a deep sleep.

Misha was gone for three days. When he finally came home, it was difficult to recognize him. He was unshaven, his suit was dirty and rumpled, and he was sullen and depressed. He went into the bedroom to Ken, and Daria heard him beg for Ken's forgiveness and swear his eternal love. It was very similar to the way men in the village would ask their wife to forgive them after a drunken binge, promising never to drink again. The promises usually only lasted until the next binge.

Daria wished in her heart that her men would reconcile and would live in love and harmony. She believed that, just as the village women forgave their husbands, Ken would forgive Misha. What other choice did he have? It occurred to her that family life is the same everywhere – in Russia, in America, and even with homosexuals.

Chapter Twenty-five

Daria was impatiently looking forward to the moment when the plane would land at the international airport in San Jose. She dreamed that little Michael would hug her. It was strange, but this little boy had firmly taken a place in her heart, as if he were her own child.

Elizabeth and Solomon met Daria at the airport. They drove her to Elizabeth's apartment where Tanya and the children were waiting for her. Susana was clearly excited to see her. "Hello Daria! I am so happy that you came to visit us!" she exclaimed.

Michael was shyly peeking from behind Tanya's back. He had forgotten Daria and he looked at her with trepidation. Daria held out her hands, but the child didn't go to her.

"Michael, darling, don't you remember me?" Daria asked excitedly.

He is unaccustomed to people," said Tanya. "He has become shy. He sits at home alone with the babysitter all day and he's afraid of people."

"Do you have a new nanny?"

"She is the third once since you left. No one as faithful as you, dear Dasha, ever came along. Now we have another new baby sitter – an elderly lady, angry at the whole world because she was not given refugee status by the authorities."

Daria sat on her haunches and held out her hands toward Michael. Tanya nudged him, and he reluctantly went to Daria. She caught him, hugged him, and kissed him on the cheek.

"What about me?" asked Susana.

Daria had to let Michael go back to his mother and she hugged Susana. The girl clung to her trustingly.

"I love you," said Susana.

"I love you too." Daria's heart melted in delight. She hadn't expected such a warm greeting. It seemed to her as if she had returned to her home after a long absence.

Elizabeth put food on the table and the whole family sat down to dinner. Daria was seated at the head of the table as if she were an honorary dear guest. She felt awkward with such attention.

"Don't be modest, Dasha," Elizabeth said. "We all missed you. On the one hand, we remember and appreciate your affection for Susana and Michael, but on the other hand you are a relative of ours now."

"What, a kind of cousin?" asked Daria.

"A relative anyway," said Tanya. "In addition, we are very proud of you. To obtain a master's degree in such a short period of time doesn't happen to everyone. This is evidence of true talent."

"I was lucky. They counted my teacher's diploma."

"It's not luck. You studied hard and earned a diploma above a Bachelor's degree. For a Bachelor's degree, you usually have to study for four years, and you spent five years of study in the Soviet Institute."

"Is it the number of years that matter?" asked Daria. "In Russia, I studied a completely different profession. At the institute, I certainly didn't study many subjects that I needed for this degree. The university showed kindness, and I was allowed to take the special classes that I didn't take in the institute. The first year was very difficult; the double class schedule was a burden."

"We are very proud that you overcame the difficulties and achieved success," said Tanya. "What are your plans now?"

"I would like to find a job in San Jose or in the vicinity," Daria said.

"Your union with Misha didn't work out?"

"No, Misha's okay." Daria dropped her gaze.

"He's busy with his friend Ken? Isn't that it?"

"It's not my business." Daria didn't want to discuss the matter of Misha and Ken.

"What's to hide?" Elizabeth said sadly. "We can

guess. We have always understood it, but we hoped that you could change it. Now it is evident that there is no hope."

Tanya chimed in. "You know, Dasha, we have long suspected that Michael is gay. We see now that it cannot be undone."

"Yes, it cannot be undone," Daria confirmed reluctantly.

"Dear Dasha, we sympathize with you," Elizabeth said with tenderness. "We understand how difficult it is to marry a person and discover that he is gay. This is a tragedy."

"It is not a tragedy. Misha told me in advance. He may be gay, but he is an honest man."

"You immediately rush to his defense. This says something good about you. Yes, we don't criticize. We refer to him as a patient."

"It is not a disease. I am very grateful to him. He got married just to appease his mother, and he never deceived me; he was always honest. I respect him for what he is. And I ask that you also take him as he is."

"You don't have to persuade us. We blame that heinous Ken. How I hate him!"

"Well, that's not true. Ken is very thoughtful and a good man. I respect him very much," Daria said.

"Women, please change the subject!" protested Solomon. "This topic doesn't interest me. Daria, is your resume ready?"

"Yes, I have a resume."

"Give me a copy. I will show it at our company."

"Thank you. I wanted to ask you about getting the address and phone number of head hunting agencies."

"I have a whole file full of them. I will give it to you."

"That would be wonderful. I want to call the agencies."

"In addition to that, I recommend that you buy the Sunday edition of the local newspaper and check out the job ads."

Solomon had changed the conversation in order to stop the discussion about Misha. Daria didn't want to discuss Misha either. She was much more interested in learning more about what the children were doing.

"Tell me about the children," Daria said to Tanya.

"Susana is in school, in the kindergarten class."

"Susana, do you like school?" asked Daria.

"No," said Susana firmly.

"Why? Don't you like the teacher?"

"I like the teacher. I just don't like going to school."

"Why?"

"I don't know. I love it at home."

"You'll love the school soon," Daria insisted gently.

"No. They say I talk funny."

"Who says so?"

"All the children."

"Don't listen to them. You will lose your accent soon," Tanya said. "And you know *two* languages, but they only know one."

"Aunt Dasha, you're a teacher. Teach me in our house, can you?"

"No, Aunt Dasha no longer works as a teacher," said Tanya. "She wants to work for a company, like your dad does."

Chapter Twenty-six

When Daria returned to Los Angeles, Misha and Ken were not very receptive when they met her at the airport and she felt offended. She knew Ken dreamed of the day when he and Misha would be alone. He would be happy that she wanted to relocate to San Jose, thus making his dream come true.

Misha was also not very cheerful and Daria wondered what the cause might be for such a dismal greeting.

The men took Daria for breakfast at a small restaurant near the airport. They sat silently around the table, burying their gaze in the menu. Daria, upset with their sullenness, couldn't concentrate.

"What happened?" Daria asked Misha. "Why are you both so gloomy?"

"Dear Daria," said Ken. "We have big trouble. I've tested positive with the AIDS virus."

"Are you sure?" Daria asked in horror.

"To know for sure, the doctor is going to retest me."

"Don't be discouraged. I am confident that the repeated analysis will be negative."

"I am hoping so."

"I'm sure," Daria said.

Now it was clear as to why the men were so tormented. She thought suddenly that if Ken had AIDS, it would mean it was only Misha who could have infected him. Misha went to bars and met with unknown gays.

Daria looked into Misha's eyes. "Misha, did you take the test too?"

"Misha did. The results were negative. He is healthy," explained Ken.

"Is it true?" Daria asked, looking suspiciously into Misha's eyes.

"Yes, my test came back negative," Misha confirmed.

"Well then, you should test negative too, Ken." Daria said reassuringly. "You cannot get sick if Misha is healthy!"

The conversation didn't improve Ken's mood. It was evident that he was still painfully thinking about the possibility of the disease.

"Anything can happen," said Ken sadly.

The following couple of days were troubling for Daria. It was necessary to solve several problems at the university and to say goodbye to Harry, to Mirra, and to the other members of Misha's big family, all of whom had accepted Daria as their own. How to explain to them why she was leaving Misha?

Daria turned to Misha, requesting that he promptly talk to his relatives. But Misha still refused to open up to his family.

"Do you want me to tell them that I just stopped loving you? Maybe you want me to say that we just didn't get along? I haven't the slightest desire to quarrel with your family."

"And what did you say to my Aunt Lisa?"

"I didn't have to invent anything. They guessed the reason immediately. The only bad thing was that they accused Ken. I couldn't convince them that Ken is worthy of respect."

"Tanya also knows?" Misha interrupted.

"Not only Tanya, but Solomon too. I think that, in Los Angeles, everyone guessed. If I were in your place, I would have opened up to the family long ago. They are your family. They would curse you and then forgive you."

"You told Aunt Lisa! How could you?"

"I repeat to you that I didn't say *anything* to them. They guessed. They all knew."

"What should I do?" Misha was shocked.

"Are you asking me? I think you should build up the courage and announce to your family. It will facilitate your life."

"Who asked you to discuss me with Aunt Lisa?" Misha couldn't stop.

"Believe me, I didn't discuss anything. They all guessed. They figured things out even before you decided to appease the family by marrying me."

"It cannot be!" Misha was in despair.

"Don't think that people are fools. They see and they draw conclusions."

"You think so? Does the whole family know?"

"I can't speak about everyone in the family, but I am sure that many people know. They don't discuss it with you and your parents only out of courtesy."

Misha was upset and didn't know what to do. Ken was busy with his own emotions. Daria herself was sad and sick at heart.

In any case, she needed to have a conversation with Misha's father Harry about her departure because she was in a hurry to finish the business in Los Angeles and get back to San Francisco.

Daria rang the doorbell of Harry's apartment, worrying about what to say to him. She heard shuffling steps from behind the door.

"Who is it?"

"It is me, Daria."

The door opened. Daria's attention was drawn to the fact that Harry had become much older looking since Dora's death. His eyes were dim and his shoulders were slumped. Even his apartment seemed sad. It had lost the coziness it once had when Dora was there.

The old man was happy to see Daria. In his lonely existence, anyone visiting was like a holiday.

Daria cut the Kiev cake that she had bought in the Russian store and boiled water for tea. She and Harry sat down at the table and Harry began the conversation.

"I spoke to Lisa. She said that you want to work in Silicon Valley, where Solomon is working. Go, daughter. It is easier to find a first job there."

"I came to tell you about it. I'm hoping you will understand me correctly and support my wish to work."

"My daughter, do you think I don't understand how hard and sad it is for you to live with two men? I see that the venture, invented by my Dora, did not work out. Oh, she had set her hopes on you! Such a beautiful woman! So smart and kind! Why didn't Misha see this? Forgive us for getting you into this hopeless undertaking. Why did God punish us like this?"

"I don't consider my marriage as something regrettable," said Daria. If I were in Dora's place, I would have made every effort to distract my son from his lifestyle. I have to apologize to you that I was not able to fulfill the mission that you had for me."

"We realized this as soon as we learned that Ken would live with you in the same apartment," Harry replied.

"It would be a great relief for Misha if his life

was recognized by the whole family. This would make Misha happy and Ken too."

"Don't tell me about that American! I don't want to see his nasty face!" Harry said angrily.

"You are wrong about that; Ken is not to blame," said Daria. "If not for Ken, it would have been someone else. Ken is a very decent man; the problem is not him. I have read a few books on the subject. Their behavior is not usual but it is natural. They are not as we are; they are different. And this difference is natural for a small percentage of people."

"We must treat it as a disease, an incurable disease," said Daria, trying her best to explain. "We cannot blame Misha or Ken."

"Why did this disease happen to our son?"

"I don't know the answer to that. However, I know for sure that Misha's life would be much easier if he could openly tell everyone in the world the truth about himself. You have to help him!"

"What will people say?"

"You should not care what people will say. The people who love you and Misha will not say anything, and those who are hostile to you will gloat. You should not care about those people. If you ask me, I will always treat Misha with respect."

"Thank you. Dora was right. You are a very good person. I will always treat you as our daughter."

Daria told Misha all about her conversation with his father. Misha couldn't believe his ears. He was sure that the old man had been completely in the dark about his personal life. Harry had never indicated to Misha that he had guessed the orientation of his son.

The message that Daria brought was actually good news. Misha finally realized that the continued secrecy didn't make any sense. It was time to officially announce to the family that he was gay.

Then Ken literally burst into the apartment and he was excited. It was so unlike Ken that

Misha and Daria both ran into the living room to meet him.

"Let's celebrate!" Ken cried out loudly. "I got the result of the second test and it was negative! I am not sick!"

"Hooray! I was sure of it!" Misha declared, smiling.

"I didn't doubt it," said Daria. In reality, she had been worried about Ken. He had taken the first analysis so close to heart that she couldn't stop sympathizing with him.

To celebrate, the three of them went to the same restaurant where they had recently celebrated Daria's graduation. This time the atmosphere was completely different. All three were joyful. Misha joked a lot, hilariously translating into English the old Odessa jokes. Ken didn't understand all the jokes, but he was happy to laugh.

How easy it was to laugh when there was no immediate threat to life! In the midst of the fun, Misha suddenly announced that he had decided to reveal his secret to the whole family in the coming days. If his dad knew, he figured that all the others probably knew too.

Ken was very happy. He ordered an expensive bottle of wine and insisted that Daria drink some wine to celebrate their new open life.

The next day Daria collected her things. It was amazing how easy it was to accumulate things in America. It seemed that while she was in Los Angeles, she had lived a very modest life, and yet in two years she had accumulated a mountain of things.

"Don't be surprised, Miss Daria; in America everyone gets rid of their old things. You can donate your old clothes to charities, and they then sell them for pennies," explained Ken.

"Who would buy them?"

"The needy. People who cannot afford to shop in retail stores."

"Why don't they give these things to the needy people for free?"

"How would the charitable organizations exist then? They also have to pay a salary to their employees."

"I thought that people worked as volunteers at those organizations," Daria said.

"They do, but volunteers can't do all of the work. There are expenditures for equipment, vehicles, the rental of the facilities, and other things. Everything must be paid."

Daria looked at her computer and asked, "What do you recommend I should do with my computer?"

"Your computer was outdated when Misha gave it to you," said Ken. It should also be given to charity."

"But won't I need a computer?"

"At work, they will give you a computer. Then for use at home, you will eventually need to buy one. Computers become obsolete very quickly. What operating system are you using on your computer?

"MS DOS. Why?" asked Daria.

"Now all computers use Microsoft Windows. Soon you will not even be able to buy programs for MS DOS and you will be forced to change your computer. There is no sense to keep your computer any longer."

Daria had filled two large suitcases. Misha looked at the suitcases and grinned. "You have a heavy load! I think it would be good if someone can meet you at the airport and help you with your bags."

"I am uncomfortable asking Solomon for help. He has done so much for me!"

"I'll call him and ask. For you, asking is uncomfortable; for me, it is very easy."

"No, Misha! It will look like I am asking. I'll manage by myself."

"Drop it! I will arrange it."

Lily arrived at the door. She had come to find out if Daria was really breaking off her relationship with Misha.

"How can you do this?" she asked Daria reproachfully, looking at the display of suitcases. We had our hopes set on you! Is it so hard to seduce Misha?"

"You are talking about me as if I were not in the room," Misha said. "No woman can tempt me. I don't react to their spells! Can you understand that, Lily?"

"Why? Don't you want a normal family and children?" Lily queried.

"I love Ken and I want a family with him! You would not understand," Misha said.

Lily left the apartment very upset.

"That is why I was so scared!" Misha said. "Look at her reaction!"

"Lily loves you and she will forgive you," said Daria. "It will just take time for her to get used to the idea that you are gay."

Misha grimly left the living room. He called Solomon to request that he meet Daria at the airport.

The farewell evening was very sad. Daria had grown accustomed to Misha and Ken, and the fact that they were there to help her in so many ways. She was also sad to leave the friendly city of Los Angeles.

On the other hand, she looked forward to the future and she was full of hope.

Chapter Twenty-seven

In San Jose, Solomon met Daria and drove her to Elizabeth's home. Elizabeth lived alone in San Jose not far from the airport. She had a two-bedroom apartment, and she invited Daria to stay with her until she earned enough money to rent her own apartment. Daria was very grateful.

Solomon had prepared a list of employment agencies for Daria, and he recommended that she begin searching for a job the next day. Daria was grateful that Elizabeth and her children were so friendly to her, as if she were their close relative. She couldn't explain this generosity.

Daria found her first job through an agency. A small new company needed an assistant to the director of marketing. Her first duty was the preparation of a brochure describing the company's new product.

Mr. Singh, Daria's boss, showed her a preliminary sketch of the device. It would be used for gluing a silicon microchip to a copper base. He explained that with the current technology they had to dry the glued product in an oven overnight. Their engineer, Mr. Pezhabd, had proposed a way to speed up the process

by using microwave heating, and a group of enthusiasts led by Mr. Pezhabd had established the company.
They had already produced a prototype, tested it, and
found that drying the adhesive could be reduced from
24 hours to 15 minutes without sacrificing quality.
The company had received funding from a venture
capitalist to hire people and start the development of
the device. Now the development was in its end stage,
and it was necessary to start marketing it to potential
customers.

Mr. Singh was an amazing man. Dressed in an
elegant three-piece suit, he wore a magnificent tur-
ban on his head, and he spoke with great emphasis.
It turned out that all the company management, the
same group of five enthusiasts who had founded the
company, came from India. The president of the company was Mr. Pezhabd, and the four other members
of the group had the rank of vice-president. Mr. Singh
was a relative of one of the vice-presidents and served
as the company director.

A middle-aged American of German decent,
Mr. Rudy Schwartz, led the work on the design of
the device. The young draftsman, a relative of Mr.
Pezhabd, was his only assistant. When Daria went to
Mr. Schwartz to get the data for the device, he complained to Daria that he had to do all the work himself. He said he received no help from his assistant,

but he couldn't replace his draftsman with a more useful candidate due to the fact that he was a relative of the management.

It took a couple of months before Schwarz finished his design of the dryer and started its production. Meanwhile, Daria had designed an attractive brochure to be presented to potential buyers. She designed the brochure without any help from Mr. Singh. In his position as Director of Marketing, Mr. Singh knew very little about the machine or its application. Fortunately, Mr. Schwartz had explained to Daria, in detail, how to describe the invention.

Before Daria gave the brochure to the printers, she asked Mr. Singh to approve its contents, and Mr. Singh submitted the brochure to the president of the company, Mr. Pezhabd. The president liked the brochure and told Daria to go ahead with printing. Rudy advised Daria to contact several printers to get their estimate and then order the print job from the least expensive printer.

Daria was very grateful for Rudy's help. It seemed to Daria that without Rudy's help, she would have had a lot of problems and possibly been dismissed for professional incompetence.

Their working together led to a close friendship, and Rudy discussed with Daria his relationship with Mr. Pezhabd, the president. Their relationship had become complicated when Rudy found out that the microwave effect of accelerating the drying process was actually a bluff, because in the tested prototype, the microwaves were actually shielded from the microchip and copper base by a solid graphite plate. The microwave field heated the plate, and the heat from the plate dried the adhesive. Being a straightforward individual, Rudy reported his concerns to Mr. Pezhabd, pointing out the measurement of the microwave field in relation to the plate, and the position of the microchips during the drying process. Mr. Pezhabd shouted at him and ordered him to design the machine and forget about the measurements.

Rudy dutifully stopped his measuring, but he couldn't stop his desire to understand the cause of the acceleration of the drying process. He continued to think about it, and he needed somebody to talk to about the issue.

Rudy realized that Daria was the most suitable person. He was confident that she would not repeat their conversations to her superiors.

The company wanted to present their new machine at the upcoming Semiconductor Show and they rented a small booth in the exhibition hall for the duration of the show. The purpose of the show was to advertise products to companies that rented equipment for manufacturing semiconductors. Daria was instructed to contact design firms and order a suitable design for their booth at the exhibition. Mr. Pezhabd expected to establish contacts at the exhibition that would be potential buyers of their products. Daria called designers in the San Francisco Bay area, but they were all busy with orders from other companies, so she had to negotiate with a company based in Los Angeles.

The machine designed by Rudy was gradually assembled and tested. It worked perfectly and Mr. Pezhabd was very pleased.

Daria congratulated Mr. Schwartz. "You can probably expect an increase wages," she said with a smile.

"What are you saying, Miss Daria? I think I will be rewarded with a dismissal. The task for which they hired me has been completed, so now they don't need me."

"It cannot be!"

"Such things happen. The funny thing is that the companies who dispose of their equipment developers usually fail. Things tend to fall apart soon after the departure of the designer. Even a seemingly negligible question can become a complex problem."

Daria couldn't believe Rudy. She decided he was probably just in a bad mood.

Mr. Pezhabd called Daria in for a conversation.

Daria took a seat at the small table that stood next to his desk and Mr. Pezhabd sat down next to her.

"I asked you in, Miss Daria, to discuss the upcoming exhibition with you." His tone was gentle and trusting, as if he were talking to his beloved daughter. "This is a very important event for our company and we hope to meet with a lot of people. However, our set-up doesn't look particularly attractive, and so to attract visitors, we have allocated money for souvenirs. We *must* attract visitors to our booth."

"Yes," said Daria, "I understand."

"You will be on duty at our exhibition," continued Mr. Pezhabd, "and your task will be to meet visitors and answer their questions. Those questions that you cannot answer you should divert to Mr. Schwartz, who will also be on duty at the exhibition. Now,

I apologize for my tactlessness, but it is very important that your appearance attracts visitors to our booth. A mini-skirt, cleavage, and an effective hairstyle can very definitely help in this process. Don't think that I don't see that you are attractive in any attire; but the exhibition is a special case, and we need you to help us."

Daria didn't like her superior's desire that she wear a mini-skirt and a low-cut blouse to the exhibition. She was not a schoolgirl or a flirt, and she didn't want to appear in front of the business world giving the wrong impression. Also, she was now worried that she had succeeded in getting her position only because of her appearance. It was humiliating. Like a fool, she thought that they had valued her diploma and her experience; but what experience did she have really? She actually had no experience in this type of work. She concluded that she had been hired only for her looks and that was humiliating!

She complained to Rudy and he listened to her fears with a smile. "Well, think about it, what's wrong with that? You have an advantage – beauty opens the door, and then you can get to the top because of your brains, your work ethic and your knowledge. Is that so bad? It is an advantage that God gave you, and it would be a sin not to use it. And regarding the mini-skirt, my advice is simple: ignore his request. Buy yourself a simple but classy dress with bare shoulders – something attractive but modest. Did they offer you compensation to purchase the dress?"

"No, they didn't." replied Daria.

"They don't have the right to make these demands unless they pay for it," Rudy said.

"They believe that if they pay a salary, they have the right."

When Daria got home, she discussed the president's requirement with

Elizabeth. Elizabeth decided that Rudy had

given her good advice. Daria bought a rather expensive dress and Elizabeth altered the dress at the waist so it emphasized Daria's figure. Daria also bought several transparent silk scarves to go with the dress.

Elizabeth walked around Daria saying, "What a fool our Misha is! Such beauty he didn't notice!"

Chapter Twenty-eight

The exhibition was a success. Many visitors stopped by their booth and Daria barely had time to serve those requesting a souvenir. Very few of the visitors were interested in the drying machine, but an Asian man listened carefully to Daria's explanations and then asked to speak with the company's management. Mr. Pezhabd was close by and the man handed Mr. Pezhabd his business card. Mr. Pezhabd smiled as he studied the business card and he began to explain the essence of his invention. After the explanation, Mr. Pezhabd invited the man to visit their company and see the machine in action, and the Asian man agreed to visit.

"This is very good, Miss Daria!" Mr. Pezhabd said. "We may have paid for the show. This man is a representative of the largest Taiwan company producing semiconductors. If they make an order for the machines, our company will be saved. You can take a day off after the exhibition."

The first day of the exhibition was very tedious. By evening, Daria's feet were swollen from hours of standing in heels, and her eyes were tired from surveying the motley crowd of visitors. Daria was glad to come home to Elizabeth and lie down on her bed. She was so tired she didn't even want to eat or drink.

The next morning, Daria came to the exhibition an hour before the official opening so as to tidy up her booth, and many of the other exhibitors were also there early. As she adjusted a stack of booklets on her table, she suddenly felt that someone was staring at her. She turned her head and saw that it was Tom, the young man that she had once had a date with in Calistoga.

"Hello Daria," he said.

"Hello Tom." Daria smiled at him.

"Do you represent the company Heat Wave?" Tom asked in surprise.

"I do, as you can see."

"But the company is headquartered in San Jose," Tom said, pointing to the company poster on the booth. "Are you back in the Bay area?"

"Yes, I am."

"Can I call you? Would your husband mind?"

"You can. And I have no husband."

Daria handed Tom her business card. He took the card and smiled. "I'll call you," he said.

"I'll look forward to your call," said Daria, also smiling.

A young man came over to Tom. Tom looked back at Daria as he followed the young man through the exhibition stands.

The next day the exhibition ended and Mr. Pezhabd confirmed that Daria could take a day off.

She decided to use the day searching for apartments. She didn't want to overstay her welcome at Elizabeth's, and now that she had a steady job, it was time to obtain independent lodging.

Elizabeth was distressed; she didn't want Daria to leave. Living with Daria, she didn't feel lonely. She suggested contacting the manager of the apartment complex where she lived and asking if there was an apartment available in one of the buildings. In that case, they could live separately but be close to each other, and they could see each other often. Daria was touched by her proposal and she went to the manager to inquire. It turned out that in a week, one of the apartments in the same building where Elizabeth lived would be available.

Having agreed to rent the apartment, Daria hurried to tell Elizabeth. They were both very happy that things had worked out so well.

Chapter Twenty-nine

Daria was feeling elated as she hurried to work the next morning. It felt good to come back to the team where her work was appreciated and where she had been successful.

Inside the building, she was struck by the silence. Where was everybody? Daria went to Mr. Pezhabd's receptionist to find out what had happened. He was sitting at his desk, crying.

"What happened?" Daria asked.

"I am dismissed," he said in tears. "I came to work and they gave me an envelope and told me to go home."

"How come? It cannot be!"

The office door opened and Mr. Pezhabd looked out into the reception area.

"Come in, Miss Daria," he said.

Daria entered the spacious office. Mr. Singh, Daria's boss, was sitting near Mr. Pezhabd's desk. Mr. Pezhabd offered her a seat next to him and Daria felt the tension in his movements and in his voice. The idea that the company was satisfied with her work disappeared from her mind.

"I want to thank both of you for your good work," said Mr. Pezhabd. "Yesterday we had a meeting with the representatives from the Taiwanese company and we had high hopes for a large order. But to get an order will take time, and in the meantime our company is in a difficult financial situation. So the company's management has decided to eliminate a number of positions. Your department has been eliminated, and I will take on the marketing responsibilities myself. Once again, I want to thank you for your diligent work."

Mr. Pezhabd handed each of them an envelope. Daria realized that she had found herself an apartment in vain. Being out of work now, she couldn't afford it.

Both she and Mr. Singh left the office in a very bad mood. They met Rudy Schwartz, who was carrying a pile of books in his outstretched hands.

"As I expected," he announced. "The Moor has done his duty, and the Moor can go."

"Are you also fired?" blurted Daria.

"You are in good company. Did you not expect this? Learn, baby, about American life.

Nothing is more temporary than a permanent job. Did you earn enough for unemployment benefits?"

"I don't know. I worked for only three months."

"Then it's bad for you. To get unemployment benefits, six months of work in one year is required."

"I worked at the university too."

"Then go to the unemployment office tomorrow and apply for benefits," said Rudy.

Daria was despondent. She had just mastered this job, and now she had to find a new one. Returning home, she walked from corner to corner not knowing what to do or how to act. When Elizabeth came home from work in the evening, she found Daria crying.

"Calm down, my dear! We will survive this. You will find another job. I will contact Solomon."

"How can this be? Yesterday I was praised for my good work and today they don't need me? How can that be?"

"Anything can happen! You shouldn't think about it. We must concentrate on finding you a job and not thinking about your past work. Forget about it!"

The next day, Daria went to the state unemployment agency and registered. Her work in the university qualified her to receive unemployment benefits, and the agency promised to send a check within a week.

In the afternoon, Daria studied the ads in the Help Wanted section of the Sunday newspaper that was lying on the coffee table. She found an ad from a job agency that attracted her attention. It declared that it was the employers who paid for their agency services. Daria decided to call them, and the pleasant female voice on the phone strengthened her desire to turn to this agency for help.

The receptionist at the agency gave Daria some application forms to fill out. She settled at a table next to a pretty black woman who was busy filling out the same forms. The woman was nervous. She made a mistake on one of the application forms and had to ask the receptionist for another blank. Watching the woman, Daria also began to worry. "Nervousness can be passed from person to person like an infection," Daria thought. She moved to another table to calm herself.

"Don't you like me?" asked the black woman, angrily.

"It's just that your nervousness was passing itself on to me," explained Daria.

"You would be worried in my place too. I need a job, but nobody offers black people a job."

"It cannot be so," said Daria.

"All the good work is taken by immigrants, and then we have no place to work," the woman retorted.

Daria decided to remain silent. Was it worth it to enter into a discussion with a hostile person? The secretary, who just then invited the black beauty to meet with a certain Miss Patricia, rescued the situation.

Daria waited for about an hour. To ease the waiting, the receptionist brought her coffee. Finally, the time came for Daria to cross the threshold of Miss Patricia's office.

Miss Patricia got up from her desk and walked toward Daria.

"I'm sorry that you had to wait so long. I managed to get an interview for Miss MacPherson at the Intel Company."

"She told me that nobody wanted to employ black people," said Daria.

"On the contrary. Most companies are happy to employ black people, but not many black people have the necessary education and skills. All companies are suffering because they have bad race statistics, so I'm sure Intel will offer her work, even if she is not very suitable. I cannot promise the same to you; potential employers will not offer you any concessions. Therefore, we need to work hard to find you a job. Start with telling me about your work history please."

Daria gave details about her work as a teacher, a university assistant to a professor, and the short-term work experience in the company of Mr. Pezhabd.

"Not much," said Patricia sadly. "I really want to help you, but an application for a job in marketing requires at least three years of successful work experience. Do you have a guarantor?"

"What is a guarantor?"

"This is a man or woman who knows you and can give you a recommendation."

"I can ask Mr. Solomon Glikshtein to vouch for me."

"Tell me about Mr. Glikshtein."

"He works for a company called Applied Technology."

"I just received a request from a company for an experienced employee in the field of marketing," said Patricia. "Contact Mr. Glikshtein and ask if he knows Mr. Norman Chen. Maybe he will be able to help us place you."

Daria felt uncomfortable contacting Solomon for help. She didn't even tell Elizabeth that Miss Patricia had recommended that she talk to Solomon. Daria felt that it was Patricia's job to call Solomon.

Patricia did call, and she asked Solomon about Daria and whether Solomon was willing to speak to Mr. Chen.

Solomon was genuinely surprised by Patricia's call. He himself, at Elizabeth's request, had thought about how to help Daria. He was confident that the lack of work experience would prevent Daria from getting a job in their company.

Solomon's conversation with Patricia was long. She questioned him in detail about the nature of his work, and learning that Solomon was working under the direct supervision of Mr. Chen, advised him to think seriously about Daria as a candidate for the position. She liked Daria and she thought that Daria could easily learn the new job.

Influenced by Patricia, Solomon decided to talk with Norman. Solomon found Mr. Chuck Jennings, the head of the design team, in Norman's office. He spoke to the men about Daria, frankly admitting that he doubted the possibility of employing her due to her lack of experience.

Quite unexpectedly for Solomon, Norman thought that Daria's lack of experience was a plus. Chuck Jennings supported Norman's opinion, saying that the most important thing was the ability to learn.

Chapter Thirty

Daria was thrilled to have a job again and she spent her first day at work organizing her workspace. Within the large office, there were cubicle style sections, designed as offices, for each worker. A technician installed a computer in her cubicle and connected it to the company network. Daria tried to connect to the Internet, but there was no connection through the office network.

Mr. Dale, her immediate supervisor, invited her to his office, and over the course of an hour tried to familiarize her with the company's product. The company specialized in the production of disc drives – storage devices for the recording of magnetic media. This was a complex device that had been improving over time. A number of companies brutally competed in this market, trying to develop a product of greater capacity, and one that was more reliable and less expensive than their competitors' products.

Under these conditions, a good marketing plan was crucial to the well being of the whole company. Potential clients were large companies specializing in the manufacturing of computers. The success of sales to even one computer manufacturer determined the welfare of the whole company. Mr. Dale said all this dispassionately, without enthusiasm. Daria thought that if she had explained the rules of grammar in her class this way, half the students would be asleep, and the other half would be playing games.

"Excuse me," said Daria, interrupting the boring explanation. "Where can I get acquainted with the products of our competitors?"

"Why do you need to know about the product of our competitors?" Dale asked.

"I need to know the specifications of our competitors' product, versus what our company is developing, and on the basis of this knowledge, make a comparison of the characteristics. How better to convince our potential customers that our product is better, than to point out the comparative characteristics?"

"We don't need to know this. It is the task of the engineers. Let them prepare all the materials for us, and we will try to persuade the buyers. Believe me, we would never be able to prepare a presentation as well as the engineers. Our job is to invite customers to a restaurant. The most important agreements are better negotiated in an informal atmosphere. Therefore a restaurant is better than the office. Of course it is important to make a good presentation, but more importantly, to offer refreshment."

"I cannot imagine that they will make a multi-million-dollar decision at a restaurant."

"You have to understand. This is how business is done!" Mr. Dale said persuasively.

Daria didn't like the idea of the restaurant. Maybe they had hired her to do this job so she could lure potential buyers with her looks, rather than her ability to market the product?

Daria remembered the interview with Dale. She had failed the interview but they had offered her the job anyway. It looked to her that maybe she had been successful because she was suitable for attracting attention at the restaurant presentations.

Back at her desk, Daria felt depressed. She didn't study at the university to be engaged in the business of seducing customers in a restaurant.

A young woman dressed in a formal business pantsuit looked into Daria's office.

"My name is Megan," the woman said. "I am Mr. Norman Chen's secretary. He invites you to come to his office for a chat."

"Mr. Chen? Who is he?"

"The director of our department. He wants to meet you."

Daria walked into the office of Mr. Chen. The elderly Chinese man looked at Daria with a friendly smile and invited her to take a seat at the table.

"I invited you to get acquainted. Solomon has said a lot of good things about you. We hope that you will help us to strengthen our sales team."

"I'm not sure," Daria said wistfully.

"Why?"

"I don't drink wine and I don't like restaurants," Daria blurted.

"I don't understand you. What are you talking about?"

"I wanted to get acquainted with the technical specifications of our disk drives to compare them to the characteristics of competing drives, but Mr. Dale said it was none of my business. He stated that everything would be prepared by the engineers, and that our job was to invite potential customers to the restaurant presentation."

"You hit the nail on the head," replied Mr. Chen. "That's the problem with Bob. He is afraid of technology and he thinks he can sell without a serious study of the product. But it isn't so! Not one buyer will purchase our product if we don't point out the benefits. We are talking about large batches of product. In such cases, the restaurant meeting for a deal is not enough. We need you to study the product and prepare the sales presentation yourself. The engineers will help. They will teach you and explain everything, but most of the work will be up to you.

"I'll talk to Dale and ask him not to interfere with your work," continued Mr. Chen. "Our potential customers are working in a competitive environment, and they need to choose the best hardware products to compete in their market. If Dale interferes, please contact me directly. I can't afford any delays in your work. We have a month to begin to communicate with customers. Please refer to Mr. Jennings. He will appoint some of his engineers to introduce you to the product, and he'll help you with any technical issues. Get going. I have high hopes for you."

Daria felt very relieved after talking with Mr. Chen.

Mr. Jennings appeared to be a young man not more than thirty years old. He looked curiously at Daria and said, "When Solomon talked about you, he hid the most important thing. He didn't mention that you're such a beautiful woman. So you're interested in the technical specifications of our product? I will order our engineer, Mr. Pete Weiss, to take care of you. He is also Russian and he will be a big help."

Daria went to see Pete with Mr. Dale. Pete Weiss was an older engineer, an immigrant from the Soviet Union. He welcomed Dale and Daria and offered them a brief overview of magnetic recording. Bob Dale was not pleased; he had no interest in any type of theory. He just wanted Pete to prepare comparison tables that compared the company's products to the devices of competing firms.

"I run the job, and you should do what I ask you," Dale said.

Pete looked at Dale and said, "I'll do what Chuck and Norman asked me to do. If you don't like it, check with them."

"If Norman wants you to lead my group, in that case you can negotiate with the consumers without me," stated Bob Dale angrily.

"Do you want me to inform Norman of your offer that I lead your group?" asked Pete calmly.

Dale cooled down immediately, and Daria realized that her boss was afraid of Mr. Chen.

"Why hurry to report to Norman? If you must go on with this lecture, teach it to Miss

Stepanov. She won't understand anything anyway."

"That suits me," said Pete.

As soon as Mr. Dale left, Pete immediately switched the conversation to Russian.

Daria looked frightened, feeling uncomfortable using the Russian language in the workplace.

"Don't worry, darling Daria. I always talk to the Russian-speaking individuals in Russian.

Everyone is used to it."

"I think that at work we should always speak in English."

"This is true. It's a good rule. But there are no rules without exceptions. I use the Russian language only in the absence of those who don't understand me. Let us turn to the case. I would like you to learn the basics of magnetic recording. This way, you and our customers will be speaking the same language. Bob doesn't understand the main point. We are not dealing with housewives as our customers, but with *experts*. They will easily determine the level of your knowledge, and if you are illiterate, it will be immediately noted. You simply wouldn't be able to sell them anything."

Daria didn't blame Dale; he was her boss. For her part, she decided that she would diligently learn everything that Pete would teach her. Looking at Pete, Daria thought that this older and probably very experienced engineer reported to a very young boss.

"Uncle Peter, are people biased to immigrants in this company?"

"Why do you think so?"

"I'm thinking about your boss, Mr. Jennings. He is young enough to be your son, and he already commands a group; and yet you are such an experienced and competent engineer."

"You underestimate him. Chuck is young, but he is a very talented and very well educated young man. This disk drive is the result of his ingenuity and hard work. Do you know how many inventions for various improvements have been used in this project?"

"How many?"

"Nineteen. And all of them were designed by Chuck Jennings."

"Not without your help, I hope."

"No, I offered only five improvements. Chuck is the true developer of the project."

"What about Norman?"

"Norman is also a knowledgeable man. He doesn't have a PhD for nothing. But the real developer is Chuck. He is always going to Norman to discuss his ideas, and Norman criticizes them and offers advice. As a result of their discussions and arguments comes a new, more advanced version of the solution. Their joint work is bearing fruit."

"Do you give advice to Chuck?"

"He doesn't avoid asking me for my opinion and advice. He treats me with respect."

Chapter Thirty-one

Daria, sitting in the living room in her evening dress, was expecting Tom to pick her up. She glanced at the clock. Tom had promised to come at eight o'clock, but the time was half past nine and he hadn't appeared. Elizabeth, seeing that Daria was anxious, tried to entertain her.

Finally the doorbell rang and Daria hastened to open the door.

But it wasn't Tom. It was a stranger with a huge bouquet of flowers.

"Mr. Donovan asks that you forgive him. He's not able to come," said the young man. "He had a very important business meeting that he couldn't postpone, and he asked me to give you this bouquet and a note."

Daria thanked him as she took the bouquet and carried it into the living room.

"This is my date tonight." She said to Elisabeth disappointed. "Why did I dress up?"

Elizabeth took the note and read it aloud: "Please forgive me. I expected to get rid of the job before eight, but failed. We'll have to postpone our date. Sincerely, Tom."

"Why does he need me? He doesn't!" Daria said.

"Don't judge from one occasion. Maybe he is very busy. Why don't you trust him?"

"No, Aunt Lisa, I think that he doesn't need me. Why should he be interested in me?"

Her heart was sad. She felt she wasn't destined to have a happy relationship with a man. Tom was a very attractive man and there were probably many women that were interested in him. He didn't need her. How tired she was of being lonely, and how often she dreamed of having her own baby!

During the first couple of weeks at work, Daria read two books on magnetic recording, listened to a series of Pete's lectures, and lined her desk with stacks of flyers from their company and from their competitors.

She established a friendly, trustful relationship with Pete Weiss. Pete was very helpful in teaching her all the characteristics of the disk drives. He explained to her that in the hard drive, the magnetic recording is carried out by the magnetic head, which flies over the disk surface at a very small height of not more than a few microns. Due to the small gap between the head and the disk surface, the slightest vibration can cause damage to the recording head, stopping the work of the computer itself. The important feature of the drives developed in Daria's company was the fact that they had been specifically designed for use in *laptop* computers.

Pete explained that in a desktop computer, this device is installed permanently on a stationary surface, and because of this, there is no danger of it breaking. But the laptop computer is designed for carrying around and can easily be dropped. Additionally, a laptop can be used during transportation and must withstand acceleration, such as in an airplane.

"Now our competitors – Seagate and the Japanese – are working on a design of hard drives for laptop computers," explained Pete. "Everyone knows the requirements, but we believe that our latest development is far ahead of the competition. Jennings is a young genius. He has developed a drive that our competitors have never even dreamed of."

"How can you know what our competitors are preparing? Maybe they are developing an even better drive?" queried Daria.

"There are various methods involved in industrial espionage. The most simple is when an employee gets an offer to work as one of the leading developers of a competing company."

"And what happens if they invite our expert? What then?" Daria asked with a smile.

"If it happened, then we would lose. But, our people wouldn't leave us. We offer them shares in our company. By owning shares, the specialist becomes a co-owner of the company."

"You said our company offers shares. Are they free?" Daria asked.

"No. Companies cannot offer shares for free."

"What happens if the specialist doesn't have money to buy stocks?"

"Promotions are really worth the money. To encourage workers, the law allows companies to sell the shares at a 20% discount of the market price on the day of the sale. Employees can pay for shares gradually over several years, and then when the shares are paid off, the market price can be much higher than the original price. So people can earn good money this way."

"But if people sell their shares, they lose the status of co-owner of the company. So the whole idea of *keeping* the people by making them co-owners of the company doesn't work," Daria said.

"You are not right. If this idea didn't work, it wouldn't be used."

"This information about shares is interesting to me," concluded Daria.

Thanks to Pete's active help, the presentation materials were prepared in exactly one month. Daria reported on their completion to Mr. Dale. Dale frowned in surprise and asked, "Are you sure that this covers everything for our presentation?" He looked suspiciously at the folder of documents Daria had brought him.

"This is my first job," Daria said. "I think that the material is sufficient, but I am not completely confident. Please check it and I can make any corrections or additions if they are required."

"What *are* you confident about? Why do I have I such incompetent help? You have no confidence? In this case, we have a big problem. We can't go to the consumer being insecure!" announced Mr. Dale.

"I brought you copies of all the materials so that you, with your experience in this company, could determine if changes are needed; and from there, I will make corrections if necessary."

"Pete looked over your stuff?"

"Yes, he carefully checked each page."

"Is he sure that everything is in order?" asked Mr. Dale.

"Yes, he is sure."

"Show the material to Chuck Jennings. Let him check out his engineer."

"Okay, I will show the materials to Chuck," agreed Daria.

Mr. Jennings met Daria with a smile. Asking Daria to have a seat, he looked at all of the materials and said, "I think you did a good job. I was sure that such a beautiful woman could cope with the job at hand," Chuck said smiling.

"I am serious. Do you have comments and suggestions?" Daria asked.

"I have only one question. Would you share dinner with me tonight after work?"

"I'm asking you seriously," said Daria with embarrassment.

"And I'm answering seriously. I have a desire to spend this evening with you."

"Maybe another time."

"Is that so?" Jennings looked searchingly at Daria.

"Why do you embarrass me? I came here to work."

"I know, but I'd like to meet with you not only at work. You are so beautiful and so intelligent that I would like to know you better away from the workplace."

Daria didn't want to continue the conversation. She silently gathered her papers and hurried out of the office.

"Please don't be offended," Chuck said gently as Daria was leaving.

Daria returned to Mr. Dale's office.

"Did Jennings like your papers?" he asked.

"He did like them."

"Why did you come to me?"

"Jennings and Pete do not specialize in sales. I would like you to double-check everything."

"Leave the materials. I'll read them over." Dale was unhappy.

The next morning, Megan came to Daria's office. With an affable smile, she announced: "Norman asks that you visit him at three o'clock. He will be holding a meeting."

"Thank you. I'll be there," said Daria.

"Yesterday, your boss, Mr. Dale, went to Norman," said Megan. "The door was open, and I heard Mr. Dale complaining about the fact that you are still very green and that he can't trust you with the presentation.

Norman's answer was that he trusts you more than him. Bob went away in a rage."

"Dale is right. I have absolutely no experience in sales presentations," said Daria frankly.

"You shouldn't dare to say this to others. In America, it isn't right to be modest. You've got to be confident and tell everyone that you have done many presentations. People will admire you."

"Everyone knows that this is my first job," Daria said.

"I wish you good luck," Megan said with a smile as she left the office.

During the time that was left before the meeting, Daria devoted herself to rereading the materials she had prepared. She had the same feeling of anxiety as when, after graduation, she had first crossed the threshold of the classroom as a teacher.

Bob Dale, Chuck Jennings, Pete Weiss, Solomon and several men she hadn't seen before were at the meeting. Mr. Chen smiled at Daria and pointed to the seat next to Bob Dale.

Bob fussed. He busily set up the projector, pointing the beam at the screen hanging on the wall.

"Give me your papers," he said to Daria.

Daria handed him the folder. He took the folder, opened the title page and put it on the glass surface of the projector.

Daria was surprised at the courage of her boss who was about to conduct a presentation with no previous practice, and with documents he hadn't participated in preparing. She looked at Pete. Pete, remaining silent, looked at Mr. Dale.

"Start please," said Mr. Chen.

"We have prepared these materials to familiarize our customers with our new achievement – the hard drive for laptop computers," Bob began.

He proceeded to read the report prepared by Daria, page-by-page, in a monotone voice. He read the text slowly, stammering a little as he looked at the screen.

Mr. Chen listened carefully, not missing a single word.

One of the guests who sat to the left of him interrupted the reading.

"Can you just tell us about it, apart from reading the text?"

"I actually haven't studied the report yet," said Bob Dale quietly, becoming rather pale.

"Didn't you prepare it?" the guest asked.

"The report was actually prepared by Ms. Stepanov," Mr. Chen explained politely.

"Then let her do the presentation!" ordered the guest.

"Miss Stepanov, please start from the beginning," stated Mr. Chen.

Daria, listening carefully to all that was being said in the room, realized that the unfamiliar guests held a higher position in the company than Mr. Chen did.

Daria got up, walked to the table, made sure the sheets of the report were in order, and proceeded to present the report. She looked around the room at the audience and then forced herself not to worry about them, but to treat them as students in her school and focus exclusively on the report.

She knew all ten pages of the report by heart, and she didn't need to read the text. Already on the second sheet, she felt that she was able to attract the attention of the listeners. Nobody interrupted her, and when she lifted the last sheet off the glass of the projector, the same guest who had interrupted Mr. Dale's presentation, said smiling, "I enjoyed your presentation. Congratulations, Norman, on the detailed preparation."

He then got up and left the meeting. Everyone began to diverge and Mr. Chen asked Bob Dale, Pete and Daria to stay in his office.

"You rescued us, Miss Daria," said Mr. Chen. "Bob, how did you dare to make the presentation totally unprepared? And even in front of Robert! You almost ruined the meeting!"

"Miss Stepanov had never made a presentation to customers before!" said Mr. Dale, trying to justify his behavior.

"You forget that she was a teacher!" said Mr. Chen. "On Monday, we will hold our first real presentation at the PT Company. I negotiated this presentation myself, and I am planning to attend. Here, I've written my comments on the wording of today's presentation." Mr. Chen handed a sheet of paper to Bob Dale. "Ask Solomon to read the report and comment on its content. Then please make the necessary changes and bring me a copy of the corrected report. The upcoming presentation is very crucial! We must be well prepared! Any questions?"

"All clear," said Bob.

Bob Dale was very angry with himself. How had he, an experienced schemer, exposed himself by failing to present the report? How desperately he wanted to get rid of Daria, but how? She was a protégé of Solomon, so to get rid of her directly was dangerous. It would be nice if she failed the PT presentation, but even this would be dangerous. Mr. Chen would not forgive that, and he would put the blame on him.

Bob understood that it wasn't yet possible to put Daria in a bad position. He'd have to wait for another occasion. Everyone makes mistakes, and the inexperienced Miss Stepanov would make a mistake sooner or later – then he would have his revenge.

Pete was delighted with the excellent job that Daria had done of the presentation. She was modest, eloquent, and resolute. With what attention the president of the company, Mr. Morrison, had listened to her! Her position in the company would be much stronger after such a successful presentation in his presence. Pete was proud of his countrywoman.

"You did an excellent job, Dasha. It was a complete victory," he said on the way to his office.

"Who was the man whom Norman treated with such respect?"

"That was Mr. Robert Morrison, the president

of our company. The boss! Did you pay attention to the fact that he liked your report?"

"What does that mean?" she asked.

"It means that you have a good future in our company," Pete explained.

"Even if we fail at the PT presentation?"

"If we fail at PT, God forbid, then there will be *no future* – not only for you, but also for Norman Chen. Even I would have to look for a job."

Chuck Jennings came to Daria to congratulate her on the successful presentation.

She was surprised by his visit. Chuck had never visited her office.

"I came to congratulate you and to invite you to celebrate your successful presentation over dinner. We could invite Bob and Pete and spend the evening in a nice restaurant."

"Did Mr. Dale and Pete agree?"

"Pete agreed. I haven't asked Bob yet, but I'll ask him later. He's a fan of having dinner at someone else's expense."

Daria left her car in the company parking lot and went to the restaurant in Pete's car. The evening was very pleasant, although Mr. Dale tried to explain all through the evening that he hadn't wanted to offend Daria. He said that due to her inexperience, he had been afraid to entrust the presentation to her.

Chuck was in a great mood and amused everyone with jokes. He offered to drive Daria back to the office and on the way he tried to entertain her.

As they approached Daria's car, he said, "Dear Daria, I will tell you the truth. I really like you, not only as an employee. I would like to meet with you without the dull Dale and old Pete."

"What for? I am too old for you. Let's keep it a friendly business relationship."

Daria saw that Chuck's happy mood immediately deteriorated. He said goodbye and drove off. At home, Daria thought about Chuck's proposal. She liked Tom more. Why had Tom postponed their date? Why was he so busy that he couldn't spend any time with her?

Daria worked all day Saturday and Sunday so that everything would be ready by Monday. After making the changes based on Mr. Chen's and Solomon's remarks, the presentation was significantly altered. Before leaving the office late Sunday evening, she neatly folded all the copies and left them in a pile on her desk. The guard looked at her in surprise as she left; nobody had ever worked so late on a Sunday.

On Monday morning, Daria couldn't find any copies of the presentation or the original. The report had disappeared! Feeling terribly upset, she ran to Pete.

"What am I going to do? My presentation has disappeared! Last night I arranged everything on my desk, but now it isn't there."

"Don't worry! Getting excited won't help. Look on the shelves."

But there were no presentation papers on the shelf or on the desk or under the desk. Pete looked in Daria's office and said, "You saved everything on the computer, didn't you? Print more copies."

Daria turned on the computer and started printing. She was so nervous she became confused and was having trouble with the printer. Mr. Dale entered her office dressed unusually formally.

"Are you ready?" he asked.

"Nothing is ready. The presentation was missing from my desk this morning. I am printing it again."

"I knew this! You can't be trusted! I knew that you would let us down! What do I tell Norman? Because of you, I will lose my job! Why did I agree to accept you?" Bob was in panic mode.

Daria felt terrible. In her thoughts, a light flashed: "Farewell to work!"

Just then, Megan looked into her office.

"Hey, Daria, I took your presentation and the copies. Mr. Chen asked me to put each of them in a presentation cover," she said.

Daria felt a wave of relief wash over her body. "I've been going crazy!" she exclaimed to Megan. "Why didn't you leave me a note? I was SO scared. And I had just started to print the presentation again."

"Well, thank God!" Bob Dale said with relief.

Bob was genuinely pleased. If, in fact, there was no report, it would most definitely have reflected on him as well. Although it was Daria who had prepared it, he was her direct supervisor, and he too would have been held accountable.

The presentation was successful. The employees of the PT Company were impressed with the new development, and now the company's management would make the final decision on whether or not to order the hard drives.

Mr. Chen and Bob Dale were invited to a meeting with the vice president of PT. Daria stayed in the waiting room and she had to wait for quite a while before they came out.

As soon as she saw Bob's face, she realized that the trip to the company had been a success.

"This is just the beginning," said Mr. Chen. "They only ordered a thousand drives. We need to have an order for at least ten thousand. Fewer will lead to losses, so start looking for customers."

"We'll get on it right away," said Bob Dale.

Chapter Thirty-two

Daria finally moved into her own apartment in the same complex as Elizabeth's apartment. It had one bedroom, a living room and a kitchen. The kitchen was an independent room, separated from the living room by a low bar. According to American notions, it was a small apartment, but when Daria compared it to her room in the communal apartment in Moscow, it was very spacious, especially for a single woman. More important was that she didn't have to share it with other roommates. Also, the apartment had a large, well-equipped bathroom, which, to Daria, felt very luxurious. She was happy.

Elizabeth was pleased that Daria lived so close to her; it was very convenient. They could meet often to share news and also to go to cultural events together. Elizabeth often went to concerts performed by visiting Russian artists.

"Dasha, would you like to join me to go to a concert in Palo Alto?" asked Elizabeth.

"Lev Leshchenko will be performing." Leshchenko was a famous singer from Russia.

"When?" asked Daria.

"Next week, on Saturday."

"I'd love to go with you, especially to Leshchenko!" said Daria.

"I'll order two tickets," promised Elizabeth.

Daria had to buy furniture, kitchenware, and a lot of small things she needed for independent living. Elizabeth offered to help her, and she recommended shopping at the Chinese furniture store close by, where the prices for furniture were somewhat less than at other stores. The store was located in the city of Newark in a large warehouse.

Looking at the collection of furniture, Daria was horrified by the price.

"In other stores, everything is twice as much," explained Elizabeth. "Furniture in the United States is very expensive. Let us walk around and choose the things you need most."

"But I'll need to spend all my savings, and I also have to repay my loan to Ken!" exclaimed Daria.

"Don't worry. Now that you're working, you'll be able to make payments on your loan every month," Elizabeth said.

Daria walked along the halls of the warehouse. She was looking for a kitchen dining set and for bedroom furniture. She couldn't afford a rich dining set for six people, and as bad luck would have it, that was all she could find.

The sales clerk approached.

"Do you have a dining set for four?" Daria asked him.

"We have just one set available."

He summoned Daria to a small round table made of light colored wood.

"There are four chairs in this set," said the sales clerk.

"That's what we need," Elizabeth confirmed.

"It is too light in color. Is there another one?" asked Daria.

"You can cover it with a tablecloth. The price is right," said Elizabeth.

"So you think I should buy this set?" Daria asked.

"Yes, definitely, and then we can look for a bed."

They went to the bedroom section and the clerk showed them a wide variety of beds with bedside tables. Elizabeth didn't like the sets. She wanted the dining room and the bedroom set to have the same style. Then it would all fit together.

At the end of the row, they found a set that could be considered matching if one stretched one's imagination a bit.

"Wait for me here," Elizabeth said. "I intend to negotiate the price with the manager.

I want to get a twenty percent discount."

Daria sat on a chair at the back of the bed waiting for Elizabeth. Personally, she didn't like to bargain, so she was happy to let Elizabeth do the negotiating.

Two women were walking slowly along the passage. Daria wouldn't have paid attention to them if she hadn't noticed that they were speaking in Russian.

"Did you see Lisa? What is she doing here?" asked one of the women.

"I don't know. Perhaps she's buying new furniture."

"I don't like her. Her son-in-law has a high position in a company, and we asked him to help with getting my Lev a job. But he refused. Later I learned that he helped the former nanny who used to care for his children."

"It cannot be! Why would they need a nanny at their company?"

"Don't you understand?" asked the fat woman.

The women walked away, ignoring Daria, and Elizabeth returned.

"Everything is fine. He gave us a fifteen percent discount. Go ahead and pay," said Elizabeth.

On the way home, Daria told Elizabeth what the women in the store had been talking about."

"Get used to immigration, Dasha. There's always gossip, insults, slander.... Solomon couldn't help her Lev. Did his company have a foundry? No! Lev is a caster, and he isn't about to learn a new trade."

Returning home, the women saw a car parked near the front of their complex. The man behind the wheel was the same man who had recently brought Daria the bouquet from Tom.

Seeing Daria, the man got out and turned to her. "Miss Daria! Mr. Donovan just went up to your apartment."

Daria began to climb the stairs to the second floor and saw Tom coming down.

Tom was clearly delighted to see her.

"I'm sorry that I came without warning," he said. "I decided to take advantage of the free evening and pay you a visit. I know that it is impolite to just show up, but I just didn't want to wait any longer. May I come in?"

"Of course you can," Elizabeth chimed in.

Tom was delighted. He gave his friend a hand sign to leave and then followed the women into Elizabeth's apartment.

"We didn't prepare, but I think we'll find something to offer you," Elizabeth said.

The whole evening, Elizabeth entertained Tom with stories about life in the Soviet Union. Tom listened with pleasure and Daria entered the conversation occasionally. She didn't understand why Tom had come. Did he really like her? Daria confirmed to herself that she liked Tom much more than Chuck at the office. Tom seemed so solid and mature.

Tom was clearly enjoying himself as Elizabeth talked about life in distant Russia and about moving to America.

And this led to Tom asking Daria about her life. Yes, he wanted to know everything about Daria! Where was her husband? And what had led Daria back to San Jose?

Of course, what he really wanted to know was how did she relate to him, Tom Donovan? But he didn't dare ask her. Never before had he been so indecisive. Was he in love? For years, he had easily fended off women that pursued him, but this time felt very different. Why did this Russian woman attract him so much? She wasn't even trying to flirt with him. What did she have that fascinated him, and that had brought him to this house? Why was he drawn to her like a magnet?

Chapter Thirty-three

Although the company's first hard drive sale was successful, the search for new customers wasn't going as quickly as they had hoped. Several meetings with prospective buyers had turned out to be unsuccessful. Bob Dale was gloomy and troubled. Every morning, he invited all the marketing department employees to his office to discuss the potential buyers who needed to be contacted.

"The main improvement of our drive is that it is better protected against shocks, but it is not attracting new buyers," lamented Bob.

"We just haven't found those who value the advantages of our drive," said Daria.

"We must find them. If we don't find them within one month, all of us will have to look for a job," said Bob.

Bob was very worried. Every day, Norman Chen demanded a report from him, but he had nothing to offer his boss. The tension in the air thickened every day, not only for Bob, but also for Mr. Chen.

Daria felt this. With Pete's help, she put together a long list of companies who would possibly be interested in the new drive. When Daria spoke to the representatives of these companies, she realized the reason for their lack of interest. All of the potential buyers were competing with each other by lowering computer prices. Therefore, they couldn't afford to use expensive parts, such as with their hard drive. They dealt with competitors who offered drives at a lower cost and this meant that their drives were of inferior technical quality.

Daria believed that there must be applications where the *quality* of the drive was more important than the *price*. For example, in space. She shared her thoughts with Bob.

Bob chuckled, saying that for this purpose no more than a couple of hundred drives would be needed. But their company had to sell *hundreds of thousands*.

Nevertheless, Daria decided to call the Lockheed Company that specialized in the development of space travel, and she got through to one of the company executives. After laying out a detailed explanation of the advantages of their drive, Daria asked whether such a device would be of interest to the firm.

The executive explained to her that they would of course need these devices, but if she was looking for more of a mass market, she should contact the company "Progress" that specialized in computers for the defense industry. The executive kindly offered Daria the telephone number of a Mr. Kotapulos, who might be interested in their disk drives.

Mr. Kotapulos listened politely to Daria and he offered to have her come and talk to them. He suggested that she make a presentation to their technical staff regarding the drive's technical data. If they were interested, a few examples of the new drives would have to pass certain laboratory tests at Progress. Daria agreed on a date for the presentation.

Norman Chen appreciated the potential opportunity to sell to the company Progress. Of course they wouldn't need hundreds of thousands of hard drives, but they might buy ten or twenty thousand. And Progress might be willing to pay a higher price due to the need for special military requirements. The drives that would be used for regular control but did not necessarily meet the high requirements of the military could be sold more inexpensively to computer makers for ordinary consumers.

In the small hall of the Progress company, about twenty people gathered to listen to Daria's presentation. The tight group was seated in the shadow, watching the screen and listening carefully. Daria confidently described the technical characteristics of the hard drive while also explaining what technical solutions had helped to achieve those advanced characteristics. There were only a few questions.

Mr. Kotapulos invited Daria and Bob Dale to his office.

"How soon could you give us ten samples for testing?" he asked.

"We brought five samples," Bob said, "and tomorrow I can give you five more. How long do you need in order to test them?"

"I think it will take ten days."

Daria and Bob said goodbye to Mr. Kotapulos and went out into the lobby. Bob was pleased.

"We deserve lunch. I want to treat you and I know of an excellent Italian restaurant," said Bob.

Two weeks had passed since they had left the samples with Progress. Every day, Bob asked Daria if she had received a call from them. But they hadn't called. Daria could see that everyone around her was worried. Reluctantly, she decided to try to accelerate the response from Progress, and at the end of the day she phoned Mr. Kotapulos.

"Miss Stepanov, we sent you a fax today. We would like to place the first order for fifty thousand of your hard drives but with a particular condition. We need to add a special program that provides increased protection against possible attempts by outsiders to read the contents of the disc. Today I arranged an appointment between our representative and engineers from the Donco Company. This company is very successful in the development of programs that provide protection against hacker break-ins. We want your people to work with them to create a hard drive that is protected against possible cyber spies."

"Thank you. I'll tell our management about your request and get back to you," said Daria.

"Good. Tell them that we are ready to pay more for the protected drives. Additional orders for such hard drives could grow to several hundred thousand pieces."

Daria reported to Mr. Chen the results of her conversation with Mr. Kotapulos. Mr. Chen suggested that Daria and Pete join the representative of Progress for the meeting with the engineers of Donco. Daria called Mr. Kotapulos and he agreed that Daria should make a presentation to the Donco company engineers.

Pete asked Daria what she knew about the Donco company. Daria didn't know anything about the company.

"Dasha, shame on you!" said Pete. "Why are you not interested in the progress of our Silicon Valley? A young man who became interested in computer protection created Donco three years ago. Most companies create a computer network that allows company employees to share information. What this means is that a hacker, by connecting his computer to the network of the company, can then learn company secrets. As you know, these secrets have monetary value. Once connected to a company's network, the dishonest hacker scouts for secrets he can then sell to the company's competitors.

"The fight against this scourge has become a very important endeavor," continued Pete. Different ideas for protection are continually being investigated. Over the last three years, the Donco Company has gained influence even in the companies that work for defense; and this has been a great success. I think Donco Company shares will soon be offered for sale in the securities market."

"What does that mean?" Daria asked.

"It's a sign of success. The founders of the company will instantly become multimillionaires."

"Instant multimillionaires?"

"Yes, it is quite likely. The company is having a lot of success and there is great demand in the field in which they work."

In the lobby, Daria and Pete met with Mr. Kotapulos. After the usual greetings, Mr. Kotapulos said, "You may need a small change to your drive design. Are you ready for this?"

"It is undesirable," Pete said. "Our goal is to make a drive that can be used in any computer."

"We understand this, and we are willing to pay for a modified drive that you will produce specifically for our order."

"I am not authorized to make such decisions," said Pete. "I need to obtain detailed information about the required changes and then explain them to the authorities at my company. Then the authorities will make a decision about the changes."

"I agree that you need data. But I myself don't know what changes will be required by the engineers at Donco," said Mr. Kotapulos.

"We are waiting for you in the discussion room," said a young man, coming from the depths of the corridor.

Daria spoke first, using a condensed presentation about their hard drive. Her report was met with great approval. After Daria, Mr. Kotapulos outlined the requirements of the defense industry regarding the drive, and he explained that he had offered to work together on the modification of the drive.

When Kotapulos had finished his speech, a few people quietly entered the room, trying not to distract the audience. But in spite of their efforts, their arrival caused an interruption as people released seats to them in the middle of the room.

As Daria watched the small group enter, she suddenly saw Tom. Daria immediately felt uncomfortable.

It was similar to the feeling she had typically experienced in Moscow when the headmaster would suddenly come to the class.

It was fortunate that her presentation was over. She whispered to Pete, "Please, you reply to the questions. You are an expert, and it is easier for you to answer."

Pete looked at her, wondering. Usually Daria answered all the questions. This time the questions were basically about the possibility of changing the drive's internal program. Changes were necessary for the additional protection software.

At the end of the meeting, one Donco engineer concluded that they could take on the job. He looked at Tom and Tom nodded in agreement.

As Daria and Pete left the meeting, Tom blocked their way at the door.

"Hi Daria," he said.

"Hello Tom."

"Can I come by today?"

"You can," said Daria with her eyes downcast.

Pete couldn't help but notice that Daria was blushing, and he was surprised when he heard their conversation. It seemed that Daria knew Mr. Donovan. Curious.

Behind Pete, the Donco employees stood silently, waiting patiently to leave the room. Daria looked back and felt uncomfortable that she and Pete and Tom were blocking their path.

She indicated to Tom that people were waiting for them.

Tom stepped aside, and Daria and Pete headed for the door, making way for the others.

Getting into the car, Daria thought that what had happened in there was awkward. She hadn't even said goodbye to Tom. What if he was offended and wouldn't come over?

Chapter Thirty-four

Daria told Elizabeth that she had run into Tom during the meeting with the Donco Company. Elizabeth asked Daria what she knew about the young man. But Daria actually knew nothing about him, except that he seemed to be working at Donco. Daria didn't even know what kind of work Tom was doing at the company.

Elizabeth said that he most likely worked as a programmer because the company produced software.

"Do you like Tom?" Elizabeth asked.

"Yes, I do. I really like him," replied Daria honestly.

Elizabeth looked thoughtfully at the hesitating Daria. "If you like him so much, then act like it," she advised. "These days, guys don't just fall from the sky."

"I'm not sure he'll call me. I didn't even say goodbye to him."

"He will call," Elizabeth said confidently. "You're such a beauty, and it's not often that a guy can get beauty and brains all in one package."

As if in answer to the question, the phone rang.

"You see; he is ringing already," said Elizabeth.

Daria rushed to the receiver. "Hello!"

"Dasha? I'm looking for Daria Ivanovna Stepanov." The female voice on the phone was very familiar.

"Nina? Is that you? Where are you calling from?"

"Oh, Dasha, I'm so glad to have found you! I'm calling from San Jose. I returned to America! Write down my phone number. I can't speak for long."

"Your address, tell me your address," Daria said with excitedly.

Daria turned to Elizabeth and said, "This is my friend from Moscow!"

Daria carefully recorded Nina's phone number and address. Nina told her that she was free in the evenings and that she couldn't wait to see Daria.

Daria promised to come the next evening and spend a few hours with her.

Elizabeth, who had been listening to the conversation, said that she, too, would like to meet the woman who had recently arrived from Moscow. They agreed that they would invite Nina to their apartment and Elizabeth volunteered to prepare a meal.

Tom phoned later. He apologized, saying that today he was delayed at work. Daria was very disappointed. She decided to go to Nina's instead.

Nina lived in a beautiful new home in the south part of San Jose. Daria parked the car and knocked on the door. A teenager opened the door.

"Are you Daria Ivanovna? Nina Pavlovna is waiting for you," said the teenager, and she invited Daria to come into the living room.

Nina appeared in the doorway with a girl about three years old in her arms.

"Lena, can I leave Alina with you?" she asked. "Your mom will be arriving very soon."

"Don't worry, Nina Pavlovna," Lena said kindly. "I'll take care of Alina until my mother comes. Everything will be good."

Lena stretched out her arms, and the baby reluctantly passed from the hands of Nina to her sister.

"Alina! Be a good girl. Listen to Lena."

"I don't want Lena," Alina said. "I want to go with you."

The door opened and a young woman appeared in the doorway.

"Hello!" The woman said. "Are you Daria? I've been looking for your address at the request of Nina. First in Los Angeles, then here. My name is Faina, and I'm the mother of these two girls. Take Nina so she can spend some time with you. She hardly ever leaves the house, so it would be wonderful for her to get away. Please bring her back by eleven o'clock because I have to get up very early to go to work."

"Don't worry. I'll bring her back on time," said Daria.

Elizabeth lined her table with a variety of delicacies and sweets. She had never met anyone who had recently arrived from Moscow. Elizabeth always watched the news from Moscow, and she knew about all the changes in Russia. She knew that journalistic descriptions of the changes were one thing, but what a regular person thought was completely another thing.

She was looking forward to meeting Lisa and being able to share some of her own experiences.

"Lisa, meet my friend Nina!" Daria said when she and Lisa arrived.

"I am very happy to meet you," Elizabeth replied.

Nina looked around curiously. Compared to the home of her mistress, this apartment was very modestly furnished. Only the large TV in the corner of the room indicated the wellbeing of the house.

"Don't torment us, my dear, tell us how Moscow is now," Elizabeth said.

"I'm sorry, but I left Moscow six months ago," Nina said. "Life in Moscow was bad when I left. I did a stupid thing; I exchanged my currency into rubles immediately when I returned to Moscow. But the ruble had devalued quickly and I was left with nothing. I was very lucky that our friend Igor helped me to return to America. For this, I gave him the last two hundred dollars that I had saved."

"Why was it so bad in Moscow for you?" asked Elizabeth. "They say that in Moscow shops have everything now."

"That's true ... shops are full of products. The problem is not with the absence of goods. When I returned to school, everyone was very unfriendly. Even former girlfriends turned away from me. I lived there as if I were on an island. A lot of people were around but I was alone.

"My colleagues at the school didn't forgive me for taking a job in America. And Kyrill Matveyevich, the historian, asked if I was an American spy, or an enemy of the people! The old fool! He doesn't believe that it is possible to work in America and not have a relationship with the CIA.

"He used to believe that all foreigners in the Soviet Union were spies. And that every foreigner was under constant surveillance by the KGB. I lived a year in the United States and I never heard that the CIA was interested in anyone here.

"It was especially difficult to live in Moscow when they began taking our salary. Work, work, and the money was not paid. What is the use of the stores being full of goods when there is no money in your pocket? So people flew into a rage.

"And they looked at me with animosity because I didn't go hungry. I gradually spent all the money that I had brought from America on food. At home, I counted what was left, and I was horrified to find out that soon my funds would be used up. It was terrible. Thankfully, Igor helped me."

"My God! So bad!" Elizabeth said.

"I am interested in your story, Dasha," said Nina. "How did you manage to stay in the United States?"

"I got married," Daria explained.

"So where is your husband?"

"We divorced."

"For whom are you now working?"

"I managed to graduate from university here. Now I am working for a company in the field of marketing and I try to find buyers for the company's products."

"And you're not lying?" asked Nina.

"No. I'm really working in the marketing department."

"But how can anyone hire you? You're here illegally."

"No, I am now legal. As the wife of an American citizen, I got a green card."

"How did you find your husband?"

"Elizabeth betrothed me."

"Where could I find a husband, Elizabeth?" asked Nina.

"We'll come up with something," replied Elizabeth. "You need to think of what you can do in America for work. How is your English?"

"I didn't learn it. I have no need because I am working with immigrants. I don't need to talk to the Americans."

"This is bad. You need to learn English. Without it, there is no hope. You don't want to live your whole life as a maid."

"I have no choice."

"You can't be a nanny your whole life," insisted Elizabeth. "You're a linguist, a Russian language specialist."

"There is no job for this specialty. There is no work for a teacher of the Russian language and literature here in the U.S."

"I thought so too," said Daria, "but at the university there was a Department of Linguistics and they taught the Russian language."

"Get down to earth, girls!" Elizabeth intervened. "First you have to find a way to get legal status."

The conversation switched to a new topic. They discussed different ways of obtaining legalization in the country. Not finding an easy way, Nina got depressed. It seemed that everyone managed to get legal status, and she alone had no hope for the future. Elizabeth tried to reassure her, but Nina just became more upset. Daria drove her friend back to the southern area of San Jose. They rode mostly in silence.

Chapter Thirty-five

Tom called on the third day after their meeting. At first, Daria didn't realize who was calling; the voice was low and anxious. Tom politely invited her to have dinner at a restaurant. Daria accepted, and they agreed that Tom would come to pick her up at eight o'clock.

Tom was a little late. Daria was waiting for him in the living room, dressed in the evening dress that she had worn at the trade show.

Tom complimented her. "You look so charming!" He was dressed in a formal business suit and he looked pale and agitated.

At the restaurant, the waiter guided them to a small side room and offered them a place at a single table. It seemed that the room was specially designed to provide them with comfort and privacy. The light in the room was switched off, and only one small lamp lit their table. The waiter pulled back a chair, inviting Daria to sit down.

"What will you have to drink?" The waiter asked.

"I would like hot tea," Daria said.

"In that case," said Tom, "I'll have tea too. Bring me an iced tea, please."

"Did you order tea because I'm drinking tea?" Daria asked.

"No. We're going to have an important conversation, so I don't want alcohol. Also, I'm driving."

"An important conversation? About what?"

"I want to know everything about you," Tom said.

"Are you interested in my marriage?"

"Yes and no. I want to know ... did you love him?"

"Is it important?" Daria asked.

Tom looked at her directly. "Yes, it is very important to me."

Daria saw that Tom was breathing heavily and he was sweating. How sweet – and intoxicating – almost as if he were in love! Daria could feel it, and the excitement rubbed off on her. Losing her hesitancy, Daria said frankly, "I couldn't love him. He was gay. He offered me a marriage at a time when I couldn't refuse. But he had a full-time partner with whom he lived as a couple, and I was there as an extra."

"Why did he marry you?"

"He didn't do this because of me. He was gay, and he wanted to hide his orientation from his parents and the rest of the family by marrying me."

Tom sighed with relief. "I can understand him."

"We broke up when his mother died and he had no more need to hide that he was gay. He is a very good, caring person. We continue to be friends even though we are divorced now. But it is friendship, not love."

Tom felt the need to frankly share his feelings.

"I was shocked to learn that you were getting married. I tried to forget you, but I couldn't," Tom admitted. "All these years, I have thought about you. I can't live without you. You are in my thoughts all the time, day and night. Please tell me honestly, do you not find me attractive?"

"On the contrary. I like you."

"Just like?" asked Tom.

"I'm afraid to think about more than simply like."

"Really? Why?" Tom looked into Daria's eyes with hope.

"I'm afraid my soul would get burned. You always appear then disappear."

"That is because I am extremely busy at work. Work leaves me no time for courtship. I love you, and the idea that I might lose you again torments my soul and won't let me rest."

Suddenly, Tom got up from the table and went over to Daria. Dropping to one knee, he handed her a small box.

"What is it?" Daria felt both fear and hope.

Tom opened the box. On the black velvet flashed a big stone. Daria touched the stone and removed her hand in fear. Tom took the stone and pulled the ring from the box. Taking Daria's hand, he slipped the ring on her finger. Daria felt the wonderful warmth of his fingers. She looked at Tom as if asking, "What does this mean?" Tom shyly looked away, and then he asked with excitement, "Do you agree to be my wife?"

"Your wife? This is a joke! This is not serious!" Now Daria felt scared.

"It *is* serious! I'm not joking!" Tom insisted.

"I don't know. I'm scared." Daria was frank.

"I promise that I'll never hurt you, and that I'll always love you and care for you. I love you and I'm asking you for your hand."

"This is so unexpected. Can I at least think a little?" Daria asked, looking into his eyes.

Her heartbeat quickened as Tom held her hand. She felt dizzy with excitement, and Tom was no less excited.

"I can't wait. I've already waited too long," Tom said in a trembling voice.

"What do you know about me, to make such a proposal at breakneck speed?"

"I can't afford to lose you again. If you marry me, I will be with you for a lifetime. I love you!"

"Dear Tom. Why do you want to make a tie to me? I am an immigrant from Russia. I still need a lot of time to fully adapt to American life. I don't even know how to cook a single

American dish."

"What are you talking about? Did I offer you a position as a cook?"

"Did you ask your parents? Do they approve?"

"This is my life and my decision. They won't interfere! I am sure they will be very happy."

"I'm older than you!" Daria continued to argue.

"I checked. We were born in the same year. I'm only three months younger. And it doesn't matter one way or another!"

"And you know I was married before..."

"Of course I know. You said yourself that it was a marriage of convenience."

"No, I'm not talking about that. I was married in Russia. I separated from my first husband a long time ago."

"So what? None of that matters. I love you and I want you to be my wife."

Daria didn't know what arguments to add. Tom was insistent and he was convincing. As she looked into his eyes as he pleaded with her, his eyes radiated his love. His warm hand caressed her fingers.

He loved her! Feeling that she was loved was

intoxicating, and she wanted to reciprocate his love. But faced with the need to make a sudden decision, Daria was frightened.

But what did she have to lose? Why not get married right now to this handsome man? And she could have a baby! She wanted a baby badly! She liked Tom very much. He was very kind and he was very attractive. The years were running by. Could she afford to miss this chance?

"I agree!" Daria said excitedly.

Tom's face transformed. He leaned over and kissed her gently on the lips. His eyes were bright with happiness.

Daria blushed and smiled at him.

Suddenly, musicians came into the room. Waiters brought snacks and drinks. It seemed that this had all been planned in advance. As the music played, the singer sang a beautiful song and it touched Daria's heart.

Tom spoke happily about something, and Daria, still in shock from this unexpected event, quietly listened, not taking in the content at all.

At Tom's request, she drank a glass of champagne in honor of the engagement. Then he kissed her again and she happily responded.

She ate dinner, but afterward she couldn't remember what she had eaten.

Leaving the restaurant, Tom took Daria's arm and led her to the limousine that was waiting at the restaurant exit. She loved the feeling of his body beside hers.

"I decided to leave my car at the restaurant," he explained to Daria. "I'm a little drunk, and it would be better if I don't drive. Where are we going? To me or to you?"

"Everything has been so unexpected that I would feel more comfortable going to my home," said Daria. "I'm so excited. I need to calm down."

"Good. I was hoping that we could spend the night together."

"Yes, in my house," she said shyly. "I'll make some tea."

"Good. We'll drink tea and dream." Tom was happy.

Over tea, Daria asked Tom what he would like to dream about.

Tom thought about it and said, "My dream is to make you happy. What do I need to do?"

"Honestly?"

"Of course. I need to know what would make you happy."

"I want to have a son. The family only becomes real when there are children."

"And I want a son *and* a daughter. A lot of children!" Tom said.

Daria smiled. "Don't plan for too many. We're starting a family kind of late."

"Let there be as many as there will be," said Tom. "What else do you want?"

"I would like that you always love only me."

"I am monogamous. You can't even imagine how many women in the last year have tried to seduce me, but in my mind, it was always you. Only you!"

Daria's heart was filled with gratitude. She hugged Tom and kissed him.

Tom clasped her head in his hands and pressed his lips to hers.

"Come on!" she said firmly, taking Tom's hand and leading him to the bedroom.

Daria was half-awakened by the sound of running water in the bathroom. Then she remembered the previous evening. She moved her arm across the bed, and not feeling anybody, decided that everything that had happened yesterday was just a dream.

Such things are only possible in dreams. Half asleep, she stood up, put on her robe and opened the bathroom door, as usual. The bright light almost blinded her.

"I didn't want to wake you up," said Tom. "I have to go. I have an early meeting."

So it hadn't been a dream. She had really spent the night in Tom's arms.

"So early?" Daria asked.

"One who rises early gets more."

"Wait, I'll feed you." Daria said.

"I can't wait. I'll eat later. I have a meeting at eight and I have to prepare first."

When the door closed behind Tom, Daria looked at her watch. It was six a.m. Why was he running away so early? She felt fearful. She decided that Tom was no longer in love. All day long, she worried. Maybe Tom was not pleased with something, and he wouldn't come back.

Daria tried to conceal her anxiety from her colleagues, but Pete Weiss noticed.

"What happened? Did Dale hurt you?" He asked.

"No, it's purely personal."

"Then I am silent."

"Yesterday I received a marriage offer."

"Well, thank God! How do you feel?" Pete asked.

"I don't know," she answered fearfully.

"Who is the lucky man? Is it a secret?"

"Do you remember the guy who stopped us at the exit from the meeting room at the Donco Company?"

"Thomas Donovan? It can't be!" Pete said excitedly.

"That's him. What is his position in that company?"

"He is the boss! It was he who founded this company. 'Donco' means Donovan Company."

"Are you sure Tom is the owner of Donco?"

"Yes, I am sure."

"He can't be. He is too young."

"Young, but smart. He was the first who understood that computers need serious protection from hacking," Pete explained.

"Is he rich?"

"I didn't count his money. But I know that if they become a public company, Tom will become a multimillionaire."

"How many millions rich?" Daria didn't believe it.

"Hundreds of millions or more."

"Oh, dear Pete, I'm afraid."

"I'm not afraid for you. You're a clever and beautiful woman. I am sure that you will be fine."

Daria worried all day. How was it that she had so thoughtlessly agreed to this unequal marriage? Would she feel like the mistress of the house if she would be so much lower in financial status than her future husband? Did this kind of situation affect the strength of the family? She wondered....

Chapter Thirty-six

In the afternoon, the phone rang, distracting Daria from her work. It was Tom Donovan's secretary.

"Miss Stepanov, Mr. Donovan asked me to convey to you that he will be free at nine o'clock in the evening and will drive directly to your apartment."

"Thank you for calling," said Daria.

Immediately after work, Daria went to Elizabeth for advice.

Elizabeth, having heard Daria's account of the previous evening, doubted that Daria's Tom was the same Thomas Donovan, founder and CEO of the Donco Company.

Daria didn't really believe it herself. She showed Lisa the engagement ring that Tom had given her. Elizabeth took the ring in her hands and carefully examined it.

"That is a big diamond and it is beautiful! I'm sure it was very expensive! It seems that you have stumbled upon a gold mine. I am very happy for you!"

Then Elizabeth frowned. "Listen, is he purposely not married? Perhaps he's looking for a mistress! I will call Solomon. He knows everything!"

Elizabeth dialed the number of her son-in-law and asked Solomon about Mr. Donovan and did he have a wife. Solomon laughed. He explained that Tom Donovan was the most eligible bachelor in the entire industry, and that even the newspapers talked about it.

Meanwhile, Daria was worried about how to treat Tom.

"Aunt Lisa, I came to you for advice about how to treat Tom. He will be coming at nine.

I have a borsch. I think he probably has never tasted that kind of soup."

"I will help you set up the table. Don't worry about that."

By nine o'clock, Daria's table was set. In the center of the table was a crystal vase with a bouquet of roses that Elizabeth had brought over. They had set up an attractive display of appetizers, wine and ice water. And there were beautiful plates and cutlery all belonging to Elizabeth.

Elizabeth returned to her apartment so as not to embarrass the young people.

"Such a table!" Tom remarked. "When did you have the time?"

"I wanted to treat you."

They only had time to sit down at the table when the phone rang. The caller asked whether it was possible to speak with Mr. Donovan.

Daria handed the phone to Tom.

"How do you know this phone number?" Tom asked the caller.

After a moment, he said, "Is it so urgent? Well, come over here then. Write down the address."

He gave Daria's address to the caller.

"I'm sorry," Tom said to Daria. "That was Bill and I couldn't refuse him. He insisted that it was an urgent issue. I told you that I was very busy at work, and I definitely am. I apologize."

"I was hoping that you would be able to spend the evenings with me."

"I will certainly try to, and believe me, it is my hope also. But it isn't easy these days."

"I know, dear. Today I was informed of what kind of work you do."

"Who hurried with the news?"

"You don't know him. I didn't believe him at first."

"I hope it will not affect our relationship?" asked Tom, anxiously.

"It won't affect it, but it could complicate it."

"It better not. You see, I fell in love with you at first sight. When you told me that you were getting married, I decided that it was all over for me. I fell into such a depression that friends feared for my health.

"Bill saved me from that state. He would come and visit. To distract me from depression, he persuaded me to concentrate all my time and effort on the creation of a company. I had long had the idea of protecting networked computers from illegal spying, and I completely dove into my work.

"It was work that saved me; it took me away from my gloomy thoughts. Bill studied the possible market for computer programs that protected against illegal spying. He came to the conclusion that the idea of developing an effective program made sense. I bought five computers, connected them to a network, and experimented with programs that I developed. My first program allowed one computer to monitor the work of each computer connected to the network, while the rest of the computers were prohibited. The manager could check the work of his subordinates, but employees could not monitor the work of other employees or the manager. They only had access to the database, but not to the computers of their colleagues. With this program, the company Donco was born. I'm not tiring you with these details, am I?"

"No way! I'm very interested."

"Now the company employs about three hundred people. We have orders from different companies and even from the defense industry. Last year, we signed contracts for thirty million dollars. This year we've signed contracts for fifty million. We plan to bring the total orders up to two hundred million dollars in the next coming year. To expand the company we need money. Bill is busy with obtaining a loan. He's a genius on the financial end."

"Do I have to prepare something for his arrival?"

"Absolutely nothing. He's coming on business, not for a casual visit. Will you please excuse me that I have things to do? I just got into it and I can't give up halfway."

"Don't worry, I understand. I myself often work long hours if I must finish my work before the next morning. I hope our decision to marry will not interfere with my work."

"Everything will be as you want."

The doorbell interrupted their conversation. Tom introduced Bill to Daria "Bill, my friend, this is my fiancée, Daria."

"Pleased to meet you," said Bill.

"I am also pleased to meet you," said Daria, and after shaking his outstretched hand, she moved away from the men and sat in the corner of the living room.

"What is so urgent?" Tom asked.

"It is urgent because tomorrow I have to give an answer to the bank. Can you speak?" Bill looked over to the corner where Daria sat.

"I told you that Daria is my fiancée. I have no secrets from her."

"The bank is ready to give us the ten million that we asked for, but they demand in return the exclusive right to design documents for the securities market as your broker in the initial sale of shares on the market. They want to capitalize on this."

"I don't like that condition," said Tom. "What are the other ways of getting a loan?"

"I thought that this would suit us because we would need such services in the future. I didn't think about other options."

"It's wrong. We must always have a back door."

"Tom, this is a solid bank, one of the largest in America. Why don't you like their offer?"

"I don't care how big the bank is or how solid it is. I don't trust my savings to the bank to care about the strength of the bank. I am looking for a loan. I want to deal with a bank that will give us a loan for six months under a small percentage without *any* conditions. Are we not trustworthy?"

"They could transfer the money tomorrow," insisted Bill.

"If so, then let your bank give us a loan without any conditions. I don't want to be associated with additional obligations. Tomorrow, contact several small banks and determine which of them is willing to give us the money. By the end of the day, I need to know what options we have," Tom said decisively.

"How do I work with you if you never like my suggestions? Anyway, we will have to communicate with brokers for a securities registration, so why don't we agree on that in advance?"

"I don't want to take on any obligations now. The time will come and we will do it. Now I want to have the freedom of choice," stated Tom.

"Do we care who will prepare our IPO?

"I don't know. Now isn't the time to make a decision on that issue. We will make a decision when the time comes. No obligations for now!" Tom said firmly.

It was the first time Daria had seen the business side of Tom. Tom was not a spineless man. He was determined and tough. What if he would be so tough with the affairs of their family? Her gentle, compliant groom might be a tyrant when he became her husband. Had she been in too much of a hurry to agree to get married? With thoughts that happiness could turn into pain, Daria began to perspire.

Chapter Thirty-seven

Gossip spread very quickly and through completely incomprehensible channels. Almost instantly, the news about Daria marrying Tom Donovan circled throughout Applied Technology. Unexpectedly, Daria became the focus of attention. Pete Weiss, who had heard the news from Daria's mouth but kept it secret, was surprised when Mr. Chen's secretary, Miss Megan, told him the news.

"Are you sure?" Pete pretended to know nothing in order to find out from Megan the source of the gossip.

"Mary, Mr. Morrison's secretary, called me. She received a call from the Donco Company. They asked about Miss Stepanov. She didn't know anything and sent them to me," Megan said.

"And what did you say about Miss Stepanov?"

"The truth. I like Miss Daria. She is down-to-earth and friendly."

"I wish you had not talked to them."

Pete was disappointed. He was genuinely worried for his compatriot and didn't want her bones washed up in every corner of the company.

"Megan, it's better if you don't share this news with anyone."

"Your warning is too late. I accidentally told Mr. Dale."

"That is very bad."

Pete hurried to Daria to warn her that the company knew all about her relationship with Mr. Donovan.

Daria listened to Pete and said, "Don't worry, Uncle Peter. I'm not going to hide. What's wrong with the fact that Tom made me an offer?"

"Nothing's wrong with it, but people will be envious. Why is it that the most eligible bachelor in town made you an offer? What made you better than other women? They will be discussing this in every corner. Do you need it?"

"I don't need it, but how do you shut people's mouths? Let them discuss it."

Daria felt uncomfortable that she had become the subject of discussion and envy among the people with whom she needed to work. Indeed, she noticed that Mr. Dale, who usually treated her as an equal, suddenly began to talk to her in the same tone with which he spoke to his superiors.

In the evening Daria told Elizabeth about the gossip. She wanted Elizabeth's advice regarding how to behave with her co-workers.

"Lisa, what has changed now that Tom has made me an offer?" Daria asked.

"For you, nothing has changed as far as your work in the office, but for others, much has changed. Now that you belong to the elite, people who didn't notice you before will be pretending that they are your friends. And you have to think very seriously before you make them your friends. You cannot afford to put your fiancé in an awkward position if it turns out that one of your friends is an unworthy person. Any movement you make in the company will be discussed."

"What should I do? How can I refuse a person if they treat me as a friend?" asked Daria.

"To old friends, you don't need to change your attitude, but to those who had not noticed you before, you need to think carefully before taking their friendship seriously," Elizabeth explained.

"I hate to treat people with suspicion. I can't."

"It is a necessity of your new life. Caution never hurts."

When Tom came, Daria told him about her worries. He laughed. "Welcome to our club. I myself, after the company grew, became wary of people. Even old schoolmates with whom I had never been friendly acted as if they were my friend. You shouldn't abandon your friends, but it is also necessary not to promise anything to anybody."

Daria nodded.

"And there is one more thing. Obviously I will sometimes share my thoughts with you. You should never tell anyone what we are discussing. People could use it to harm us or my company."

"I definitely understand that, my dear."

"I do not want to complicate your life, but it isn't really in my power to stop that happening. Any CEO of a company becomes a subject of interest – and gossip. Even his bride becomes a public person, and she too is of interest to the press. That is just life. Can you live with that?"

"I'll try."

He looked into her eyes and smiled, and then he kissed her softly on the lips.

Daria loved his eyes and she loved his kisses.

"And I would like to remind you that it is time to get acquainted with my parents," he announced with a smile. "It is my hope that they come to love you as much as I love you."

"How do we do that?" Daria asked with some trepidation.

"The only way to their hearts is to remain exactly as you are – natural, open, sincere. My parents are people with no claim to fame or fortune. They are good people."

"I admit, my dear, that I am afraid."

"There isn't anything to fear. It is important that you and they fall in love."

"I love them already! After all, they gave me you," Daria said, smiling.

"We'll go on Friday night and spend the weekend with them."

"Good, I will look forward to it."

The phone rang, taking Daria away from her conversation with Tom. It was Nina. She said that on Saturday she would be free, and she asked Daria if they could meet.

Although she felt guilty, Daria had to decline the invitation. "It isn't a good time, I'm so sorry," said Daria.

"The call was from a friend," she explained to Tom. "She wanted to meet me Saturday, but I told her I'd be busy."

"What kind of friend?" asked Tom.

"We used to work together at the school in Moscow. Now she is in America to earn some money, and she is working as a nanny for a Russian immigrant couple."

"I don't want you to be detached from your old friends. Call her back and arrange to meet her *next* Saturday. I'd love to meet your friend."

Daria called Nina back to say they could meet the following Saturday. Then she found herself worrying about the coming weekend. It was no joke to meet Tom's parents. How would they greet her? What if they didn't like her?

Chapter Thirty-eight

Tom's parents lived in the city of Modesto, a town that was lost in the foothills and that had grown in recent years. Tom's father had played a role in the expansion of the city. He owned a roofing company, and his employees worked not only in Modesto, but also in other cities.

Tom's mother didn't work outside the home; she had always been engaged in bringing up the children and being a housewife. Now that her children were grown and had flown from the nest, she felt a void.

Tom's visit, especially with his future bride, seemed like a grand occasion. She had worried that the years were passing by, and that Tom still hadn't found a girl that he liked. On Thursday evening, she and her husband were sitting in the living room discussing Tom's pending visit.

"Dorothy, what did Tom say to you?" her husband asked.

"He said that he was coming to introduce his fiancée to us. He asked that we accept her as we would our own daughter. He mentioned her name, but I don't remember it. That's all."

"Oh, Dorothy, I'm afraid that some adventuress has seduced him in order to take advantage of his position. It was one thing before, when his company was not there yet. There never seemed to be a girl trying to win Tom's heart then. But now that his company has grown, a fiancée appears."

"So what's wrong with that?"

"I don't know, but I don't like it."

"Don't set yourself up against her. I want grandchildren."

The idea that Tom had a fiancée was a surprise to both of his parents. For many years, Tom had never mentioned an interest in women, and Dorothy had begun to worry. She was pleased that there was now a hope for grandchildren.

Joe didn't think about grandchildren. He looked at the idea of his son getting married as an extremely unpleasant phenomenon. Tom had built a company that could radically change the lives of the entire family. Friends had told Joe that Tom was practically a multimillionaire. Why share this with someone he barely knew? She was most likely just trying to get rich by marrying their son. What would that mean for him and Dorothy? Would other family members acquire benefits from Tom's new situation?

Joe felt hostile to the idea of Tom getting married. He thought they should insist on a prenuptial agreement, which would stipulate that in the event of a divorce, the wife would not be entitled to what Tom had earned before the marriage. She might not even want to marry him under such conditions.

Tom and Daria arrived very late on Friday evening. They were very tired, and passing on dinner, they went straight to the bedroom. Dorothy was disappointed that the dinner she had cooked remained untouched. Joe wasn't happy either. He had been planning to have a serious conversation with his son, but Tom had declined to talk, citing fatigue.

Tom habitually got up very early. Quietly, trying not to wake Daria, he went into the living room. Joe was already there with a cigar in his mouth. Tom winced, as he had been unaccustomed to cigar smoke for a long time.

"Dad, don't you think that it's time to stop the habit of smoking cigars?" muttered Tom.

"We need to talk," said Joe.

"Yes, we need to decide on a wedding date that will suit everyone," replied Tom.

"Wait for the wedding," advised his father. "Let her parents take care of it. We need to discuss how to protect the family from her possible future claims in case you ever want to get a divorce."

"Dad, what are you talking about!? What do you know about her? What kind of parents are we talking about? She has no father, and her mother is in Russia. I will pay all the costs of the wedding. You only need to replace her father."

"It's impossible," Joe replied.

"Why?"

"My task isn't to *encourage* this marriage, but to try to persuade you *not* to tie your life to this adventuress. It is necessary to protect the interests of the family!"

"What kind of interests? I don't understand."

"She didn't hunt for you, but for your millions."

"She never hunted me. *I hunted her.* And what about the millions? You're speaking about something that doesn't even exist yet. Perhaps I will make money, if we are successful. But who can guarantee success? My marriage has nothing to do with the millions."

"Yes, it does! Why would she rush to you hook you so suddenly? The hope of getting rich is what pushed her into it!"

"Dad! You are wrong! She didn't push anything. I was the one who chased after her. Plus she is a completely independent woman. Her earnings are not in the millions, but they're quite decent."

"Don't be a baby. It is necessary to draw up a prenuptial agreement that would shield the family from her claims to your wealth."

At this point, Daria entered the living room, and she couldn't help but hear what Tom's father had said.

"Good morning," Daria said cheerfully. "I certainly agree with the necessity of a premarital agreement. Of course it makes sense."

Joe said nothing. He didn't want to discuss anything with this 'adventuress.'

But Tom wasn't going to remain silent.

"Admit it, Dad; it is my business what I do. Everything will be as I decide. I came here to introduce you to my fiancée, and to agree on a wedding date, *not* to discuss a prenuptial agreement."

"I don't agree with you," replied Daria gently. "I believe that, so there is no misunderstanding in the future, you must specify everything before the wedding. I am pretty poor; I can't bring anything into the family; but I don't claim anything either. I don't want financial problems to come between me and your family in the future."

"No! There should not be and cannot be *any* material disputes! If I get rich, I will take care of my parents. They don't have to worry about it," Tom stated emphatically.

Dorothy came into the living room and looked around, totally aware of the tension but choosing to ignore it. Her son's bride-to-be was lovely. Her outfit complimented her tall, slim figure, and she had a lovely smile and beautiful eyes. Considering the circumstances and the conversation, which Dorothy had overheard as she entered the room, she thought that her son's fiancée was demonstrating admirable composure.

"I invite all of you to breakfast," Dorothy announced.

When they were all seated at the table, Dorothy filled their plates from a steaming pan of scrambled eggs, fried bacon and crispy slices of bread. A jug of orange juice and a pot of tea were on the table.

"Where are you from, my daughter? How did you meet our Tom?" Dorothy asked.

Daria began to talk in detail about herself, about her childhood, and about her work at the school in Moscow.

"And how did you come to the States?" Dorothy asked.

Daria told her story with humor – how, in Moscow, she had been offered a job in America, and how she had been misled to believe that she would work as a governess in a noble Russian family, but instead she had worked as a nanny for a family of recent immigrants. She told them that the host family had become her close friends, and that they had helped Daria to learn English.

She talked about how her teacher, John, had invited her for an interview regarding helping him with research for his doctoral thesis. She colorfully described how she had felt embarrassed because of her poor knowledge of English when Tom had come to visit John during the interview.

Telling all this, Daria was not embarrassed. Years had passed, and now the English words flowed freely, as if she had always spoken in English. Only a slight accent remained. Dorothy liked the accent, but Joe was irritated by it. Listening to Daria, Joe didn't believe a word of it. He was very unhappy with his son. Such a clever son, and here he was being so stupid in his personal life. Didn't he know that the money goes to money? A rich bride could not only bring a dowry, but could also have the necessary connections that would be important to a novice businessman. Additional ties to the business world wouldn't hurt young Tom.

Tom continued Daria's story. "Daria was embarrassed at the time of the interview, but this embarrassment fascinated me. I liked her immediately,"

Tom turned to Daria: "I wanted to get more closely acquainted with you, but you rushed off and got married," Tom said.

"I had no way out," Daria explained.

"What does that mean?" Joe joined. "Were you married before?"

"Yes, I was."

"Where is your husband?"

"We are divorced. He lives in Los Angeles."

"I understand that!" Joe interjected slyly. "You divided his wealth in accordance with the law...."

"We didn't divide anything," Daria said calmly. "And I don't need anything from him. Besides, I must confess, I still feel I owe him for everything he did for me. He gave me the opportunity to study and to get a masters degree in business management."

Tom didn't like his father's attitude toward Daria. He felt that his father was just looking for a way to prove that she was unworthy of his son.

The next morning after breakfast, Tom suggested to his father that they go for a walk in the garden behind the house.

"Father," said Tom firmly, "I have decided to get married and my decision is not subject to change. I don't like that your unfounded suspicions are spoiling the impression that Daria will have of my parents. And I am hurt that you don't have trust in my common sense. I chose a wife and I insist that you and Mom take her in as your own daughter."

"Why be in such a hurry? When you have advanced in society, you could find a better wife," Joe insisted.

"Forget it! This question is not up for discussion. I would like to discuss a wedding date."

"Whenever you want; I don't care," said Joe resentfully.

The conversation had not turned out well. Tom couldn't understand the reason for his father's hostility toward Daria. Why didn't he like Daria? Upset by his father's mood, he decided that they should cut the visit off as soon as possible and leave his father's inhospitable house.

On the way home to San Jose, Tom complained to Daria that his father did not understand him. Daria felt guilty about the frigid interaction between Tom and his father, and she tried to reassure Tom.

"I am the one who is at fault. I wasn't able to please your father."

"It has nothing to do with you! It's just that father imagines that I am very rich, and that I should look for a rich bride. But that has nothing to do with anything. I love you and I am going to marry you. It has nothing to do with anyone's financial situation."

All the way home, Daria worried that Tom's family did not want her. Maybe she needed to tell Tom that she had decided to refuse his offer? She was afraid that his parents' attitude would, sooner or later, ruin her life.

Chapter Thirty-nine

Tom vigorously took over the organization of the wedding. One Monday evening, Daria got a call from someone named Louise representing herself as a wedding planner. She invited Daria to come to her office so they could discuss the preparations for the wedding, and so she could show Daria a variety of necessary items.

Daria was frightened. She didn't know why anybody needed a consultant for this. Was a wedding such a complex matter that one couldn't do it without a special consultant? But she had to admit that she had no idea what the arrangements for a proper American wedding should be.

She decided to turn to Elizabeth for advice, and Elizabeth offered to accompany Daria on her visit with the consultant. After all, she had given away her daughter in an American marriage, so she had some experience.

The business where Louise worked – 'Happiness' – was a very respectable establishment of wedding coordinators. The receptionist led Daria and Elizabeth to Louise's spacious office.

Louise was a pretty girl of about twenty. Her youth confused Daria and caused her to be suspicious of her competence. Regardless of this, it was necessary to work out all the details with the agent that had been selected by Tom.

Louise began with a schedule for the wedding preparations. The first objective was to determine the date. Daria didn't want to make that decision; it would depend on Tom's schedule. Louise would have to communicate with Tom's secretary to get an answer.

While they were waiting to solve the date question, Louise brought out an album with samples of wedding invitations and asked Daria to pick the one she liked. A basic examination of the samples took more than half an hour. Daria chose one of the simplest invitations, announcing that the invitation was on behalf of the parents of the bride and groom.

Suddenly Tom arrived. "I hastened to the rescue as soon as I realized that there are questions that Daria has no idea how to answer," said Tom. "I'd like to hold the ceremony in the next few days."

"It's impossible," said Louise. "First of all, it's necessary to invite the guests, receive their response, order the bride's gown and the suit for the groom, pick the bridesmaids and determine the groomsmen, order all the same suits and choose the dresses, choose a church, arrange something with the minister, and reserve a restaurant. All of this will require a lot of time."

"In order not to delay the wedding, we'll send invitations to guests but won't wait for their response. Who will come, will come. We'll order all the gowns and tuxes for friends and girlfriends from Hong Kong, and we'll send them all the sizes and ask to have the outfits sent to us by air. We'll buy the wedding gown in Los Angeles. I have a tuxedo. A preacher friend of mine will preside over the ceremony any day we choose. We'll conduct the ceremony in the banquet hall of the golf club, and after the ceremony, the same golf club will cater the banquet for the reception. Do you agree, dear?" asked Tom.

"I have no objections. Do as you wish. I don't have any idea about all of this," replied Daria.

"What is the budget you plan to allocate to the ceremony?" Louise asked.

"I don't want to limit you too much, but try to keep it within a hundred thousand."

Daria was shocked at hearing such a figure. It was a fortune! Throw away a hundred thousand dollars on a one-day party?

"Can we have a more modest ceremony?" she asked.

"This is very modest," Louise replied. "First of all, your gown can cost a quarter of that amount."

"I don't want such an expensive gown! replied Daria. "It's not necessary. There must be gowns that cost much less...."

"You can't wear a gown from an ordinary shop!" Louise insisted.

"Oh, but I can," insisted Daria.

"We certainly aren't going to skimp on your gown!" stated Tom. He turned to Louise. "My beautiful wife will be in a beautiful gown," he declared.

Louise nodded.

Daria turned to Tom and asked quietly, "Why is that, Tom? I am not a young girl and my parents cannot participate in the financing of the wedding. I am categorically against such an expensive gown. It's impractical to spend that kind of money on a thing that I will wear only once."

"It is impractical, but it is necessary," Tom said. "The day after the wedding our photos will be in all the newspapers. I want everyone to see how beautiful my wife is."

Elizabeth supported Daria. "Don't worry about that. Our Daria will be beautiful in any gown!"

Daria turned to Tom. "Please understand me, my love. I don't want a costly gown. I'll buy a wedding gown in a store and buy it at my own expense."

Tom took Daria's hand in his. Elizabeth was pleased to see that he was being patient and understanding with Daria.

"At the wedding there will be a lot of people with whom I am not very close, but whom I must invite whether I want to or not. Among them may be people who are hostile toward me. I just don't need to give them reason to gossip and speculate."

"How would they know that the gown was bought in a store, and not ordered from an expensive designer?"

"They would know. They know everything. But I think that your desire is more important to me than gossip. Buy the gown in a store if that is your wish. My only request is that I would like to go with you for this purchase."

"I have no objections, of course. The most important thing is that you would have to like the gown as much as I do."

Louise waited patiently for the discussion about the gown to end and then chimed in. "I need a list of invitees and their addresses as soon as possible. It's also necessary, first off, to determine the exact date for the wedding."

"Can your agency negotiate a contract with the preacher, a printing house, the golf club and banquet hall, and generally coordinate all other technical questions?" Tom asked.

"Of course we provide these services."

"That's fine. I am asking that you contact my

secretary with any questions. Please contact my bride only when absolutely necessary."

"That's fine," said Louise. "You need to sign a contract with our agency. I'll send it to you tomorrow."

"Agreed," said Tom.

Tom apologized to Daria for the fact that he had to return to work.

Chapter Forty

Daria had a lot on her mind.... She didn't understand what was happening to her. Just a few months ago, Tom had been a pleasant but distant memory of a trip to the local resort town of Calistoga. He hadn't stirred up any feelings in her heart and soul. Even the decision to accept his proposal of marriage had been made spontaneously. What was happening now? Why was she, day and night, thinking about this man? His love and respect for her had broken through her armor, and all her thoughts were about *him*.

Daria was afraid of the feelings that arose within her. And she was frightened about the inequality of their social status. Would she fall into complete dependence on this person? It was her belief that a strong family should be based on the equality of the two partners, on respecting each other. How to achieve equality if she was just starting her career as a specialist and he was the owner of a successful company? She needed to pay back her debt, and he was willing to spend a hundred thousand on just one celebration? Daria knew that her excitement was much more pleasant than worrying about loneliness, poverty and despair, and yet her heart was restless.

Daria thought about what an interesting man her Tom was. How gentle he was with her! How attentive he was! How could she not fall in love with this man? He was bright, handsome and skilful. She felt happy. But it was not clear to her how it had happened that she was so lucky. It was very scary for her to think that just as easily as she had found her loved one, she might lose him. How many beautiful and rich women were in the world? One such woman could easily rob Daria of her groom. It would be so easy for many women to love such a guy.

Despite these thoughts, Daria happily went to work in the morning. Everything was going very well for her. She loved her job and was ready to make every effort to succeed at work, where friends surrounded her. It seemed that the whole world was friendly and nice.

With such thoughts, Daria approached the Applied Technology building. A tall young man stopped her at the entrance.

"Are you Miss Stepanov?" he asked.

"Yes, I'm Daria Stepanov."

"I am Jim Candels, representative of Immigration and Naturalization Services. We have a question for you. I am asking that you come with me."

The young man pointed to a car standing at the edge of the sidewalk. Daria had no time to recover before she was in the car, separated from the driver with metal bars. What did this mean? Why? She decided to be patient. This was a misunderstanding. She had the legal status of permanent resident, and after checking, they must let her go.

They stopped at the entrance of a familiar building – the Department of Immigration and Naturalization Services – in the center of San Jose. Daria was led out of the car. At that moment, the flash of a camera blinded her. An unknown photographer in a shabby T-shirt managed to take a few more shots while Daria, accompanied by agent Candels, entered the building.

"We have received notification that you are living illegally in the United States," the agent said, as they sat down in his cramped office.

"I live in the country legally. I have a document issued by your office."

Daria found the cherished green card in her purse and handed it to the representative. He took the card from her hands and began to examine it closely.

"Hmm," he muttered. "It looks real. We have learned that, in Russia, they know how to make fake documents look as if they are real. By whom and when was it granted to you?"

"The card was issued by the Department of Naturalization Services in Los Angeles. The exact date, I don't remember. You will find it on the card itself."

Their conversation was interrupted by a knock on the door.

"Who's there? Come in," said agent Candels.

An official looking elderly man in a formal business suit entered.

"Jim, are you once again checking on unfounded denunciations?" asked the man. "I am representing the interests of Ms. Stepanov, and from this moment on all your questions should be asked through me. Do you have a judge's permission to detain Ms. Stepanov?"

"I will have permission from the judge on this case by noon," Agent Candels replied.

"So, you don't have permission from the court?"

"I will."

"When you obtain the court order, *then* you can detain her. But now you have to let Miss Stepanov go."

"Here is the official summons." Agent Candels handed the paper to the lawyer.

"We'll be in court at the appointed time. Come with me, Miss Stepanov."

"I can't let her to go. What if she doesn't appear in court?" said the agent.

"I'm sorry, what grounds do you have for detention? She has committed no violation; you'll have to let her go."

"We're leaving via the emergency exit," the lawyer said to Daria. "I don't want the paparazzi to meet us at the door. You are lucky. I was here in the building when Mr. Morrison phoned me. He asked me to take care of your business."

The lawyer led Daria out the back of the building and walked with her to a cafe on the next street. She could see that he was a frequent visitor to the café, as they were immediately led into a small empty room where the table was set.

"I didn't have breakfast earlier. You don't mind if I eat breakfast while I talk with you, do you?" he asked.

"Please eat. I am not offended. I don't understand what I did wrong. What claim do the authorities have?" Daria asked.

"First, let me introduce myself. My name is Sam Flistein. I am a lawyer who specializes in immigration issues. Your company, Applied Technology, is my customer. I need to be prepared for your protection. We have a couple of hours for this. In the afternoon we have to be in court so as not to give Jim a chance to arrest you."

"I don't have any secrets. I'm in the country legally. I have a green card."

"Start from the beginning. When you came to the country, on what basis did you receive a green card?"

Daria recounted her life from the time of her departure from Russia and her arrival in the United States. She told him that Misha had proposed to her and that he had hired a lawyer who obtained for her an absolutely legal green card. She told him about her studies at the university, and she told him everything except for the recent events that involved Tom. She didn't want to implicate Tom, but it turned out that her boss, Mr. Morrison, had told Sam about Tom.

Sam asked Daria cautiously about her relationship with Tom Donovan. Daria said that they were planning a wedding, if the interference of the Immigration Service didn't prevent it.

At noon they were in the judge's office. The judge gave the floor to the prosecution and Agent Candels turned to the judge.

"Your Honor, we received a call from the company Applied Technology that Miss Stepanov is an illegal immigrant, and that she began working with false documents. We are asking your permission to detain Miss Stepanov during the investigation of this case."

"Did you check her documents?" The judge asked sternly.

"I inquired, your Honor. Her green card, issued by our office in Los Angeles, is genuine. We have a suspicion that our workers in Los Angeles were misled by trusting her false marriage as real."

"What are the grounds for such suspicions?"

"Miss Stepanov lives in San Jose, and her husband is in Los Angeles," Jim said.

"Yes, that is suspicious. What else?"

"Nothing yet, but we will continue to investigate."

"Miss Stepanov, what can you say?"

"Your Honor," interrupted Sam, "I'm here on behalf of the company Applied Technology to represent the interests of Miss Stepanov."

"Please, your explanation."

"I don't understand what claim the Agency has regarding my client. The prosecutor himself acknowledged just now that Immigration Services issued Miss Stepanov the document that gave her the right to reside and work in this country. The charge is that the agent has suspicions. But suspicions are not evidence, and as such are not recognized by law. Miss Stepanov is a known person, and wouldn't hide from the authorities. We ask you, Your Honor, to deny charges of the right to custody of Miss Stepanov. Suspicion cannot be the basis for arrest in the absence of any evidence."

"It's true. You warrant that she wouldn't hide from the court?"

"Excuse me, Your Honor, where can she hide? It would be nice to hide her from the paparazzi surrounding the exit from your office. The detention of Miss Stepanov will be the sensation that will be in all the papers in the Bay area tomorrow," said Sam.

"Is Miss Stepanov so important that newspaper reporters are waiting for her on the street?

"It's true, Your Honor," confirmed the clerk of the court. "It's difficult to get out of our office because of the invasion of reporters."

"The request of the accusations is rejected. Miss Stepanov can go free."

"Thank you, your Honor," said Sam.

Leaving the office, Agent Candels caught up with Sam and Daria.

"Sam, tell me please, why is Miss Stepanov so famous?"

"Why explain to you, Jim, if you so easily took on this libel at face value? Read the newspapers tomorrow."

Sam took Daria's arm and led her through a gauntlet of reporters and camera flashes to his car.

"Sam, do you want to say something to the press?" asked the reporters.

"I have nothing to say. Nothing happened. It was an error of the Immigration and

Naturalization Service. That's all."

Sam quickly opened the car door and helped Daria into the back seat. He then drove off.

Daria thought: As in the morning, but no bars.

Chapter Forty-one

Nina dressed little Alina. She was going with the baby for a walk in the nearby park. Actually, it was a stretch to call the small area with grass and a pair of green trees a park. The only attraction was a brightly painted construction designed for children to play on. Alina loved it. She loved to climb the ladder to the bridge, and from the bridge jump onto the pipe and reach the other side of the structure.

Lena asked, "Aunt Nina! Can I go with you? I want to read outdoors."

"Of course, Lena! It would be more fun for Alina to walk with you."

Nina sat on a bench in the shade of a young tree. The entire area in which they lived had been built only recently, and the trees hadn't had time to grow yet. The shade from the trees barely covered half the bench and Lena sat under the scorching sun.

"It is so hot today," Lena complained.

"Yes, it is very hot in the summer here, and there is no snow in the winter. Have you ever seen snow?" asked Nina.

"I don't remember snow, but I probably saw it in Russia," Lena replied.

"Look, Lena, there are boys where Alina is climbing. They could hurt her."

"Don't be afraid. They are little boys. They also want to play." said Lena.

A man in T-shirt and jeans came to the bench.

"My name is Joe," he said in English.

"What does he want?" Nina asked in Russian.

"He said his name is Joe," Lena explained.

"Why do we need to know his name?" asked the worried Nina.

The man, listening to the Russian language, decided that Nina had agreed to listen to him.

"I am a news reporter from the local paper," he said.

Lena translated his words. Nina became scared. Her visa had recently ended, and she was afraid of any government official. She didn't want to get on the pages of a newspaper! It could end with quick eviction.

"Lena, take Alina and return home quickly."

The reporter saw fear in Nina's eyes.

"Miss, please tell her that I'll give her a hundred dollars for a short interview. A hundred dollars for thirty minutes!"

Lena translated. Nina looked incredulously at the man. The man smiled affably.

"Oh, I do not believe it." Nina said. "It is better to leave."

"Don't be afraid. He wouldn't hurt you. I'm interested to talk to this reporter," said Lena.

"You may be interested, but your mother and I are going to have trouble."

"Don't be afraid, Aunt Nina. I'll ask him what he wants to know." Lena was curious.

Joe interrupted them. "Do you know Miss Stepanov?" he asked.

"He asks if you know Miss Stepanov."

"Daria?" Nina queried.

"Yes, Miss Daria Stepanov."

"I know her. Daria is my friend."

"Tell me about her and I'll pay you the money," insisted Joe.

"Oh. Lena, this is not good. What does he want from her? I don't know about this."

She resolutely took Alina's hand and started toward home.

"What's wrong, Aunt Nina? You could earn a lot of money," insisted Lena, but she reluctantly followed Nina.

Nina phoned Daria as soon as she got home. There was no answer. Then she called

Elizabeth. Elizabeth, who had also been contacted by a reporter, told Nina not to say a word about Daria to anyone. She explained that any information Nina might give to the media could be used to harm Daria, and sooner or later would hurt Nina too.

Lena watched the street. Joe stood near their home for a long time, waiting for someone to come out. Two hours later, he got into his car and drove off. Nina sighed with relief when she learned that the reporter had left, but her anxiety remained. God forbid if he called the Immigration Service! She would be expelled from the United States quickly.

In the evening, when Faina came home from work, Nina discussed the appearance of the reporter at the park and what Elizabeth had said.

"You know, Nina, in America we say that there is no free lunch. They offered money for something the paper needs. They hunt for a sensation that readers would be interested in so they will buy the newspaper. Suppose you say that Daria Stepanov is worthy of respect, that her talent helped her to achieve the position that she occupies. That would hardly interest the readers of the newspaper. They want something dirty or bad. You should definitely not get involved. Do you know why he was interested in your Daria?"

"I am not sure why. I can't say anything bad about Daria, and I don't want my name to appear in the newspaper. The Immigration Service would expel me from the country."

"I agree. We are useless to him," Faina said.

"What if he comes back tomorrow?"

"Consult with Daria."

Chapter Forty-two

Daria approached the Applied Technologies building cautiously. She feared that the events of yesterday would be repeated. But she didn't see the Immigration Service agent in the parking lot, or at the doors of the company. With relief she walked straight to her office. Out of habit, she turned on the computer, but she could not bring herself to get started. Pictures of the day before kept coming to her head. Who could write a denunciation to the Immigration Service? Jim said that the accusation had come from the Applied Technology company.

So this meant that somebody she worked with had turned her in. Did the company's management want to get rid of her? Why would they? Maybe it was Pete Weiss? No, it was hard to believe that Uncle Peter, whom she trusted completely, would do that. Maybe it was Megan, Mr. Chen's secretary? She could be jealous of the fact that Tom had proposed to Daria. Does that mean that she would write a denunciation? Unlikely. So who did? Maybe it was Chuck, out of jealousy? Perhaps it was Chuck. Who else would do such a thing?

The phone rang, interrupting her thoughts.

"Miss Stepanov, Mr. Morrison asks that you to come to his office," said Mr. Morrison's secretary.

"I am on my way. For what reason? Do I need to take something from the documents?"

"I have not been told anything about documents. Mr. Morrison asked me to invite you and didn't explain why."

Daria decided that the company wanted to get rid of her. Why did they need an employee who might be evicted from the country?

She entered the spacious office of the company President. Mr. Morrison stood up to meet her, motioned for her to take a seat, and said, "Miss Stepanov, there was a misunderstanding, and I, on behalf of the company, want to extend a sincere apology. I am asking that you sit closer to me please."

Mr. Dale sheepishly entered the office. Mr. Morrison pointed to a chair near the wall. Mr.

McPherson, the head of the personnel department, entered last.

"Everyone is here." Mr. Morrison said. "Please, McPherson, report to us."

"Company Information Service, at our request, checked the contents of the computers of all employees who have been associated with Miss Stepanov and found the source of the unpleasant denunciation."

Mr. Dale suddenly interrupted McPherson. "That is a violation of workers' rights! I will file a complaint!"

"There are no policies excluding the study of content on company owned computers," Mr. McPherson said calmly. "It has been established that a letter to the Immigration and

Naturalization Service department was written by Mr. Dale. He took advantage of the company's letterhead to print the denunciation. As a result, the letter was almost as if it were a formal request by our company's management. No one in the company had authorized Mr. Dale to do so."

"Immigrants come here and grab the best work!" shouted Dale.

"I didn't give you permission to speak," Mr. Morrison said. "We gave you the opportunity to show us your talent and your performance. You instead proved your lack of loyalty to the company by putting us in a bad light. And this could lead to the disruption of the public order of our drives. In the interest of the company and for ethical reasons, I release you from your duty. Mr. McPherson, please make sure to personally see that Mr. Dale leaves the company premises within half an hour. He can leave the company pass on my desk."

"I won't leave so easily! I will sue you!" Dale cried.

"It's your right. Frankly, I wouldn't recommend it, if you want to get a job elsewhere."

"This is a challenge! I'm not leaving without a fight!"

"Give me your pass and get out of my office!" said Mr. Morrison.

This whole scene shocked Daria. She had not expected the denunciation would have come from Mr. Dale. She had actually pulled together all the work for which he was responsible. And he had always let her know that he was grateful for her good work. He had said that, thanks to her, the whole group looked good in the eyes of the management. Why did he denounce her?

"Miss Stepanov." Morrison turned to her after Dale and McPherson had left the office. "I beg you not to take the denunciation to heart. In this country, we are all immigrants. My great-grandfather and great-grandmother fled the famine in Ireland in the mid-nineteenth century. Back then, some people here met them coldly. My great-grandfather worked hard to show that immigrants always benefit the state. I've kept an eye on your work. You are an excellent worker. Our country needs immigrants such as you. I am sure that you will bring great benefit to our company."

"Thank you," said Daria. "I will do my very best."

Mr. Morrison continued. "Dale's act had no justification whatsoever. To our good fortune, I learned about your arrest very quickly. I immediately phoned Sam Flistein and instructed him to take your case. Sam called me in the evening and said that you have nothing to worry about. He says that Dale's denunciation is not worth a damn. I ask you to just continue working and not worry about the incident."

Mr. Morrison's sweet speech did not calm Daria. She knew that she was guilty because she had received her green card when she married Misha. From the very beginning, Misha had not planned a real marriage with her, and because of that, Bob Dale was right. She had used the deception to receive the right to reside in the country. If that was revealed in court, she could be expelled from the country.

She had brought only trouble to Tom. With melancholy, she thought that perhaps it was not worth venturing into marriage? She didn't want to become a constant source of trouble for Tom. Last night, when she had called Tom, she had decided not to tell him about the incident. She was scared.

Daria felt guilty, and today, as she thought about the situation, she decided that it would be better if Tom found out the truth about Misha from her. The truth is always better than a lie. If he loved her, he would understand, and he would help her.

She called Tom. His secretary answered. Learning that it was Daria calling, she immediately put her through to Tom.

"What happened, my honey?" asked Tom.

"I urgently need to talk with you."

"What is so urgent?"

"It's very urgent for me," Daria said.

"Can it wait until the evening?"

"I don't know."

"Then I'm coming. I'll be at your company in half an hour."

"Thank you, dear." Daria said.

Pete looked into Daria's office. Noticing Daria's eyes filled with tears, he said, "Why are you worrying? There are such people as Dale in any company. Forget him."

"I'm not thinking about him. I am thinking about Tom. I bring him nothing but trouble. Now the gossip will go on without mercy throughout Silicon Valley."

"So what? He will survive. In his situation, there are always the envious. The most important thing is that in our company the management and I won't let someone like Dale offend you."

"I am ashamed because I thought that it was maybe your boss Chuck who deceived me."

"Of course he is disappointed that you have turned out to have such a prominent groom, but he is an honest man, and he has no meanness in him. He is extremely talented, and he believes the classics: 'Talent and villainy are incompatible.'"

Tom arrived quickly, as promised, and Daria was waiting for him at the door of the company.

She was still upset, thinking about how to explain to Tom that she worried about his involvement with her. She wanted Tom to take her to a place where they could speak freely, without witnesses, because she needed to express her thoughts.

The door of the company opened, and Mr. Morrison's secretary called, "Mr. Donovan, Miss Stepanov, would you be so kind as to come to Mr. Morrison's office?"

"Okay!" Tom said.

He took Daria's arm and led her through the lobby. Mr. Morrison met them at the threshold of his office and suggested that they go to a meeting room next to his office.

"You will be comfortable here. I'll tell my secretary not to let anybody disturb you. I see that Miss Daria continues to worry. There are no grounds for concern. Our lawyer will decide the case. Don't worry."

"What's the matter?" Tom asked when Morrison left the room.

"I was arrested yesterday and threatened to be expelled from the country."

The Land of Milk and Honey

"For what?" Tom asked.

"I was accused of deception ... that I have no right to reside in the United States."

"What nonsense!"

"It's not nonsense; it's a serious accusation. The fact is that I really married Misha in order to stay in America, knowing that the marriage was fictitious. My visa at that time was over, and I agreed to a fictitious marriage only because I dreamed to study in the university in America!"

"I don't see any guilt in your actions."

"But you're not a judge. The court may decide that I lied to the authorities."

"I'll hire the best lawyer."

"Mr. Morrison hired Mr. Flistein, the lawyer, to take the case. He is the company representative at the Immigration and Naturalization Service. It was he who helped me yesterday. If not for him, I would be in jail right now. The judge allowed me to wait for the decision."

"I will hire the best lawyer to help Flistein. We will make the case that this should be shut down before it goes to court."

"Dear Tom. I didn't call you to discuss my case. I'm afraid that I'm bringing you a lot of hassle and trouble. You should think twice before finally binding your life with me."

311

"Is that what you think? I love you, and I won't let anyone get in my way! The rumors and gossip won't stop me. I'm not afraid of this; I will fight it. I will get a victory, and I will not let anyone offend you. By proposing to you, I voluntarily took on the obligation to protect you."

Finally, Daria started to calm down. With Tom she would survive. How lucky she was in life to have met Tom! Dear Tom!

Chapter Forty-three

Tom didn't want uncertainty about Daria's immigration to distract them from preparing for the wedding. However, he had not forgotten about his decision to back up Sam Flistein with the best lawyers. On the advice of Sam, he contacted the well-known law firm of Maksnou Chesley, who had become famous in Hollywood for solving immigration problems. Mr. Sean Chesley took up the matter personally.

Tom and Daria's wedding was scheduled for the end of July. Daria asked Tanya and Nina to be her bridesmaids, and the ceremony was also to include Tanya's daughter Susan as the flower girl. Daria invited Misha's partner, Ken, to act as the father of the bride. He had already given her away in marriage once, so now Daria wanted him to participate, and this time it would be a joyful celebration.

She phoned Ken and asked him to take part in the service. Ken didn't want to participate. He said he didn't like noisy ceremonies or large groups of people. And the possible publication of his name in the newspapers embarrassed him. Daria explained to him that with all due respect to his desire to avoid the press, she was still asking him; she had no one else to turn to. She could ask Misha, but Misha was too young for the role of her father. In addition, the press knew that she had been married to Misha. In the end, Ken agreed.

The most difficult thing for Daria was to write to her mother about the wedding. Oh, how she wished that her mother could come to the wedding! But how could she do that? She shared with Tom her wish to have her mother at the wedding and how difficult it was to solve this problem. He told her that he would think about it. His company had representatives in Moscow, and he would discuss with them what could be done.

Elizabeth was enthusiastic about the upcoming wedding and she actively helped Daria with all the organizing. She was also able to fend off the journalists who were interested in the details of Daria's life; they were not able to extract a single word from her. She also instructed Nina in how to reject a request for an interview. As a result, the local newspaper's exploitation of the episode of the Donovan bride arrest was illuminated mostly with Mr. Dale's words. In all fairness, the newspapers ended up publishing a negative review of Mr. Dale, stressing that it was he who had made the denunciation, and that his words should be taken with a grain of salt.

In early July, a judge ordered a review of Daria's case. The representative of the Immigration Service presented his proof of the state of deception, based on the fact that Daria's marriage was a fake and that she had entered into marriage only to fraudulently obtain the right of residence.

Mr. Sean Chesley, who represented the interests of Daria, asked, "Your Honor, the defense confirms that the marriage of Miss Stepanov and Mr. Michael Fishman was unusual. But Miss Stepanov did not deceive the state. Rather, she was deceived by Mr. Fishman. If Miss Stepanov married a US citizen to obtain a residence permit, or in other words, for the sake of personal gain, then she would have had to compensate for all the financial costs of such a marriage.

"Please attach to the case the copies of the checks that were used to pay for the different expenses of the marriage. Here are the payments for the services of the minister conducting the ceremony and for the hotel accommodation during the ceremony. All expenses were paid by Mr. Fishman. And he paid the bills to the attorney, Alex Brodmann, to petition for the right of residence in the United States.

"So why was the marriage a sham? Mr. Fishman, when dating Miss Stepanov, hid from her the fact of his true sexual orientation. Please attach to the case this letter from Mr. Fishman, in which he wrote in detail the reasons that prompted him to ask for the hand of Miss Stepanov. Faced with a beautiful, intelligent woman, Mr. Fishman sincerely hoped that it would distract him from his harmful attraction to the male sex. It was he who was fascinated by her and persuaded her to marry him. Neither he nor Miss Stepanov had any thoughts about cheating the state. It's a pity that his plan failed. He was not able to turn away from his desire for male sex. This is the reason that his marriage with Miss Stepanov was not successful.

"Now a few words about Miss Stepanov.... Miss Stepanov is a model immigrant for our country. She didn't waste time in vain during her marriage to Mr. Fishman. She enrolled in a university, got a degree in business management, sought employment, and proved that she is a specialist in her field. She is a benefit to her new homeland. During the years that Miss Stepanov has lived here, she has regularly paid taxes. In addition, she has had no clashes with the law.

"The Immigration and Naturalization Service has legitimately issued a document to assure Miss Stepanov as a permanent resident of the country. There was no desire to circumvent our immigration laws. There are no grounds for the review of the decision previously taken. We ask you, Your Honor, to reject the accusations and to restore the fair name of Miss Stepanov."

The judge had listened carefully throughout Chesley's speech. "The court will consider the materials presented by Miss Stepanov's side and make a decision in two days," he announced. "This meeting of today is completed."

Mr. Chesley resolutely went to the desk of the judge.

"Your Honor. May I talk with you?"

"Come to my office, please."

Daria waited in the hall with Mr. Flistein.

"Don't worry, Miss Stepanov, don't worry," said Flistein. "Chesley has a bomb to drop on our friend Jim."

"I don't understand," said Daria. "What kind of bomb?"

"He has a letter from the management of the Immigration Service, in which they blame Jim for presenting the case to court while bypassing the management of Applied Technology, just for the sensation of it. The head of the department that employs Jim finds no grounds to question the decision made in Los Angeles that granted you permanent resident status in the country. Sean didn't want to declare this letter in open court, in order to avoid giving the press more grounds for sensation."

"Why not close the case without a trial?" asked Daria.

"We need a court order to prevent any further instances of raising the matter again. All the materials are considered in the case, and the court has to make a final decision."

After five minutes, Sean Chesley came quietly from the judge's office. He carried with him the court order to dismiss the case due to lack of evidence. The case of the expulsion of Daria was closed.

At the exit of the courthouse, the journalists were waiting. Mr. Flistein said politely, "Press representatives, as I told you earlier, the charges were a mistake. The Immigration and Naturalization Service admitted its mistake and they have abandoned the charges."

"Is it true that Miss Stepanov's husband was gay?" asked a reporter.

"I'm not going to discuss any details. I have nothing to add to my statement."

Chapter Forty-four

Daria's mother, Antonina Nikolaevna, was cleaning in the cowshed when she heard the voice of a neighbor loudly calling her.

"What happened, Dunya?" asked Antonina.

"Somebody is looking for you," the neighbor said.

Antonina came out of the cowshed, wiping her hands on her apron. She looked around and was immediately surprised. Behind her fence was a large black car of an unknown make. A respectable looking young man in city clothes exited the car to meet her.

"Are you Antonina Nikolaevna?" he asked politely in Russian.

"Yes I am," said Antonina nervously.

"My name is Anatoly Ivanovich. I came to you at the request of Mr. Donovan."

"Who is this mister? I don't know him," Antonina said.

Her heart clenched in fear. Now were they accusing her in connection with some American mister? Dasha did not need to go to America; it would bring trouble to the family.

"I'm sorry, dear Antonina Nikolaevna, but did you not receive the news of the upcoming wedding from Daria Ivanovna?"

"What wedding?" Antonina decided that the young man wanted to provoke her.

"Your daughter Daria Ivanovna Stepanov is going to marry Mr. Donovan."

"Marry? Marry to whom?"

"Mr. Thomas Donovan, president of the company Donco. I have a letter here from him. Mr. Donovan has instructed me to organize your travel to the United States to attend the wedding of your daughter."

Antonina Nikolaevna had never expected an invitation to the United States. And in general, for her, a rural teacher, visiting the United States was something completely unrealistic. She knew that her daughter lived there, and that she had achieved success there; however, in her mind, the United States remained the "Yellow Devil" country, where the common man is better not to go.

It was enough to analyze life in Russia in the last few years. After the collapse of the Soviet Union, in connection with the transition to capitalism, people's lives had changed rapidly, and these changes were not for the best. Who could have believed that teachers' salaries wouldn't be paid for six months? What would it have been like for her, if not for the help from Daria? The people became poor to the extreme, and meanwhile a bunch of modern-day capitalists were emerging fast and furious.

Antonina was terribly afraid of America. "How would you organize the trip?" she asked. "And what if I don't want to go? I have a cow and no one to care for it, except me. I should take care of my garden too. What would I do without potatoes next winter?"

"Dear Antonina Nikolaevna, it is better to discuss this around the table. Do you have cup of milk?" asked Anatoly.

"Come in, please."

Antonina invited Anatoly into the house and her neighbor Evdokia slipped in behind him. Antonina didn't want her neighbor to listen to the conversation with this stranger, but she felt awkward excluding her friend.

Anatoly continued the conversation when the three of them were seated around the dinner table. "I think that you, Antonina Nikolaevna, should not refuse the trip," he said. "Why offend your daughter and your son-in-law too? The question with your farm is not difficult to resolve. For good money, people will take care of your garden and your animals."

He turned to the neighbor. "Here you are. What is your name?"

"Evdokia," said the neighbor.

"Do you agree, for three thousand rubles a month, to care for Antonina Nikolaevna's farm?"

"For three thousand a month?" she queried.

"Yes, three thousand rubles a month."

"For such money, I will be happy to work," stated Evdokia.

"There, you see, Antonina Nikolaevna, how simple it is to resolve this issue." Anatoly smiled.

"And where do you think I will get three thousand rubles?" Antonina asked.

"This is not your concern. I will provide the money and Mr. Donovan will pay me back. So what do you say? Shall we go to America?"

"Go, Antonina, you must go!" said Evdokia. "Your daughter is going to get married! How could you not to go for the wedding?"

"It's easy for you to speak," retorted Antonia Nikolaevna. "I'm afraid. I do not know a word of English. I studied English in the teachers' institute, but that was a long time ago, and there is nothing left in my head now. What will people think of me?"

"You'll be with your daughter. Don't worry about the people. I would be happy if I had a chance to go!" Evdokia said.

"I would like to think more," said Antonina.

"We have no time for that," said Anatoly. "We need to solve many things before you can go. Do you have a passport?"

"A passport for travel? No, I don't have a passport."

"You see, you don't have a passport. I will have to start from this point. A passport can only be obtained in the district capital city. We must not hesitate. You could be late for the wedding. I'll go now to the village council for the necessary documents. Then we'll drive to the city for a passport. Then we will not return here, because we will drive to Moscow as soon as we obtain your passport. So here, Evdokia, is your first three thousand rubles. This is the salary for the month ahead. Get to work."

He drew a wad of money from his pocket, and counted out three thousand rubles.

Evdokia watched in disbelief.

"Will we not come back?" Antonina was terrified.

"From the district capital we will go directly to Moscow to apply for the visa at the American Embassy. And from there, we will board the plane to America."

"So soon?"

"I have the hotel booked in Moscow. The visa will take time. I was ordered to take complete care of you," said Anatoly.

Anatoly stood up. "And now I have to go to the village council."

Antonina sat at the table, stunned. "That was like a dream," she said to her friend. "Was it real?

"You are lucky, Antonina," said Evdokia. "Your Dasha is getting married to a serious person. He sent the businessman here to arrange everything. And I am lucky too. Where, in our time, would we earn this kind of money?"

Evdokia was happy.

Chapter Forty-five

Morning burst into the bedroom with the sun ablaze. Daria opened her eyes and abruptly sat up in bed, fearing that she was late. Whether it was this movement, or whether it was from fear, she suddenly felt nauseated. She covered her mouth with her hand and hurried to the bathroom. Nausea was a good sign; it could be a sign of pregnancy.

Daria wanted a child and she would be happy to endure nausea if that was what was happening.

Daria cleaned the toilet, washed herself, and returned to the bedroom. Tom opened his eyes and smiled.

"It's time to wake up?" he asked.

"Lie down. It's only quarter to six. I got up because I was nauseated. I think I am pregnant."

"Really, my darling? That would be happy news!"

Daria smiled.

"So maybe your first wish is fulfilled."

"And yours!" She smiled.

"I want a lot of children," said Tom.

"I'm afraid of being late at the airport. Today my mother arrives." Daria said.

"Don't worry. You have enough time. What is she like, your mom?"

"You will see. She is easy, very down to earth. I hope you will like her."

Tom went with Daria to meet her mother at the airport. He had planned to get a hotel room for her mother, but Daria didn't want to do that. She believed that her mother would be happier in her apartment. Elizabeth's apartment was next door, and Elizabeth would help her mother and make sure she didn't get lonely. Mama, who didn't speak English, would be lonely at a hotel.

Daria had moved into Tom's condominium some time ago. She would have liked to settle her mother in their condo, but she and Tom were very busy and Daria wouldn't be able to pay attention to her mother.

They waited for her mother to appear at the customs exit, and it didn't take long before Antonina arrived, pushing a cart with a suitcase in front of her. Daria thought that her mother had aged a lot in the past few years, and her rustic outfit in the fashion of the sixties strengthened the impression. Daria felt guilty.

"Mommy!" Daria cried, kissing her mother. "I'm so happy that you came for my wedding! This is my husband Tom," she said, speaking in Russian.

Antonina smiled at Tom and gave him her hand to shake. Tom took her hand, kissed it, and said, "Welcome to America! Thank you for coming to visit us!"

"Mama, Tom welcomes you and thanks you for agreeing to come to our wedding," said Daria, speaking in Russian. "And please meet Elizabeth Isaakovna. Elizabeth is the closest person to me in America. She's my guardian angel!"

"Welcome Antonina Nikolaevna!" Elizabeth said, also in Russian.

"Hello!" Antonina said. "I am very grateful to you for taking care of my Dasha."

Tom picked up Antonina's suitcase, and the group went to the garage where Tom had parked the car. On the way back from the airport, Tom asked Elizabeth to please take care of Daria's mother. He wanted Elizabeth to take Antonina to a good store to buy clothes for Antonina, all the clothes that she would need, and he would give her the money when they arrived at the apartment. Elizabeth gladly agreed to help in this matter.

Antonina Nikolaevna was listening to the English speech without realizing what they were saying. She was pleased that she had been met so sincerely, but she was a little uncomfortable by the fact that she did not understand their conversation. Daria explained to her what was being said.

A table was waiting for them at Daria's apartment. Nina was on duty as the host. Daria had agreed with the idea that during the time of Antonina's stay in the United States, Nina would live with her in this apartment. It was school holiday time, so Lena could look after her younger sister. Daria said that she would pay Lena for it, but Lena refused payment. Instead, she wanted Daria to let her take Alina to the wedding. In response to this request, Daria invited all their family to the wedding.

Tom wanted to spend the evening with Daria and her mother, but his company was waiting for him at a meeting. He had to say goodbye.

"I don't want to leave," apologized Tom. "How much I wish that Daria could work at Donco. Then we would have more time together."

Daria translated for her mother, and then she asked Tom: "In what position?"

"I'll think about it. I have an idea, but the idea is still incubating. When I have thought through the idea more, we will discuss it."

"Okay, honey."

When Tom left, Daria asked her mother, "Do you like my fiancé?"

"He looks nice. My concern is, whether he will be good to you. Is he a capitalist? I don't like capitalists. Oh dear, I'm afraid that you bind your fate to a capitalist."

"Mama, what is this nonsense about capitalists?"

"When I was in Moscow, Anatoly, the representative of your Tom, said that your fiancé is a capitalist, and the owner of a company. I thought about it all the way here. Capitalists cannot be trusted! They are only interested in money. I've seen enough of our new rich people. They don't care about people, and the people are suffering."

"Mom, why do you compare him with the New Russians?"

"What is the difference between our New Russians and your capitalists? Both are enemies of the working class. We, the common people, are as dirt to them."

"Oh, Mom, how strong the Soviet propaganda has stuck to you! Aunt Lisa, please help to explain this issue to my mother!" asked Daria.

"Do you know, Antonina Nikolaevna, I'm also a capitalist," Elizabeth said.

"You? It cannot be!" Antonina looked at Elizabeth with disbelief.

"Yes, it can. I bought shares in the company Microsoft a couple of years ago."

"And now you're the owner of this company?"

"Yes, along with thousands of other shareholders. I just own a tiny piece of it."

"How can that be?"

"Microsoft is a public company. Its shares are freely traded on the market. Everyone can buy them. I bought shares worth two thousand dollars with the calculation that they will be worth more in the future. And indeed, I can now sell these shares for *three* thousand dollars if I want to. Once I have shares, I am a capitalist, but this does not mean that I should not work and live only on the dividends. I will continue to work. There are millions of such capitalists in America. I am proud that I have successfully invested part of my savings in stocks."

"And our groom too?"

"That is another matter. He has set up a company and it is very successful. He works in the company as a leader, and he is doing an excellent job. I don't see anything wrong with that," said Elizabeth. "He is very intelligent and he works very hard."

"I'm worried about Dasha."

"It's natural. I too, was worried when my daughter was getting married."

"And did she marry a good man?" asked Antonina.

"Very good. I love him as a son. I like Tom, too. I think that he will be a good husband for Dasha."

"And it's not terrible that he doesn't know a word of Russian?"

"Dasha has no problem communicating with him."

Nina joined the conversation: "I would have found a groom for myself too if I could understand English like Dasha."

"What's stopping you?" Elizabeth said. "You're a young, good looking woman. You are too young to limit yourself just to the duties of a nanny. You must build your future."

"How can I learn English if everyone with whom I talk to, talks to me in Russian?"

"How Dasha learned! Go to school."

"I'm afraid. I am illegal here."

"Yes, Nina," Daria said. "You definitely need to learn the language. We'll think of something so you can continue to stay here."

"You should not. I am tired. I want to go to Moscow. As soon as my contract is over, I will return to Moscow," Nina said.

"But how long will your earned money last?" asked Daria.

"I don't know. I'll still go home. I don't want to lose the room I have in Moscow."

Chapter Forty-six

Ken and Misha arrived the day before the wedding. As a first duty, they went to get acquainted with Antonina. Ken thought that because he had taken the role of the bride's father at the wedding, he had to meet with her mother. Misha acted as the interpreter. Antonina liked Ken, such a gentle, quiet man. Misha also made a good impression on Antonina and she could not understand why Daria had parted with this beautiful man and married some American. She was too shy to ask Misha this question. She decided to ask Nina, but Nina didn't know either.

Antonina was tired after visiting various expensive department stores with Elizabeth. She also worried about the unusually high cost of her clothes. She decided that this capitalist would not spend the money for nothing. He probably wanted something important from her. But what? She didn't know any Russian state secrets. She was a simple village teacher. Could it be that he loved Dasha so much? She could not believe this. She was sure that capitalists loved only money. So there was something else. And because she didn't know what he wanted, she had no peace of mind.

All that she had seen, heard and learned over the past couple of days since she had landed in San Francisco shocked Antonina. She had never seen such an abundance of products, especially in the large grocery store where Elizabeth had taken her. There were so many types of meat, and all kinds of strange fruits and vegetables, and lots of canned food in boxes and bottles. Antonina was amazed that anything you wanted to buy, you could simply choose and put it in your cart. And what a variety of cheeses! Elizabeth said that simple people, not just rich ones, were buying these things!

Elizabeth told her some unbelievable fairy tales about America! Pensioners over 65 years old could receive state benefits and live independently of their children. In Russia, you couldn't live on an earned pension, but here, even people who had never worked in this country could live without worries.

Why did this Elizabeth praise America so much? Probably she is afraid of the CIA, concluded Antonina, and so she tells me tales. She leads me especially to the shops for the rich to brainwash me. But I don't believe her; she won't fool me. I know that here are a lot of homeless people.

Antonina had read in the newspapers back home that in America there are a lot of poor people and a lot of unemployed. Why did Elizabeth not say anything about them?

Antonina decided to share her thoughts with Nina. She trusted Nina more because Nina worked as a nanny and she understood the needs of the poor.

"You are wrong, Antonina Nikolaevna," said Nina. "You should believe Elizabeth. All that she told you is the truth. If I had the chance, I would stay here."

"So do the old men, immigrants from the Soviet Union who have never worked here, have a decent living?" asked Antonina.

"Yes. Those who work in Russia can envy them."

"Is it true? Why is America so kind to immigrants?" asked Antonina.

"They have a law to protect elderly people."

"And what about the homeless?"

"There is some homelessness here, it's true. But they have mostly themselves to blame. They don't want to live in shelters."

"Why not?"

"The shelters prohibit alcohol and drugs. So they feel they have no freedom."

"America is a strange country!" concluded Antonina.

"It is a very strange country from our point of view. It's a pity that America is not for me," Nina said sadly.

"Why does my future son spend so much money on my clothes?"

"They ordered a dress for me too. He wants the

guests from the bride's side to be nicely dressed. You know, to make a nice impression.

"It's a waste of money. So many hungry and poor in the world, and they spend the money for nothing."

"My boss told me that Tom is a very important person. He earns a lot of money."

"One word: he is a capitalist! People, I suppose, work hard for him, and he just rakes in the money."

"Here you are mistaken. He works very hard. Dasha told me."

"She protects her capitalist. I don't believe her. If you have a lot of money, why would you work? You would spend your money and enjoy life."

"Why do you think that he got his money easily?"

"He is young and already so rich," said Antonina.

"Young, but very smart. Not everyone could invent a new company."

Antonina didn't believe Nina. Nina had been spoiled here in America. Antonina believed that there were no honest capitalists. Such capitalists didn't exist. Nina had obviously forgotten what she had been taught in school.

Elizabeth drove Antonina to a beauty salon. Daria had asked that she order a manicure and a new hairstyle for her mother. It was especially difficult to clean her hands. Because of all the hard work, they were covered with thick calluses. A woman in the salon steamed Antonina's hands a long time, and then rubbed them with a pumice stone, but she could not scrub the ingrained dirt from under her fingernails. She had to stick on artificial nails and then polish them. Antonina was not pleased with the fact they were busy with her for so long. She was not used to someone fussing over her.

Elizabeth laughed in response to Antonina's grumbling. "Dear Antonina Nikolaevna, you're a beautiful woman. You need to look lovely at the wedding. Dasha wants her mother to be beautiful," explained Elizabeth.

"But who needs me?"

"Don't say that. You could attract a lot of men yet, and it could happen that you will get an offer of marriage."

"Don't embarrass me, Lisa," said Antonina.

Her hairstyle was another ordeal. Antonina was frightened when the stylist lowered her seat and asked her to bend her head back.

Elizabeth reassured her. "Don't worry, they always wash the hair before doing a perm."

"Do I have a dirty head?" asked Antonina.

"No, it's just how they do it."

Leaving the salon, Antonina looked at herself in the mirror. She stared at a youthful, pretty woman and she recognized herself with great difficulty.

"Now I'm a city woman. Our women at home won't want to know me."

"Get used to it. You are now the mother-in-law of Thomas Donovan."

"That sounds like 'a thief in the law.' Can I just be mom?"

"Whatever you want."

Chapter Forty-seven

The wedding day finally came. Daria was so excited. Everything that had happened to her seemed like a fairy tale. Even when Ken solemnly took her by the arm down the aisle of the church, she couldn't believe that everything was happening in real life, and not in a sweet unimaginable dream.

The church was full of people, a sea of faces that to Daria was like a far away scene in a painting. She focused her gaze on the group of people standing near the pulpit, illuminated by soft lights. Suddenly, among the women dressed in identical dresses, she saw Tanya. Their eyes met, and Tanya smiled kindly at her.

Her smile soothed Daria. She turned her head and saw Tom's eyes shining. She smiled approvingly at Tom, and the ceremony began.

When the priest asked if there was an objection to the marriage, Daria waited to hear a voice from the audience with some unknown objection and worried that their marriage wouldn't happen. But no one spoke against the marriage, and the ceremony ended with the happy announcement that Tom and Daria were now husband and wife.

Tom's sweet kiss returned Daria to reality. Then Tom took her by the arm and led her out of the church. At the exit, photographers and television reporters surrounded them. Thomas Donovan's wedding would be in the news on the local TV stations. Daria smiled approvingly at Tom.

In the banquet hall, Daria saw that her mother was sitting next to Ken. What a pity that Ken was not interested in women. They could be a lovely couple, Mom with her amazing hairstyle and the strikingly handsome Ken.

Guests lined up to congratulate the newlyweds. Mr. Morrison came with his wife. "I am very glad that we have found you a bride on our team," he said. "Now our companies are connected."

"I am very grateful to you, of course," said Tom. "I don't want to disappoint you, but I found Daria long before she became your employee."

Morrison's wife looked carefully at Daria and said, "I have heard so many good things about you. I hope that we will be friends."

After that, a lot of people, unfamiliar to Daria, approached them with congratulations. Daria and Tom shook their hands and politely thanked them. Chuck Jennings, waiting his turn, came to congratulate the newlyweds. Daria introduced Chuck to Tom with, "Honey, this is our engineer, Chuck Jennings.

My friend Pete says that he is a genius, and I have no doubt that this assessment is valid."

"Nice to know you!" Tom said.

"Mrs. Donovan, please don't exaggerate," Chuck said.

That was the first time somebody had called her Mrs. Donovan! It was extremely pleasant.

Chuck continued, "I would like to congratulate you and Mr. Donovan. You're lucky, Tom. You have an unusually beautiful and intelligent woman."

Sam Flistein came to congratulate them. While shaking his hand, Tom said, "I want to ask you to help us change Daria's name on her green card. We decided that my wife will change her last name from Stepanov to Donovan and we need to change all of her documents to her new last name."

"I would be honored to take care of this. Do you want us to just change her green card and her Russian passport too?" Sam asked.

"Do you help in the Russian consulate too?" Daria asked.

"Yes, we deal with them too."

"Yes, I would like to change my last name on my Russian passport as well," Daria said.

Daria wondered why Pete Weiss didn't come to congratulate her. Had he taken offense to something? Daria didn't want anybody who was her friend before her marriage to think that their relationship had changed in any way. After the first dance with Tom, Daria went in search of Pete. Pete and his wife sat modestly in a corner of the hall.

"Uncle Peter! Introduce me please to your wife. I don't want you to sit in the corner," Daria said in Russian.

"Dear Dasha, don't embarrass us, the old people. We will sit modestly in the corner."

"No, you are one of my most welcome guests, and I want to introduce you to my mother."

"We will be glad to meet your mother," Pete said.

Antonina was still sitting next to Ken. Daria summoned Peter to her and introduced him.

"Mother, this is my best friend and mentor, Peter Danilovich. He has taught me everything and I am very grateful to him for that."

"Thank you," said Antonina. "I'm still worried about how my daughter is doing here in America!" she confessed.

"This is understandable," Pete said. "Your daughter is a very good worker and a good person. Such people are very much appreciated in America. You see, Mr. Donovan appreciated her so much that he decided to join his destiny with her."

"Oh, I'm still afraid of this capitalist!" Antonina said.

Daria left them to talk. She hurried over to Tom and his friends. It was necessary to make sure that people who were close to her husband would also become close to her.

Daria had not forgotten that Tom's parents hadn't wanted this wedding. Feeling nervous, Daria went to her father-in-law. Surprisingly, Joe met Daria with open arms. Kissing his daughter-in-law, Joe said, "I congratulate you. I hope that you will visit us in Modesto. Are you leaving your work?"

"I love my job and I would like to keep it," she said.

"You look so beautiful!" said Dorothy, her eyes shining, and she gave Daria a warm hug.

Daria was grateful for her obvious approval.

"I have good news for you," she said, addressing both Dorothy and Joe, "I am pregnant. You can expect a grandchild in eight months."

"Congratulations!" Dorothy was clearly thrilled. "I have dreamed of this!"

She embraced Daria again. Quietly she said, "Don't take offense with us. Joe was completely wrong."

"I'm not offended. I believe that he was right to worry. But I didn't marry Tom because of material considerations. I only learned that he was the CEO and owner of Donco after he had proposed to me."

Misha came up to Daria and distracted her from Tom's parents. He invited Daria to dance.

"Are you happy, Dasha? You conquered America."

"You are wrong, Misha. I am far from it."

"Really?" Misha looked at her doubtfully.

"I still have a lot to achieve. I have yet to find the right approach to Tom's parents, his friends, and his business partners. Life is a complicated thing and I'm not sure that Tom's love will be enough to withstand the turbulent flow and pitfalls of real life, and that I didn't damage the fragile family boat. I don't expect an easy life ahead."

"Tom's parents are against your union?" Misha guessed.

"*Were* against."

"Difficulties exist, but I have no doubt that you will overcome them all. Today, I have to say that you achieved the American dream! I was sure of you, but I didn't expect that you would achieve such success so soon."

Nina sat at the same table as her employers. Daria walked over to her.

"Dasha," said Nina. "I've decided to fly back to Moscow together with your mother."

"Maybe you can stay longer? Why do you hurry?"

"I cannot. This country with rivers of milk and honey is not for me. I miss Moscow," Nina said.

"It's sad news. I will miss you," said Daria honestly.

"I want to keep our friendship. I hope you won't forget me. Please write me occasionally."

"Of course I will," said Daria.

Tom came up and asked Daria for a dance. Daria apologized to her girlfriend and went with her loved one. Her wedding was not a place to talk heart to heart with her friend.

Immediately after the banquet, a limousine took Daria and Tom away to the city of Monterrey, where they spent a week in a beautiful room in a local hotel near Fisherman's Wharf.

When Daria and Tom got back to San Francisco, they saw Antonina off at the San Francisco airport. Daria hugged her mother and kissed her goodbye. Antonina's eyes filled with tears.

Daria tried to calm her. "Don't cry. I'll come to visit you, Mama."

"Will your husband let you?"

"For sure! I will arrange it with him. He is a very good person."

"I still worry. I will pray to God for you!" Antonina said.

Nina was also leaving. She hugged Daria and said, "Goodbye, Dasha. I won't set foot in America in the future. There is no luck for me in America."

"Write to me, Nina. I don't want to lose you," Daria said.

"I will," said Nina sadly. She took Antonina by the arm and walked to the gate where only the passengers were allowed. Daria and Tom watched them until they were lost in the crowd.

Tom reached for Daria's hand and said, "They are gone in the crowd! We should get back to work. I have accumulated a lot of unresolved issues."

"And I have my duties at Applied Technology too. Don't forget that I am now in charge of the marketing of our division," Daria said smiling.

– The End –

About the Author

Viktor Shel was born in Odessa, the USSR. He immigrated to the USA in 1980 and from 1998 settled in city of Dublin, California. He began writing in 1998 using his native Russian language. Viktor's writing based on his experience in Soviet Union and USA. Being the immigrant from the Soviet Union, he dedicated his short stories to the lives of Jewish people from the Soviet Union in their former homeland and in the USA. In year 2005, his short stories were published in the emigre newspaper "East – West" distributed in San Francisco, Denver and Toronto.

In year of 2007, collection of these stories came out in the Canadian publishing company Trafford Publishing as a Russian language book. At the same time, the same publishing house published the result of many years of hard work – novel "Оксана" (*Oksana*). The novel is an epic, describing history of a one family from 1941 until 1995.

In subsequent years, Viktor Shel published two more major works on the lives of his contemporaries – novel "Молочные реки" (*Milk River*), 2008 and the trilogy "Превратности судьбы" (*The Vicissitudes of Fate*), 2013.

Viktor Shel always had interested in history. His first historical novel "Лёвушка" (*Leo*) was written in 2008. It refers to events at the end of the nineteenth century in Russia, and described adventure of young Jewish boy who was kidnapped and managed run from kidnapers.

The historical novel "Острые клыки овец" (*The Sharp Fangs Sheep*) written in 2010 highlighted the adventures happened in the early sixteenth century. The young converts from Judaism escaped from persecution of the Spanish Inquisition and joined the Mediterranean corsairs in fighting with Spanish crown.

Currently, Viktor completed story in which the events happened in the first century AD.

In 2013, Viktor Shel translated the novel "Лёвушка" into English and published under the title "Young Leo".

Now Viktor dedicates all his time to translation of his works into English to make them available to English speaking readers.

LIST OF PUBLISHED WORKS

Детство Вилена (***Vilen Youth***), 2007
ISBN: 978-1-4251-2640-7

Оксана (***Oksana***), 2007
ISBN: 978-1-4251-5020-4

Молочные реки (***Milk Rivers***), 2009
ISBN: 978-1-4327-1876-3

Острые клыки овец (***Sharp Fangs of Sheep***), 2011
ISBN: 978-0-615-44692-9

ПРЕВРАТНОСТИ СУДЬБЫ
(***The Vicissitudes of Fate***)

Book 1 *Юность*, 2013
ISBN: 978-0-9890856-0-1
Book 2 *Зрелые годы*, 2013
ISBN: 978-0-9890856-1-8
Book 3 *Борьба за счастье*, 2013
ISBN: 978-0-9890856-2-5

Young Leo, 2013
ISBN: 978-0-9890856-3-2

Stories told by an Old Jew, 2016
ISBN: 978-0-9890856-6-3

Why he betrayed Jesus, 2016
ISBN 978-0-9890856-6-3

www.ingramcontent.com/pod-product-compliance
Lightning Source LLC
Chambersburg PA
CBHW051059030726
47504CB00006B/1705